The Invisible Fight

ANNA WINSON

Do not fear the unknown.
It holds the most magical possibilities.

-Anna.

CONTENTS

ACKNOWLEDGMENTS

Thank you to my readers, my family and friends. There is something so special about putting yourself and your inner world out there, and being met with such support, love and encouragement.

1

September seemed to sneak up on Ryan and me. We spent eight weeks in Dinner Plain while setting up a more permanent solution for caretaking at my chalet, Arendelle. At the same time Ryan was finishing up the ski season at Mt Hotham.

During the first few weeks back home, I found myself consumed with bringing my close friends and family up to speed on what had transpired in Singapore. I found myself in Melbourne city more and more, not only on business for Samuel Chen but also to see my family. It worked out quite well, from that respect, having Chen and I tag-team across Australasia for Huynh Enterprises Holdings.

One particularly frosty morning I planned to head into the Ski School to give my resignation to Zak officially. I couldn't help but feel guilty having forgotten to 'resign' from my job when I left for Singapore. I stepped off the front porch into the bright morning light, enjoying the crisp breeze sweeping up the mountain. I strolled through the snow to the Mountain Kitchen, eco cup in hand.

Ivan grins up at me across the counter as the door shuts behind me. I unwrap my scarf and unzip my snow jacket in the warm dining space. He finishes serving the couple in front of me before stepping out from behind the counter to envelop me in a bear hug.

'Miss Ava, how I have missed ye' face!' He chuckles down at me.

'Ivan, I saw you at Danny's campfire dinner last night!' I laugh back at him, handing over my cup.

'The usual?'

'Please,' I sigh, turning to look at the muffins and pastries on display for the morning. 'How is Marianne this morning?'

'Aye, she's doing okay. She is much happier now the sun is rising a little earlier again.' He mumbles from behind the coffee machine. I pick up a giant chocolate chunk cookie and place it on the counter, digging in my pocket for my bank card.

'There ye' are lassie.' Ivan smiles across at me, placing the lid gently on my cup.

'What would I do without you, Ivan?' I pat his hand after tapping my card against the pay pass.

'Are ye and Ryan going to stay in town in the offseason this year? Or are you headed for Singapore again soon?' His eyes twinkle across at me.

'We haven't quite decided yet, but I do need to get back to Singapore sooner rather than later. I have some unfinished business I need to settle.' I pick up my cup and cookie and wave him farewell.

I spot Zak out the front of the ski school, cleaning ice off the steps.

'Hi Zak,' I wave at him from the road. I step gingerly onto the path, having lost my 'ice legs' in the short time I spent in Singapore.

'Ava, good to see you. I take it you aren't here for your old job back?' He smiles up at me, brushing his fringe from his face with a gloved hand.

'Sadly not I'm afraid. I wanted to come by and officially resign. I am so sorry I didn't get a chance to tell you when I left earlier this year. It all happened so quickly.' I shrug sheepishly, offering him the cookie.

He takes it with a broad grin.

'Ah, it's no trouble. It turns out Hayley wanted to help out, so we've been working together since this season started. We've been doing surprisingly well together.' He sits down on the porch step, patting the space beside him. 'I must admit though, neither of us can ever get the hot chocolate to taste the way you did!'

We sit in peace together, watching the chalets come to life as the tourists begin to clamber out into the morning.

'Do you think you'll stay in DP after you get your life in Singapore sorted?' Zak asks, watching an incredibly awkward couple trying to juggle ski gear down toward the slope.

'I have no idea. I don't honestly know what I am going to do next. I just need to get through this next chapter of my life before I start looking too far forward.' I shrug.

It has been a point of contention for Ryan and me. We've been having such an incredible time these past two months. Still, he is getting crankier the closer it gets to my returning to Singapore.

'Do you enjoy living over there enough to stay there permanently? I thought you hated the heat?' Zak cocks an eyebrow, looking at me quizzically.

I wonder if he has been talking to Ryan. He keeps making precisely the same point. But things are different now. Aren't they?

'Yet another great question. I have no idea. I know I can't just walk away right now, but if the timing is right, I still haven't figured out if I can walk away.' I whisper, almost to myself. A young girl of about five years of age stumbles through the snow toward us, a rather unimpressed father in tow. Her long blonde pigtails were blowing in the wind from underneath a bubble gum pink beanie.

'Hi, Sophie!' Zak smiles across at her, holding his hand out for a high five.

'I'd better let you get on with your day,' I nod to Zak as Sophie, and her dad enter the school to pick up her skis.

'I'll see you around Ava.' He smiles at me before turning inside.

I wander back toward the chalet, my feet crunching in the snow. There wasn't much of a fall overnight, September generally marking 'the beginning of the end' of the season. It is the time of year the snow gets more dangerous, compounding into the streets as ice.

Ever since Ryan and I returned from Singapore, I have been focussed on getting back there. I feel like I can't rest until I have figured out what happened to Winnie. I also can't shake the feeling that if Tony was behind it, firing him won't be enough to deter him from pursuing his ultimate goal of taking Huynh Enterprises Holdings back.

Crossing the street toward the side road on which my chalet Arendelle sits, I spot Danny, of Danny's

Bar at the Hotel. I wave enthusiastically across at him, walking to meet him in the middle of the street.

'Ava, I see you pulled up better than most, after the campfire dinner.' He grins at me sheepishly, rubbing the back of his neck with one hand.

'I tend not to party quite as hard as everyone else,' I chuckle, sipping my coffee contentedly.

'I never got a chance to sit down with you and find out what happened after those Singaporean Mafia showed up. Ivan told me everything was fine, but he wouldn't give me any details!' He waves his hands about in frustration.

'Honestly Danny that day feels like a lifetime ago, so much has happened since then.' I shake my head, watching the memories play out in my mind.

'For you maybe, but that was the most exciting thing to happen to anyone in this town in decades.' He chuckles. 'So...'

'So, I flew to Singapore and found out that a friend of mine had passed away and left me his business to manage. There were a couple of minor disturbances, but in the end, I left it in the hands of a trusted colleague to manage it while I am back home for the meantime.' I explain, trying to leave out the unsavoury parts of the story.

Probably best not to mention that I inherited the several hundred-million-dollar international conglomerate only for evil Tony the company's General Counsel to hire another CEO to try and usurp my authority. Or that we ended up in a fistfight after I tried firing him for the fourth time, resulting in my concussion and hospital stay. Or perhaps the fact that Winnie died, leaving behind a diary containing details of him questioning his death and suggesting maybe he was not ailing of old age. I probably shouldn't mention the fact that I am trying to get back to Singapore with the second half of the journal before embarking on a mystery journey to uncover the truth about how he indeed died and if, in fact, Tony his 'trusted' lawyer, had a hand in his demise.

Yes, probably better not to mention those minor details.

'Ah, earth to Ava!' Danny waves his hand in my face, breaking my whirlpool of thought.

'Sorry, I've been drifting a bit lately.' I shrug at him, 'I've had a lot on my mind.'

'No matter. By the way, I hope you don't mind, but I put your guys' tab on your card last night. I hope that's okay?' He eyes me uncomfortably.

'Of course! I'm sorry I forgot to mention that to you when we arrived. What time did they stay out until?'

'The older one dragged, the younger one back to Carcassonne around 2 am?' He shrugs.

'I suppose I'd best go check on them,' I laugh out loud, imagining what kind of state Xi and Seal must be in this morning.

'Have a good one, Ava,' Danny waves goodbye.

As I make my way up the winding drive toward Carcassonne, I drink in the beauty that is the giant stone chalet. Two weeks after arriving back in Dinner Plain, Victoria, Jia, my new General Counsel at HEH called me out of the blue. She had just been hounded by a real estate agent who said that Winnie never came past to pick up the keys to the chalet he purchased, well over a year ago.

I drove out to Bright with my driver, Xi and personal security officer, Seal to meet the real estate agent. She explained that Winnie purchased the chalet Carcassonne sight unseen, and someone needed to sign for the keys and sign off on the continuity agreement for care and maintenance of the property.

Jia had coordinated the signing of the land titles across into my name, so all I had to do was collect the keys and drive back to town to view Winnie's purchase.

'Did you have any idea he bought a chalet?' I asked Xi as we drove in silence toward the property.

'None whatsoever, Miss Ava.' He shook his head and chuckled to himself from the front seat.

Having stayed the first few nights in the Hotel, seeing as Arendelle is far too small to accommodate two grown men in addition to myself and Ryan, Xi and Seal graciously offered to stay in Carcassonne for the remainder of our time in Dinner Plain. I stop at the base of the hill upon which the chalet stands, smirking to myself at the ostentatiousness of the 'humble chalet' Winnie had chosen to purchase. The large stone building stood upon almost an acre of land. The structure of the property somewhat resembling its European fortress namesake. Six bedrooms, five bathrooms, two spa baths and a jacuzzi. Four fireplaces as well as space to hang 12 people's skis, boards and jackets in the drying room. Carcassonne is renowned in town for being too big to be considered a chalet. Since coming into my ownership; the locals seem to have mellowed somewhat in their distaste for the place.

I walk up the drive and dig my keys from my pocket. Looking down at the large brass key in my hand, it seems more suitably fitting for a castle or palace than a chalet. I let myself in quietly and make my way into the kitchen.

I find Seal and Xi both standing in the kitchen nestled in large fluffy bathrobes.

'Good Morning, Miss Ava.' Xi bows ever so slightly.

'Stop shouting,' Seal grimaces from his place beside the sink, groaning uncomfortably. His Boston accent is much thicker than usual.

'Seems Mr Seal had a little too much lager last night, Miss,' Xi chuckles quietly, flipping a pancake on the stove. The scent of bacon and eggs wafts toward me.

'Any chance there's enough there for three?' I smile across at him, unwrapping my scarf and pulling off my jacket, laying them across an empty breakfast stool. I make my way to the sink beside Seal and rinse my empty eco cup.

'Coffee or juice?' I whisper across to him, empathising with his state.

'Coffee. For the love of god, coffee.' He stomps his way to the other side of the large grey island and flops down into a chair.

'Do either of you want me to light the fire?' I hit the button on the espresso machine and look up eyeing the cold hearth in the adjacent living room.

'You know, I never believed you when you told us you were a pyromaniac. Until we got here and now you seem to want to set everything on fire.' Seal grumbles, resting his head against his arms on the benchtop.

I hand Seal and Xi each a mug of fresh coffee and pour myself a glass of orange juice. The three of us sit down to eat when a young woman of about 25 appears at the base of the stairs.

'Hi Ava, Xi, Seal.' She blushes as she smiles at Seal. Xi and I both turn to eyeball Seal critically.

'If I find out you played 'hide the sausage' with the new housekeeper, you are going to be in serious trouble,' I hiss under my breath at Seal. He promptly chokes on a slice of pancake. That answers that question, I suppose.

'What is on the agenda today, Miss Ava?' Xi smiles across at me, pouring more syrup onto his plate.

'I'm not sure. I don't have any big plans, and as far as I can tell, there isn't any urgent business to attend to.' I shrug, sipping my juice.

'We could always fly into the city and uh, shop?' He suggests.

'Xi, if you'd like to head into the city, you are more than welcome to. I do not need the helicopter, so I don't mind if you'd like to borrow it.'

'I wouldn't be particularly comfortable with that, Miss Ava.' He slices a stack of his pancakes.

'I can't come with you today. I'm sorry. I'm meant to be having lunch with Ryan when he gets off nights. Tomorrow I promised him we'd spend the day together.' I frown at Xi, realising I hadn't planned on what we'd spend the day doing tomorrow.

'Perhaps you could both come here, watch a movie, play a round of pool,' Xi suggests helpfully. Xi and Seal have taken quite a liking to Ryan in the weeks we have been here. There is quite a secure bromance building between the three of them.

'Well, I know what I'm going to be doing. Miss Ava, I'm sorry, but you're on your own today.' Seal groans between us.

I pat him on the back gently, shaking my head. Catching sight of the giant clock hanging over the fridge, I realise I need to get back to Arendelle to start cooking lunch if I want my lasagne done in time for Ryan to finish his shift. I've never understood why he has to 'go in' when he's on nights here. Surely being on-call would be enough considering how little happens in Hotham or Dinner Plain at night.

'I have a day of lasagne making ahead of me gentlemen. If you need me, I'll be at Arendelle.' I smile at them both before taking my plate to the sink. Wrapping my scarf around my neck and dragging on my snow jacket, I blow them each an air kiss and head for the front door.

'Miss Ava!' I hear Lauren the housekeeper call from the hall. I turn to see her eyeing me speculatively.

'Yes, Lauren?' I turn toward her.

'I was wondering if it might be possible to...well...ask your permission to use the jacuzzi?' She shrugs, looking down at the floor.

'Oh, uh. Sure? As long as neither of the guys wants to use it, I don't see why not?' I smile at her, opening the front door. 'Have a nice day.'

By the time lunch rolls around and Ryan returns home I've managed to make lasagne, garlic bread and salad. I even found some fresh citrus and made up a jug of sangria, just for fun.

'Smells amazing honey,' Ryan calls from the drying room. I hear him start the washing machine and laugh at him when he enters the kitchen looking freezing in nothing but his boxers.

'It's cold out there! I'm going to take a shower,' He leans across to kiss me as I pull a face.

'Yeah, I was vomited on twice,' He rolls his eyes. He smacks me playfully on the bum before heading to the bathroom and jumping in the shower.

Freshly bathed, Ryan strolls out of the bathroom wearing nothing but a fluffy white towel around his waist and sits happily at the table, eyeing the spread before him. His beach blonde hair dripping slightly.

'Oh darling, you didn't have to dress up on my account,' I tease, eyeing his bare chest.

We fall into our usual rhythm where I tell him about my past 12 hours, and he fills me in on the gory details of his shift.

'...and that's when she threw up on me. We were honestly about to hand her over to the medical centre. This girl couldn't have waited 30 more seconds,' he grumbles, stabbing his lasagne overzealously.

'I couldn't do it,' I laugh, pouring myself another glass of sangria.

'What's on your agenda for this afternoon?' Ryan reaches across to hold my hand.

'I think I might take a nap and then I don't know what. I might call Jia or Chen to check-in. It has been a few days since I've spoken to them,' I shrug.

'You know, I was thinking. I don't have to go back to Melbourne when the season ends. I was talking to Jim at the medical centre, and he said they'd happily take me on full time to cover the Summer season too,' Ryan states conversationally. I put down my fork and take a large gulp of my wine.

'Ryan, we talked about this,' I sigh.

'And I want to discuss it again. I don't want you to go back to Singapore. Why can't we live here in Carcassonne and you can fly back and forth to Singapore as you need to? Winnie is gone, Tony has disappeared. Why go back and dig up bygones?' Ryan implores me.

'I can barely sleep at night knowing Tony is still out there and Winnie's death might be on his hands.'

'Might! Exactly, Ava. Might. This is nuts! Why are you insisting Tari must read the journal, why not get Xi or Seal to read it?!' Ryan throws his hands in the air.

'Ryan, that's not fair,' I frown.

'Not fair? Not fair? I turn up in Singapore to find you injured in the street and in the arms of that Chen no less! And you expect me to just be okay with you wanting to go straight back to him?' He stands up and begins to pace.

'I'm not 'going back to him' Ryan! He is my interim CEO, and I can't run HEH without him. I can't understand why you are making this so difficult. The sooner I can get to the bottom of this, the faster I can come home, and we can talk about the future. But I can't move forward until I know the truth.' I watch him pace backward and forward.

I wish he were wearing more clothing right now. Watching him stomp around in a towel is doing things to me that a conversation this serious really ought not to be derailed by. Ryan suddenly stops and looks at me.

'Stop giving me 'the look'. We are trying to have a serious conversation here,' He grouches, trying to avoid making eye contact with me.

'What look? I can't help the fact that you're standing here half-naked trying to have this conversation.' I bat my eyelashes innocently.

'Stop it,' he tries to keep a straight face, a grin slowly breaking out. He saunters toward me, leaning over the table until we are nose to nose.

'What do you say we 'put a pin' in this conversation until after our siesta?' His eyes twinkle wickedly.

'I thought you wanted to solve all our problems, right now?' I stare at him, wide-eyed.

'And what if this were to happen...' He reaches down and slowly tugs his towel lose, the fabric dropping to the floor in a pile around his feet.

'Oh my! What will the neighbours think?' I gasp feigning embarrassment.

Pushing my chair out from behind the table, Ryan smells of my most favourite things, alpine, snow and Ryan himself. Suddenly he ducks down, lifts me out of the chair and throws me over his shoulder until I am met with a beautiful view of his pert, tanned bottom. I squeal as I smack it playfully. Ryan slowly walks up the stairs, and suddenly all thought of calling Chen evaporates.

'You're still going to go, aren't you?' Ryan sighs, tracing his fingers down my spine as we lay in a tangled mess in bed.

'I know it doesn't make sense to you, but this is something I just have to do.' I eye him hesitantly, my face half-buried in my pillow.

'What if it doesn't just take a few weeks? What if it's months or years?' Ryan whispers, his fingers tickling my sensitive skin.

'I don't know,' I whisper back, wishing I had the answers.

'I don't know if I can wait that long,' Ryan frowns, rolling onto his back and tucking his hands behind his head.

'I understand,' I breathe, feeling like I've been punched in the stomach. I feel the hot prickle of tears, willing them desperately not to fall.

'That's all you've got to say? You understand?!' Ryan exclaims, jumping out of bed and searching for clothes. 'And here I was thinking we were doing something that 'meant something', Ava.' He shakes his head in frustration.

'I'm not saying that I don't see a future with you, Ryan, I would love that. I just can't promise when that future will start or what it looks like right now,' I sniffle, at a loss for what else to say. 'I don't want this to end just because I'm going away.'

'You're asking me to wait for you. Do you hear yourself, Ava? Do you know how selfish you sound?' Ryan runs an exasperated hand through his hair, leaving it poking out this way and that. 'I thought you said this money wouldn't change you.'

'That's not fair! This isn't about money! I'm doing this because it is what's right!' I raise my voice sitting up in bed now, anger coursing through me.

'The old Ava would never have considered gallivanting across the planet to play detective,' he fumes, finding a pair of sweatpants and dragging them on.

'I'm still the same Ava, Ryan. Besides, you didn't seem to mind the money so much when you needed the helicopter to get to Melbourne for Greg's bucks party!' I'm seeing red now. 'Or when you wanted to give up your rental to save money and live here with me!'

'Well forgive me for wanting to have an excuse to come back to Dinner Plain every night. I can see now that it was a mistake.' Ryan drags on a t-shirt and storms downstairs. I drag the comforter up off the bed and follow him downstairs, tripping and stumbling the way down.

'So that's it? You're just going to walk out and never come back?' I cry harder, finding any possession of Ryan's I can lay my hands on and launching it toward him.

'Yeah, I guess so. Do me a favour, get Xi or Seal to come by and get my stuff. I'm going to finish the season from their place.'

'Newsflash buddy! 'Their place' IS MY CHALET TOO!' I fling a beanie toward him.

I watch as he storms out the door, throws his bag in the bed of the truck and drives up the laneway toward Carcassonne, the tyres slipping on the ice. I stomp back upstairs and run a bath in the large copper tub. Digging around in my handbag, I grab my phone and text Xi.

> Give Ryan Seal's keys to Carcassonne.
> We're going back to Singapore tomorrow,
> can I ask you to make the arrangements?
> -A

Not a minute later, Xi's reply comes through.

> Consider it done.
> Seal and I will pick you up at 8 am.
> Xi

Pouring an array of scented oils into the bathtub, I watch it slowly heat and spread across the surface. Sliding into the steaming water, I wonder how today possibly went so wrong. I guess I knew all along that we'd either survive this or we wouldn't. I suppose Ryan decided he didn't want to wait to find out.

The tears continue to trickle down, dripping off my chin into the tub. I turn and look at Winnie's ring sitting safely on the bench beside the tub. The large pink centre diamond reflecting the afternoon light. Does he have a point? Is learning the truth about Winnie's death just destructive and unnecessary?

I shake my head to myself.

No, it isn't unnecessary. If Tony had anything to do with Winnie's death, he needs to be held accountable, and without a body for an autopsy, I am Winnie's only hope for justice.

2

The flight back to Singapore seemed to take far longer than previous trips. Perhaps it was my anxiety to get back to Tari and get to the bottom of the conundrum that was Winnie's death, but I found it difficult to sleep or relax, with so many thoughts whirring around in my head.

Did I overreact to Ryan? Did he have a good point? Am I just digging up pointless drama over Winnie's death?

I thumb frustratedly through the journal, watching the pages glide from one side to the other.

With the look on Ryan's face as he walked out the door, burned into my brain, I could see it every time I closed my eyes. The anger, the betrayal.

Was Ryan, right? Was I eager to get back to Singapore because...I scarcely want to finish the thought, knowing how guilty it made me feel...to get back to Chen? It wouldn't matter, even if I were eager to see him again. Chen is promised to Mei. Nothing can ever happen between us.

Images of Chen begin to flip through my brain like a Rolodex, his hands in his silky black hair, standing with his jacket slung over one shoulder, his perfectly narrow waist with a crisp white shirt tucked into his pants. His long slender fingers as they thread between mine, palm to palm. I shake my head, trying to rid myself of the imagery. I get up and begin pacing for the hundredth time. Seal and Xi having given up watching me wear holes in the carpet, no longer felt the need to offer assistance or advice. I can tell they are both feeling bereft at the thought of their newfound 'brother' Ryan, being exiled from the family. I have taken to thinking of them, in these past few restless hours, as children of the divorce. Seal sits moping in a recliner, watching a movie with headphones in—his hangover from the previous day still haunting him. Xi stretched out in the sleeper cabin, peacefully snoring. I pace in time with his breath sounds, whoosh, whistle, whoosh, whistle. Listening to Xi's breathing reminded me of watching my grandfather nap. So peaceful, so relaxed. The absolute opposite to how I am feeling. I sigh heavily and abandon my pacing, deciding on a peppermint tea before a nap.

After landing in Singapore, I instruct Xi and the after-hours guy to head straight for Spago in our big black SUV. Not only was I in desperate need of a cocktail, but I couldn't imagine being in Singapore a second longer without seeing Tari, how I missed her support and encouragement these past two months.

Arriving at the Marina Bay Sands hotel, I manage to contain myself and avoid elbowing people out of the way to get into an elevator sooner. Stalking out into the rooftop bar, I feel my heart sink.

I knew I should have checked to see if she was working tonight.

Glumly, I step up to the bar and flop down into a chair. Xi and Seal join me quietly, one perched on either side.

'Not a worry Miss, we will find Miss Tari, tomorrow,' Xi pats my hand on the bar top. The sound of a familiar cackle draws our attention toward the far corner toward the lounges. There, with a high ponytail and extremely short dress, sits Jia. I can barely contain myself, jumping from the bar and launching myself across the space at her. After momentarily catching her unawares, she hugs me back fiercely.

'Ava?' She laughs down at me.

'Oh, Jia. I have missed you!' I cry, only to be tapped on the shoulder. Turning around, I realise Tari is standing beside the lounger carrying a tray of cosmopolitans.

'Tari!' I squeal, throwing my arms around her, almost causing her to drop her wares.

'What on earth are you doing back here, girl?' She frowns at me.

'It is such a long story, but I found the journal,' I whisper, looking around the room for curious eyes and ears.

'Okay,' she whispers back, humorously.

I flop down into the lounger beside Jia and for the first time in days, feel at peace.

The next morning, I awake in my bed in the Beach

Street penthouse. Rolling over I check the time on the alarm clock: 8.00 am.

Ugh, I suppose I had better get up. I wonder if Xi let Gladys know we were coming home. I hope so; I could desperately use scrambled eggs and bacon this morning.

After showering and dressing, I apply a little makeup and make my way downstairs. The smell of bacon and fresh espresso coffee tells me Gladys is in the kitchen.

'Good Morning, Miss Ava!' She greets me with the brightest of smiles. 'I have missed you these past weeks.'

'I have missed you too Gladys,' I smile across at her, taking a seat and sipping my pre-poured orange juice.

'Do you have a big day ahead?' She turns to hand me a cup of coffee.

'To be honest, I don't even know if anyone else knows I am back in town. I suspect it might be quite a shock for some people.' I smirk into my coffee cup.

'Mr Chen came past last week to enquire as to when you might be returning, Miss Ava.' Her eye twinkles as she delivers this news.

'Did he now?' I ponder this piece of information.

I wonder why.

By 8.30, Xi and Seal promptly arrive, both suited and very handsome as always.

'Good morning, gents.' I smile at them both as I join them at the elevator.

'You seem to be in good spirits this morning Miss Ava.' Xi smiles at me appraisingly.

Upon arriving at the office, I notice HEH tower

has an entirely different vibe from the last time I left it. Without Tony's poisonous presence, the space felt cleansed somehow.

'I heard Jia had someone burn sage in the Legal suites.' Seal smiles, observing that he too felt the space had changed following Tony's departure. Sasha greeted us at the executive suite entry on the top floor with a colourful bouquet.

'Welcome back, Miss Ava!' She smiled at me broadly, passing across the bouquet and leading me into Winnie's office. 'I have so much to tell you!'

'Let me settle in for a bit Sasha, and when we have lunch you can tell me all about it!' I smile at her, dragging off my coat to hang in the coat nook. Following my old routine, I dig out the laptop, papers and Monty and place them all on the large oak desk in the centre of the gargantuan window. I head to the cupboard concealing the wine fridge and withdraw a bottle of sparkling water. Sipping contemplatively, I wander to the window and look out across Singapore, the vista so perfectly capturing the Marina Bay Sands building and the Singapore Flyer. Even though the weather was slightly overcast, the day outside looked stunning.

An unexpected arrival behind me draws my attention away from the view. Turning, I spot Samuel Chen standing on the precipice.

'I had not expected you back yet.' He frowns, his silky black hair falling across his face. He tucks it behind one ear with slender fingers, his eyes taking in my black slacks and silk blouse before coming to rest on my loose curls and face. I suppress a shudder; I'd forgotten what it felt like to be appraised by his gaze.

'I decided it was time to check-in, in person.' I smile back at him, stepping forward to lean against Winnie's desk. 'How have things been here?'

'Peaceful. Without drama, you could say,' he smirks at me as he paces toward the lounges, perching on the edge of the tall wingback.

'I presume you mean since Tony's departure,' I enquire.

'Presume away,' Chen chuckles, scratching his jaw. The sound does things to me in very unprofessional places. 'How long are we to enjoy your company before you jet off again?' I can't help but note the slight twinge of sadness in his delivery.

'I don't anticipate going anywhere for the foreseeable future. Tari and I have a bit of detective work to complete, and I can't see how that would take us out of Singapore.' I take a sip from my sparkling water.

'Can I persuade you to join me for lunch today? I haven't been to Newton Circus since our last visit, and I'd appreciate the company.' He eyes me hopefully.

'I am sorry, Chen, but I have promised Sasha, we will have lunch together. Perhaps we can visit the hawker centre together later this week?' I try to offer a reassuring look, but it seems to fall short.

'Of course, Miss Ava,' Chen looks down at his hands.

'How is Miss Mei? I haven't seen her or your family since the...ball,' I realise that I haven't asked Chen what happened at the ball following Tony and my rather dramatic departure.

'She is well, as are my parents,' he doesn't look up to answer me.

'Did I leave you with much of a mess to clean up after I was taken to the hospital?' I frown, looking across at him.

'No. Abbie and I took care of it; most guests left the event none the wiser to the goings-on that night,' he sighs disapprovingly.

'Why do I get the impression you are still angry with me for the way the evening unfolded?' I cross my arms, frowning harder now.

'Will you not admit it was all a little unnecessary?' He rolls his eyes, staring at the table before him.

'Unnecessary? Tony gave me a concussion after I caught him trying to sell our Foundation land to a private developer!' I stare at him, flabbergasted. 'Are you intentionally trying to rile me up?'

'And what if I were?' His cheeky smile returns, his baby blue eyes sweeping up to meet mine.

'Then I'd say it is working,' I grumble, eliciting a sexy chuckle from Chen.

'Seeing as you inquired after my family, it is only right that I ask how Golden Boy is?' Chen grumbles politely. 'Pining no doubt for your timely return to the alps? I personally cannot fathom your interest in the place; I can scarcely imagine anything less appealing than the sodden wet that is snow.'

'Ryan and I had a disagreement which is partly why I returned to Singapore. As far as I am aware, he is no longer interested in me.' I take another sip of my water, taking extra care not to choke on it.

'Ah well, I am sorry to hear that,' Chen eyes me curiously, a slight embarrassment creeping into his cheeks.

'I'm sure you are,' I state bluntly. 'Do you have anything business-related to report or did you just drop in to exchange pleasantries?'

'Straight to the point as always, Miss Elias. I did want to discuss one matter with you; that of your new General Counsel.' Chen eyes me warily.

I sigh heavily. 'What about Jia, Chen?'

'Miss Chang is doing an excellent job, and I approve of her employment,' he delivers with a straight face.

'Really? No snide remarks, no minor disapprovals?' I cock an eyebrow at him, wondering what his game is.

'No tricks, no quid-pro-quo. I think Jia is a good match for HEH and I believe you chose well. I just wanted you to know I respect your decision.' He smiles warmly up at me.

'Well then, thank you for taking the time to let me know. I am glad you are finding Jia suitable to your needs.'

'Do I dare ask what this 'detective work' is that you plan to embark upon?' He smiles wryly at me.

'I don't think Winnie's death was due to natural causes and I intend to find out once and for all.' I nod to myself.

'Didn't Winnie have his body cremated?' Chen frowns up at me.

'He did.'

'Then, without a body, how do you intend to prove what happened to him?' Chen laughs.

'I'd have thought you'd be pleased with my new-found occupation. The more I am focussed elsewhere, the more autonomy you have to run HEH.' I smile down at him, trying to derail the conversation.

'Is that your way of telling me to 'butt out'?' Chen

smirks.

'Yes,' I laugh. Chen stands gracefully and glides toward the desk. Taking my hand, he kisses my knuckles.

'A pleasure to have you home, Miss Ava.' He breathes. Standing so close, I am reminded of the day we spent in the markets together, holding hands and drinking iced lime juice. But so much has happened since then.

'Chen...' I whisper, my gaze locked on our hands. I turn my hand and intertwine my fingers with his.

It would take but a second to lean forward and kiss him. Just one second, and no one ever need know, right? Why does this feel so alluring, so illicit, so sexy?

A knock at the door causes him to drop my hand and step away from me. I know I have no right to be, but my body is disappointed about the interruption.

'Miss Ava, I'm sorry to interrupt, but Mr Chen's office called to remind him about the meeting in Conference room 1.' Sasha bobs an apology and departs again.

'Care to sit in and scrutinise my meeting?' Chen chuckles.

'I'd be delighted to,' I laugh, grabbing Monty and my compendium before following Chen to the elevator.

I watch Chen dreamily as he conducts the meeting. He speaks with such confidence, such enthusiasm. He commands the space easily, comfortably.

Maybe that's what being a Harvard graduate gets you? Maybe that's just what being a Chen gets you?

I zone out, mesmerised by Chen's body as he speaks; observing his every little movement. The way he straightens his cuffs when he has waved his arms around too enthusiastically or the gentlest rise of his chest when he breathes, pausing in between sentences.

Why do I feel like a schoolgirl with a crush on a senior? What is it about Chen that feels so unobtainable? Is it because I know he's off-limits? Is it because he feels exciting and illicit?

Images of Ryan's face as he walked out of Arendelle pop into my mind. I miss him. Strong, steadfast, reliable, Ryan. Sexy, stubborn, charismatic, Chen.

Trying desperately to rid myself of the overwhelming sense of nostalgia, I distract myself by trying to imagine Chen in unfamiliar situations and attire. Scuba diving, bare-chested and glistening, knee-deep in crystal blue water. Hmm.

As a doctor, in dark blue surgical scrubs with a stethoscope around his neck, his silky black hair peeking out under a scrub cap. The image morphs suddenly, too close to home to Ryan in his dark green paramedic jumpsuit, shoulder mounted radio, and his stethoscope tucked into his back pocket. That was not an image I had to imagine. I'd seen it many, many times.

Come to think of it; I'd seen Ryan in a tuxedo as well as wearing board shorts at St Kilda beach.

I frown to myself, deciding perhaps the best distraction was listening to Chen discussing the latest Profit and Loss statements.

Damn, how does he manage to make even that sound sexy?

3

I could scarcely contain my excitement as Monday rolled around. These past months I had missed my dinners with the Invisible Women. Before Xi has come to a stop in front of Margot's warehouse, I launch myself out of the car. I feel Seal racing to keep up behind me. Barging into the cavernous bar space, I am met by three sets of curious eyes. Jia, as usual, perched behind the bar making cocktails in a copper shaker. Her long ponytail sweeps this way and that as she shakes the mixture enthusiastically. Linah sits perched on the sofa, her bright eyes framed by her sharp black bob. Margot stands frozen, halfway down the stairs from her studio. Her glasses were teetering precariously from the tip of her nose.

'AVA!' She cries, launching herself toward me, her blonde curls billowing behind her. I catch her in a firm embrace, giggling at her excitement.

'I can honestly say, I never thought you'd be this happy to see me,' I laugh at her.

'Come, come, come.' She grabs my hand and drags

me toward the sofas. I lean over, and air-kiss Linah before sitting on a cushion by her feet and kicking off my heels.

'I am always caught by how beautiful this place is, Margot,' I smile up at her, taking in the copper pendant lights and red brick facade.

'It hasn't been the same without you,' Jia pipes in, carrying across a large tray of dirty martinis.

'Or Seal,' snickers Margot, reaching for a cocktail. Jia smacks her hand playfully while loudly shushing her, looking around to check if Seal was within earshot.

'About that, Jia. You might wanna make sure he's been tested before you let him near your cookie jar,' I frown, trying to count in my head how many ladies I recall 'visiting' Carcassonne.

'Noted,' she nods thoughtfully.

'How is that possible? You've only been gone for two months! Who manages to find people in a remote alpine town to sleep with when they're only in the country for eight weeks!' Linah laughs confusedly.

'You'd be surprised how many people go on ski vacations looking to let loose and experience a romantic fling,' Margot nods sagely from the wingback. The three of us turn to look at her.

'What? I lived a little before I met my man.' She shrugs before reaching across and taking a glass from Jia's tray.

'Now Ava, fill us in on what happened since we saw you last. We're dying to hear!' Linah pats my shoulder.

'Where to begin? I guess in an abridged version; I found the second half of Winnie's journal and Ryan and I broke up,' I shrug, uncertain how else to phrase it.

'No!' Margot gasps. Linah and Jia exchange looks.

'He wasn't happy about me coming back to Singapore to 'chase ghosts'. He said he didn't appreciate me expecting him to wait for me.' I take a large gulp of cocktail.

'But did you ask him to wait for you?' Linah frowns.

'Not really, I told him I didn't want things to change and that I'd be back as soon as I could,' I sigh, taking another drink.

'Well it's his loss,' Jia states firmly, leaning over to top up my glass. Just at that moment, the buzzer sounds signifying the arrival of dinner.

'What are we eating tonight?' I smile at Margot as Jia heads for the door.

'Spanish Tapas,' she winks at me, playing delicately with my hair.

'I'm sorry about Ryan. I know how you felt about him,' she whispers gently.

'Thanks, Margot. I realised I couldn't fight him on it. He wasn't wrong; I suppose in a way I was asking him to wait for me,' I shrug.

'He's a fool; you are far too precious to let go of so easily.' She pats me tenderly. 'Let's go console ourselves with grilled everything and fried cheese sticks.'

'Sounds like the perfect consolation to me!' I smile up at her.

'...so then Chen says, 'maybe we should ask Ava',' Jia laughs, popping another spicy meatball into her mouth.

'I can't believe what a 180 he's done! It doesn't even sound like the same man.' I shake my head, dipping a fried mozzarella stick in chilli capsicum sauce.

'Ever since the ball he's been different. We even noticed it watching him on the news, didn't we Margot?' Linah nods in agreement, 'less cocky somehow.'

'But still just as beautiful,' Margot sighs, sipping her cocktail. I can't help but smile to myself.

'I think if Ryan has left the picture, then you really should investigate your options with Chen,' Jia states matter-of-factly. 'Don't look at me like that Linah. She said there was a spark last time; maybe it'll come back?' She winks across at me.

'Is he still supposedly betrothed, or promised or whatever to Mei Yang?' I look around the table quizzically.

'Oh, well yes, there is that small inconvenience,' Margot chuckles. I roll my eyes and laugh.

'Have you had a chance to see what the journal says? Does Winnie state in it that he thinks Tony was trying to kill him?' Linah stares at me wide-eyed.

'I haven't had a chance to read it with Tari yet. We're catching up tomorrow night to take a look.' I shrug.

'What are you going to do if you find something in there? I told the others; I haven't seen nor heard from Tony since the ball. He completely disappeared off the radar. Chen too admitted it was eerily quiet without him,' Jia states, stabbing at an olive aggressively with her fork.

'I don't know what I'll do. I just know that I need to find out what happened. Otherwise I will never sleep soundly again!' I sigh, exasperated.

'We are all here if you need anything,' Linah smiles encouragingly across at me.

'That's about all there is from me! Please tell me you all have far more exciting news?' I look around at them all. We fall into easy conversation and pick back up as though no time had passed.

The next night Tari came across to the penthouse after her shift ended. She brought food from the restaurant, which gave Gladys my housekeeper a night off.

'What do we have here?' I smell the takeaway bag appreciatively.

'Dim sum, duck pancakes, those fried crab ball things you like,' she smiles across at me, handing me a plate.

'You are my angel.' I place the plate down and grab a bottle of prosecco out of the wine fridge. Munching away in silence, Tari flips through the pages at the beginning of Winnie's journal.

'Hm,' is all she says.

'Hm, good or hm bad?' I eye her impatiently.

'Well if you're waiting for him just to come out and say 'Tony killed me' you're in for a disappointment.' She cocks an eyebrow at me.

'He doesn't put it that plainly?' I sigh, deflated.

'Nope, he is mostly journaling his symptoms and his arrangements for his passing and your takeover.'

'I hate that word.'

'Passing?'

'Takeover.' I roll my eyes.

'I'll take it home and look at it side by side with the other one and see what I can suss out.' She pats my hand encouragingly. 'Do you want me to tell you about something funny I read in one of his other journals?' Her eyes twinkle mischievously.

'If it will make me laugh, sure,' I smile at her, shoving a whole dim sim in my mouth.

'In one of his journals from about 30 years ago, he went on this partying rampage through Europe.' She stares at me straight-faced. I nearly choke on my dim sim.

'What?' I garble. 'Winnie? A partying rampage?'

'Yup. That's exactly what my face looked like when I read it. He details these 12 weeks he spent travelling across Europe, and if I didn't know any better, I would think he...' she trailed off, looking at me uncomfortably.

'He what?' I stare at her open-mouthed.

'It feels weird talking to you about this; he kind of feels almost grandfatherly to you,' she shrugs, embarrassed.

'Don't leave me hanging! What did he write about?' I frown.

'I think it might have been the uh, 'notches on his bedpost'.' She grimaces awkwardly.

'Wha....?' I frown before it clicks. 'Oh my god, Tari! Seriously? His conquests?' I whisper. She nods enthusiastically.

'How...wait, maybe I shouldn't be asking this?' I frown at myself, embarrassed.

'How many?' She raises her eyebrows at me.

'Do I want to know, or am I going to lose my dinner?' I bury my face behind my hands.

'Three,' she states categorically.

'Three! He bedded three completely random women, in how many weeks?' I exclaim.

'12 weeks. One in France, Spain, and Switzerland.' She smiles at me cheekily. 'Who'd have thought Winnie would have a fun side.'

'He did name his jet 'Screaming Eagle'. I had to assume there'd been some 'wild rides' on there at some point,' I cringe, giggling at the bizarreness of this revelation.

Well, Winnie, I'm glad to know you had real fun at some point in your life, before it was overtaken by business obligations.

'Tell me more about this trip; I've always dreamed of visiting Europe!' I giggle at Tari as I dip a crab ball in chilli jam. 'But maybe skip over the illicit trysts!'

'Oh Ava, he writes so beautifully, reading his journal is like being there!' She laughs, sipping her Prosecco. We spent the rest of the evening trawling through images on the internet of Paris, Budapest, Rome and Zurich.

As a few weeks passed, life in Singapore settled into a comfortable routine. I began sitting in on Chen's meetings as an observer. I watched the way he interacted with the staff and stakeholders with deep curiosity. After drawing one meeting to a close, Chen waited for the other staff to depart before turning to me.

'As you can see, nothing much has changed in the time you were away,' he smiles down the table at me. 'But I can tell you that everyone is happy to see you back.'

I smile at the compliment, 'Thank you, Chen. That means a great deal to me.' I look down at the notes in my compendium, 'There was one thing I wanted to clarify?'

'Please?' Chen walks over to take a seat beside me. Sitting so close, I can smell everything that always reminds me of him—mint, his aftershave and simply Chen.

'Has a new contract been drawn up for the Port of Oman? After the Pirate incident earlier this year, I'd like to double-check the nitty-gritty of the next one.' I turn to look at him, realising just how close he is. I can see the slight ring of dark blue that encircles his iris. His long black lashes fan onto his cheeks when he blinks.

'Great question! Let's go see Jia and find out, shall we?' He smiles broadly at me, a cheeky smirk playing at the corner of his lips. Arriving at Jia's office, we notice she seems rather flustered.

'Jia, are you okay?' I step in the door, shutting it behind Chen.

'I've had better days.' She paces backward and forward, her ponytail swinging erratically.

'Tell us what's troubling you, and we will see if we can help,' Chen offers, unbuttoning his jacket and taking a seat opposite her desk.

'Ava, you might want to sit down for this too,' Jia states, pointing to the second chair.

'You're starting to worry me, Jia, what's going on?' I frown, sitting as directed.

'I received an envelope today via courier. It is a court summons.' She stops and turns to look at us. 'To contest Winnie's Will.' I feel the world fall away at my feet.

'I beg your pardon?' Chen grinds out through clenched teeth.

'I told you it was bad.' Jia sits behind her desk and leans toward me.

'Ava, are you okay?'

'On what grounds?' I stare at her.

'Paternity. A man has come forward claiming that Winnie is his biological father, and therefore is entitled to an inheritance.' Jia frowns, looking back down at the papers in front of her. I silently hold out my hand for the package. Jia reluctantly acquiesces, passing it across the desk. I flip through the pages, holding them aloft for Chen to peer over my shoulder.

'What precisely does he want?' Chen grumbles, his minty breath fanning the side of my face.

'Everything,' Jia growls.

Fuck.

'Winnie always told me he had no family. Surely this is just some whack-job looking for his five minutes of fame?' I shake my head, confused.

'Five minutes of fame is correct, the rest - I'm not so sure about. It is not unheard of for a man to sire a child he knew nothing about. Or sire one and ignore their existence.' Jia stands and commences pacing again. 'The case isn't our biggest problem. As soon as he knows we've been served the papers, I'll bet he goes to the media.' I freeze and turn to look at Chen. His face is as anxious and frightened as mine.

'Trust me, Ava, this is bad news for all of us. HEH really can't afford another scandalous media scrum after the pirate incident. Thank god they never got word about your little scuffle with Tony.' He rolls his eyes, running his hands through his hair.

'We need to get the PR team in a conference room immediately, to talk about a strategy and what we plan to say when this gets out.' I look between Chen and Jia, feeling my head begin to pound.

Chen and I ride the elevator down to the conference rooms in a tense silence. Chen sighs beside me, his hands finding his hair once again. 'I'm ashamed to have to ask this of you, but do you know if there is any chance...' He whispers. I shake my head, staring at my feet.

'I have no idea, Chen. Winnie was no monk, but I can't imagine he would be reckless enough to father a child without caring for it.' I can barely get the words out. For what feels like the tenth time since I met Winnie, I sense the instability of the world beneath my feet. Chen quietly drops his hand, entwining his fingers through mine in a silent gesture of tenderness. I turn to look up into his eyes, a sea of turmoil staring back at me.

'I don't even know where to begin, Chen,' I whisper. He hesitates before he leans over and sweetly places a kiss on the top of my head.

'We'll figure it out, I promise,' he whispers into my hair. As the elevator ticks toward the conference floor, we slowly disentangle our fingers and step apart. It is beginning to get harder to ignore his advances. I wonder if Chen feels it too?

The meeting with the PR team did not leave me with much hope for 'spinning this to protect HEH'. I stare down at Winnie's ring as the meeting begins to wrap up, the emerald cut centre diamond glinting up at me.

'Ava?' I look up to see Abbie and the rest of the room staring at me; Chen's face plastered with a familiar humorous smirk.

'I'm sorry, pardon?' I shake my head in apology.

'Do you have anything of Winnie's that might be able to be used for a paternity test?' Abbie repeats her question, looking at me expectantly.

'Uh...,' My fuzzy brain refusing to cooperate.

'It would help us to at least show the media we are cooperating. A hairbrush or comb? A hat containing fallen hair?' Abbie nods at me reassuringly. One of the other Executive Directors pipes up, interrupting my train of thought.

'You might want to check with a scientist about that. I read a lot of crime fiction, and for hair to be viable for a paternity test it has to have the follicle, not just the shaft.' He looks around the table to a series of confused faces. 'It's the part that grows from the scalp, not just the 'hair' part...' he tries to explain, pointing to his head.

'Mr Adams, thank you for your contribution, and yes, we should clarify the requirements with a professional before making any public statements.' Abbie's gaze returns to me.

'I understand what Mr Adams is referring to, and come to think of it; yes. I think I can find something that might help.' I smile to myself, staring at Monty in my hands. The star diamond in the lid, glinting as I roll the Mont Blanc pen between my fingers.

'Okay, spill the beans, Missy,' Chen chuckles down at me in the elevator. I look up at him in surprise.

'What?'

'What has you grinning like you're the cat that got the cream?' I feel the heat radiating off him as he leans in close. I take a deep breath, trying to slow my racing heart.

'I want to preface this by saying; I haven't entirely

forgiven you for your behaviour before I went away. But why don't you come to the penthouse for dinner tonight and I'll explain it to you?' I look up at him, feeling the heat of his gaze upon me. He reaches up, with one long finger to brush a curl behind my ear, tracing a line back down my cheekbone. The elevator comes to a gentle stop as the doors open before us.

'Mei.' I frown, looking toward the door.

'Please don't ruin the moment, Ava,' Chen whispers.

'No. Mei is here,' I state firmly, stepping out of his reach and exiting the elevator. I stand in the lobby where Mei Yang had been standing moments before. Looking about the space, unable to see her, I turn and walk out the front door toward the street, spotting her beside the flower bed.

'Mei?' I approach her apprehensively. She turns toward me, a face of thunder. I look around, hoping no one is within eavesdropping distance.

'Do you know who I am?' She leers at me.

'Yes. We've met...' I choke.

'Do you know that the Yang and Chen families have been planning our marriage since before I was born?' She seethes, her eyes welling up with fury.

'I had read that somewhere...' I whisper sheepishly.

'Chen and I may not have feelings for one another, but we understand the obligations we have toward our families. If the two of you are to continue 'carrying on', I'd appreciate it if you'd do so with more discretion in future,' she spits, blinking back tears.

'I cannot apologise enough for our behaviour. I wasn't entirely certain of how absolute your future betrothal was,' I frown, feeling myself blush.

'I am sure Chen led you to believe that it is not set in stone; however, our families' expectations are too great for us to disobey.' She turns to look me in the eye. 'I have no intimate designs on Samuel Chen, and so if you wish to pursue an intimate relationship, I will not make a scene. I only ask that you do so in privacy, out of respect for our impending 'marriage'.' All I can bring myself to do is nod mutely.

'If you will excuse me, I have an event to get to.' She nods curtly at me before turning on her heel and stepping into a sleek black Mercedes town car. I feel like I've been kicked in the stomach.

What was I thinking? I have no right to be making eyes at Chen. Besides, I don't even know how I feel about him as a person right now. But, did she just permit me to sleep with her fiancée? I turn slowly back toward the door to come face to face with Chen, his face contorted in anguish.

'So now you know,' he frowns, staring at my feet. I step forward and try to catch his eye. He evades my probing gaze.

'Why are you upset?' I ask, reaching up to touch his face only to remember Mei's warning. We are in a public space. I drop my hand limply to my side. At a loss for what else to do, we stand there uncomfortably.

'It's getting late. I don't want Xi to miss dinner with his family,' I shrug, taking one last look up into Chen's pained face before turning toward the door.

After grabbing my handbag and coat from Winnie's office, I'm about to head for the door when I hear the glass slide open behind me. I turn to see Chen standing in the doorway, suit jacket in hand.

The top buttons of his crisp white shirt sit undone, giving him a sexy, dishevelled look. He runs a hand through his hair before tossing his jacket across the back of the tall wingback chair.

'Chen?' I frown, watching his movement as he stalks toward me in long determined strides.

'I just have to know...' He joins me but does not stop; he reaches his hands up into my hair and holds my face tenderly. Our eyes meet, Chen allowing me one last chance to object before lowering his lips to mine. Surrendering to his embrace, I drop my bag and coat to the floor. Deepening the kiss, Chen runs his hands down my back until they come to rest at the base of my ass. Lifting me gently, he places me on the edge of Winnie's desk, leaning in between my parted legs. My hands clench into fists in his hair as we cling to each other like it is our last moment on earth.

Chen eventually pushes himself away from the desk, sucking in a breath like he's run a marathon. Leaning over, he rests his hands on his knees.

'What are you doing to me, Ava?' He breathes, his wide eyes looking up at me. I feel the creep of a blush up my neck and across my cheeks, my breathing matching his. I feel my heart pounding erratically; by some miracle, Chen doesn't seem to hear it.

'What...was that?' I frown, frozen on the edge of Winnie's desk.

And why do I so badly want to do it again? I'm so confused.

'I saw the way you looked at me, after Mei told you...' Chen whispers, anguish evident in his voice. I step down from the desk, approaching him slowly.

'Saw what?' I frown, reaching for him.

'Pity for a man who cannot even convince his

fiancée to want him.' He whispers wincing.

'Chen? I do not think that at all. That look was my conflict from the relief that I had permission to be with you and yet knowing all that has happened in our past,' I whisper, reaching down to his face as he slowly straightened to stand. He captures my hand in his, placing a gentle kiss on the inside of my palm.

'You weren't ashamed of me?' He frowns, the vulnerability evident in every fibre of his being.

'How could I be ashamed of you for that? Chen, do you not feel the tension when we are in the same room together? How could I possibly deny that spark?' I shake my head, smiling up at him. 'You are the reason HEH has not sunk into oblivion these past months and other than the Tony thing, or the Tari thing, you've been good to me.'

'Mei does not want me,' he whispers into my hair, hugging me into a tight embrace.

'I'm so sorry, Chen,' I whisper back, my face buried in his chest. Through his shirt, I can hear his heartbeat returning to normal.

'What are we going to do?' He leans backward, looking longingly into my eyes.

'I have no idea what the right thing is anymore. But I know what I want to do,' I whisper, reaching up on my tippy toes to place another kiss on his lips. He chuckles deeply, the sexy sound resonating through me as his hands begin to explore.

4

Flashes of the night before come back to me as I doze lazily in bed the next morning. Chen and I arriving at the penthouse, relieving one another of items of clothing as we make our way upstairs to the master suite. Champagne and bubble bath as Chen's strong hands massage the knots from my shoulders in the warm tub. Sitting naked on the floor of the kitchen at midnight as we eat leftovers from Gladys' dinner.

I will not feel guilty for this. This doesn't mean I approve of Chen's prior behaviour, nor does it mean we will be doing it ever again. Most likely not. Maybe.

I roll over, satiated from our sunrise tryst to see the curve of Chen's muscular back peeking out from under the bedsheets. I quietly lift my hand to trace my fingers down his spine, relishing the opportunity to enjoy the view uninterrupted. I feel the deep rumble of a chuckle before Chen slowly rolls over, his bright blue eyes catching mine. A smirk evident on his face.

'Enjoying yourself there, Miss Elias?'

'Not in the slightest, Mr Chen,' I giggle back as he catches my hand, placing gentle kisses on each of my fingertips. My stomach growls hungrily between us, causing Chen to chuckle once again.

'I guess that signifies the end of sexy time?' He laughs, leaning down to drag the sheet below my navel to place a tender kiss on my belly.

'Shower time before breakfast time?' I smile playfully at him before rolling over and sauntering toward the bathroom.

After the room began to fog, I stepped into the steaming stream of water, wondering if Chen had picked up on my invitation. I didn't have to wait long before strong arms wrapped around my waist from behind, Chen placing open-mouthed kisses from my neck down to my shoulder.

'Hm, I could wake up like this every morning,' he smiles down at me as I turn and start to soap his chest and arms.

'Me too,' I smirk up at him, relishing the sensation of my hands running up and down his toned physique.

Once we were both sufficiently washed and dried, Chen and I made our way to the kitchen for breakfast. Gladys barely bat an eyelid as we made our way to the island bench and took our seats.

'The usual, Miss Ava?' She smiles knowingly at me before turning to enquire after Chen's request for breakfast.

'Thank you, Gladys,' I smile across at her, picking up my orange juice to sip it thoughtfully.

A sudden ruckus from the elevator bay suggests Seal has arrived for the morning. Stomping in, he plonks himself in a chair on my other side, peering down the counter at Chen.

'Interesting choice Ava,' he winks at me before tossing a bundle of mail in my direction. 'The guys downstairs asked me to give these to you.' He leans over and pours himself a glass of orange juice as he bids Gladys good morning.

I look down at the small pile of envelopes in my hands: some body-corporate letters, others postcards from loved ones back home. One envelope in particular catches my attention, as I turn it over to see no return address. I flip it over a few times, noticing Chen watching me with curiosity as he sips his coffee.

I run my butter knife under the inside of the seal, digging out the single page inside. There before me, like some crude B-grade horror movie, sat a letter composed of cut out magazine and newspaper words, glued poorly onto the page.

'What the...?' Seal leans across, taking in the scene.

'YOU ARE BEING WATCHED. YOU HAD BETTER WATCH YOUR BACK,' I read out loud. 'Are you kidding me? What the fuck is this?' I turn to look at Seal quizzically.

'If I didn't know any better Miss Ava, I'd say you just received your first death threat. How interesting!' He ponders as he turns back to sip his juice.

'Are you not going to do something about this?' Chen demands incensed, looking from the page to me and then to Seal.

'Oh, would you like me to take it to my little crime lab and dust it for fingerprints? How about I test the sticky bit for DNA from spit where they licked the envelope?' He rolls his eyes sarcastically, taking a plate of pancakes and bacon from Gladys.

'Shouldn't we be taking this seriously?' Gladys stares wide-eyed at our trio.

'Do you know how much money private detectives cost?' Seal asks before shoving a fork full of pancake in his mouth.

'Yes,' Chen states bluntly.

'Ah, well....then...' Seal garbles. He swallows and takes a sip of his juice. 'Let me save you some time. How many people know Ava lives here?' He leans on his elbow and eyes us both.

'A handful?' I frown.

'Exactly, and half of us are currently in this kitchen. Unless you suspect Tari or one of the other Invisible Women, there is only one logical explanation.' He turns back to his plate and slices more pancake.

'You're referring to Tony, I imagine,' Chen grumbles.

'What do you know, ladies and gentlemen? He's smarter than he looks.' Seal waves his fork in Chen's direction. Chen makes to stand before I grab his arm and force him to sit back down.

'You think Tony is sending me a terribly put together death threat?' I frown, turning toward Seal.

'Yes, Miss. I do.' I sigh heavily before standing and excusing myself from the kitchen.

'If you don't mind Gladys, I might grab something at the office. I seem to have lost my appetite.'

Back upstairs in the master suite, I busy myself with putting on makeup and finding clothes to wear to work for the day.

'You're not surely planning on going to work after this?' Chen stares incredulously from the doorway.

'What else am I meant to do? Sit around here sulking about the man trying to steal my company and the idiot trying to threaten my life?' I raise an eyebrow at him in the mirror.

'What if he's serious, Ava? I'm worried about you.' Chen whispers as he sidles closer and wraps his arms around my waist, burying his face in my hair.

'I'll be fine; I've got Seal,' I shrug.

'Yes, because he was so effective last time.' Chen rolls his eyes at me in the mirror. I shake my head, giggling at the memory of Seal running down the street toward Chen, Ryan and I after Tony's assault; my bleeding head causing me to collapse in the street, as he shouted: 'They wouldn't let me in because I wasn't on the guest list!'

'Do you mind if I ask you something?'

'Sure.' I smile at him in the mirror as I attempt to apply makeup with his arms around me.

'What did Seal mean by 'the Invisible Women'?' He frowns at me in the mirror, his chin resting on my shoulder.

'Oh, um. Well, when I first arrived in Singapore, and Tony announced you as CEO, I needed to find some allies who knew what I was going through. To find people who had been 'silenced by their male counterparts' as I felt I was by Tony.'

'And by me...' Chen's arms begin to fall. I turn to face him, waving my foundation brush in his face.

'Now listen here, you. That was before I'd even met you. The Invisible Women were people I sought solace in before we came to our agreement to work together.' I smile reassuringly up at him.

'Why are they 'Invisible'?' His frown deepens.

'The same sort of reasons; they had male superiors

who placed male colleagues in the spotlight for recognition of the ladies' work.' I shrug, uncertain what more to say.

'And they too feel that they are being sheltered from their full potential by their male counterparts?'

'I never said I was being sheltered by you. I know full well that HEH would never have ridden out Winnie's passing as well as it did without you at the helm.' I reach up on my tippy toes and place a chaste kiss on his lips.

'Have a little faith in me, okay?' I smile back at him, wrapping my arms around him, hugging him tighter to me.

The day at the office seemed to run smoothly until Sasha came screaming in just before lunchtime, Jia hot on her heels. Sasha picks up the remote to the large flat-screen TV, switching it on to the news channel.

'And following up on our headline story, Mr Marcus Evans sat down with reporter Linley Norman, announcing he is the love child of the late Mr Huynh Li, of Huynh Enterprises Holdings. Channel 5 News reached out to current CEO, Mr Samuel Chen, for comment earlier today with no response.' An ill-fitting suited man appears on the screen talking and holding up a photograph undeniably containing Winnie and a barely identifiable woman.

'Mr Huynh met my mother whilst travelling abroad in Europe, where my mother resided. They spent a few weeks together and I was born as a result of their love.'

I stumble back and sink into the couch. Suddenly Chen barges into the room, trailed by Abbie and several other PR team members.

'I can assure you Mr Chen; we received no request for comment. We would have contacted you immediately if that had been the case!' She states shrilly.

'Everybody get out!' Chen storms to the whiskey trolley and picks up a decanter. The entire room jumps immediately, funnelling out the door. Jia takes a seat opposite me, rolling her eyes at Chen's back, causing me to smile.

'Chen, we knew this was going to happen at some point.' I aim for reassuring.

'This asshole thinks he can turn up out of the blue and claim something like this!' He waves his arms around before taking a long sip and sitting down heavily.

'As soon as I could get through to his attorneys yesterday, I demanded he submit to a DNA test. Ava told me about the diamond, and so I knew we'd likely have a leg to stand on,' Jia nods at me confidently.

'Diamond?' Chen stops to stare at us both.

'Oh, I meant to tell you about that last night.' I blush, remembering what we were doing that led me to forget to mention it. Jia looks between us, a knowing twinkle in her eye.

'Winnie was contacted about a decade ago by a guy who wanted an investment into a company that created carbon diamonds. He made Winnie pull a chunk of hair from his head and when they didn't use it all they sent some back in a glass vial. Does that about cover it?' Jia turned to look at me expectantly.

'Yes. Because Winnie pulled the hair from his head instead of cutting it, we know it should have the follicle as well as the shaft. That is what Mr Adams was talking about yesterday. Apparently, paternal DNA can only be tested using the follicle,' I finish, turning to look at Chen to check he is following along.

'Are you telling me that the diamond in the top of that pen you're always carrying around was forged using Winnie's hair?' He gulps uncomfortably.

Good thing I didn't tell him about Winnie's ring.

Jia and I exchange glances, clearly thinking along the same lines.

'Yes, but the point is, we have Winnie's DNA, and if this guy refuses the paternity test, then we've all but caught him in the lie,' Jia smiles triumphantly. 'His only option is to consent to the test; otherwise, the second his case hits the courts, they'll throw him out.'

'So now all we have to do is wait and see if the guy refuses the test?' Chen frowns, sipping his whiskey.

By that afternoon, we had our answer. Mr Evans' attorney contacted Jia to advise he was refusing the paternity test and that they would see us in court.

Jia and I sat glumly at Tari's bar at Spago as Jia relayed to her the events of the day.

'His lawyers came back to us. They said their client believes that being forced into taking a DNA test 'impinges upon his rights to bodily autonomy'.' Jia rolls her eyes, slumping further down into the chair beside me.

'But surely that proves he's lying! If he were telling the truth wouldn't he want a DNA test to prove undeniably that he is Winnie's son?' Tari leers from across the bar.

'We can't force him to take a paternity test, and the court has now set a date for the preliminary hearing in

December,' Jia sighs frustratedly.

'December!' Tari and I exclaim in unison.

'All we can do is sit tight and hope that the court throws him out immediately, knowing that he refuses the paternity test.' She pats me absentmindedly on the arm.

'There's nothing else we can do? We have to sit here and wait for two and a half months to find out 'if the Judge will take the case seriously' or not?' Tari throws her tea towel down in disgust.

'Be thankful they managed to find a date before the Christmas closure. If anything happens and their dates back up, we're looking at February at the earliest.' Jia scolds our apparent lack of gratitude.

'I can't believe there is nothing else we can do. We have to wait while the media continue to have a field day and HEH sit in the headlines for all the wrong reasons?' I drop my head onto my arms on the bar top. 'Even Chen isn't going to be able to resuscitate this one.'

'Honestly Ava, short of finding the woman who birthed the man and getting her to publicly confess that he is making it all up; there is nothing that we can do,' Jia sighs, taking a large sip of her whiskey.

I slowly lift my head from my arms and lock eyes with Tari.

'Are you thinking what I'm thinking?' Tari grins wickedly at me.

'I think I might be!' I squeal.

Jia looks between us like she's watching a tennis match in a mental asylum. She was partly intrigued, partly afraid for her safety.

'What on earth just happened here?' She frowns, waving a finger between the two of us.

Tari leans forward, whispering to us both. 'Winnie left us a journal from 30 years ago depicting three rendezvous with different women in Europe.'

'How do you know for certain that they are the only European women he ever slept with?' Jia frowns deeply.

'Oh, I'm pretty certain. Just take my word for it.' Tari nods at her reassuringly. 'How old did you say this guy was again?'

'29 or thereabouts.' Jia frowns.

'Aha! It is possible that if Winnie did get someone pregnant that the dates when he was in Europe line up!' Tari states excitedly before frowning, realising the implications of that.

'And let me guess, you two geniuses have it in your heads that you're just going to turn up at the houses of these women - who are probably all in their 50s or 60s might I add! And ask them if they birthed this man who is now trying to blackmail you into giving him your company?' Jia cocks an eyebrow sardonically.

I look at Tari, Tari looks at me.

'Yep.' We both smile at her.

'And what happens if he isn't the child of one of these women and simply a random stranger?' Jia's eyebrow travels further up her forehead.

'He stood at that press conference holding a photograph of Winnie and an unidentifiable woman. I wouldn't be surprised if Winnie did know the woman in question, but I doubt he fathered her child,' I state, a glimmer of hope growing inside of me.

'Also, if it turns out it is a complete waste of time, then we will have had a nice few weeks in Europe!' Tari adds, beaming across at me.

When Tari's shift ends, we return to the penthouse together to plan our European 'investigation'.

As we ride the elevator up, Tari looks across at me.

'Are we just doing this to distract ourselves from the fact that we haven't deciphered Winnie's final diaries about his death?' She whispers.

'Honestly Tari, I have no idea. I suppose it does feel a little like running away, doesn't it?' I frown to myself.

'We are not running away! We are running forward!' She giggles. 'Now, the first thing we need is a map of Europe,' Tari states as the elevator reaches the top floor.

'No, the first thing we need is wine!' I giggle as the door opens.

We make our way into the kitchen on the first floor, spotting Gladys standing on the terrace talking to someone.

'Were you expecting anyone tonight?' Tari turns to frown at me.

'Nope,' I shake my head, turning toward the fridge to find a bottle of wine.

'Ah, Miss Ava. I hope you don't mind, but Mr Chen came to see you.' She smiles at me anxiously.

'Thank you, Gladys. It is no problem at all.' I turn to find us a pair of wine glasses as Gladys heads for the stairs. Silent as the wind, Chen appears at the doorway, stopping when he sees Tari.

'Oh, I'm sorry. Do I need to show you my 'guest pass'?' She cocks an eyebrow at him, pretending to fumble in her jacket pocket.

'I guess I deserved that,' Chen concedes quietly.

'You think? You know what Ava, it looks like your lime wedges are running low. Should I replenish them?' She glares across at Chen.

'Ava, are you going to say anything?' Chen stares at me, imploring my intervention.

'Don't look at me. You were a right ass to Tari last time she saw you. From what I gather, you never bothered going back to apologise either...?' I cock an eyebrow at him, pouring wine into the stemmed balloon glasses.

'I...' Chen stands on the threshold looking lost. 'I am sorry for my behaviour toward you. It was unacceptable.' He runs a nervous hand through his hair.

'Wow, you should see your face,' Tari laughs uproariously, 'Lucky for you; I have thicker skin than that. Besides, from what I hear, Ava seems to think you have some redeeming qualities. Somewhere.' She rolls her eyes in my direction. 'I also recall getting back to the bar after the two of you left to find an obscenely generous tip.' Chen blushes slightly, 'It was all I could think to do.'

I hadn't heard about that. I shake my head.

What is it with these people and thinking money fixes everything?

'Great, now that we aren't going to stab each other with salad forks; what are you doing here, Chen?' I eye him through the bottom of my glass as I take a large gulp.

'I wanted to check you were okay after everything that happened today.' He hesitantly steps further into the room.

'Did something else happen? Other than the guy refusing the paternity test?' Tari frowns, looking confusedly between the two of us. Chen turns to look at me speculatively. I roll my eyes and dig the collaged magazine letter out from my handbag.

'What is this? Some sick joke?' Tari shakes her head, looking up at me, holding the page aloft.

'It turned up this morning. It's no big deal. Even Seal agreed.' I shrug, sipping my wine.

'Well, we all know how helpful Seal was the last time you 'required assistance'.' Tari rolls her eyes, catching the look on Chen's face.

'Whoa, and Mr Silver Suppository agrees with me! There's a first,' she laughs, Chen's face quickly transforming into one of shocked embarrassment.

'Tari and I have a plan to see if we can speed up the paternity battle,' I interject, trying to derail the conversation. 'We are going to go to Europe, find his mother and get her to tell us the truth about Mr Evans' father.'

'That is absurd,' Chen states flatly.

'Besides, it will mean I am out of the country and therefore out of harm's way.' I nod to myself.

'But you only just returned.' Chen frowns, stepping toward me. I notice Tari disappear quietly into the living room.

'Chen. What happened last night aside, you are still marrying Mei. Whether you want each other or not, I don't know that I can ever bring myself to do that again. It feels...wrong.' I frown, looking down into my wine glass.

'You didn't...enjoy...it?' Chen frowns, his hands finding his hair once again.

'I did enjoy it. But that's not the point. Mei's permission or not, that won't be happening again.' I look up into his eyes, seeing the hurt and resentment.

'I thought you said you were starting to forgive me for what happened with Tari and with Tony?'

'This isn't about that!'

'It isn't?' His eyes implore mine.

'You're engaged to another woman!' I place my wine glass down and throw my hands in the air.

'Mei gave us her blessing!' He hollers back.

'To have sex with each other Chen! Nothing more! Why can't you understand that?' I frown, shaking my head at the madness of the situation.

'So I shall forever be doomed to a loveless marriage merely for the sake of saving face with my family?' He sinks into a chair at the breakfast bar.

'That is a decision you will have to make, Chen. But I will not be here to warm your bed and help ease the guilt of making a decision you know won't make you happy,' I whisper.

'I was born into the Chen family, and with that comes certain obligations. To marry for mutual advantage is but one of them,' he sighs, burying his face in his hands. I walk around the island and kneel beside him.

'Chen. I think it is important that I go away. It will give you time to figure out what you want to do with Mei and place distance between us.' I gently pull his hands from his face, devastating baby blue eyes piercing my soul.

'If Mei weren't in the picture...?' Chen eyes me with the smallest hope.

'I can't answer that honestly; there are still so many other issues we would need to work through first.'

'Because you don't trust me,' he states bluntly.

'Because I have seen glimmers of this smart, considerate, sensitive man. But I have also seen dark, belligerent, elitist aspects of you that I don't know if I can overlook in the long term.'

Chen nods slowly, as if in confirmation of something internal.

'I am going to be better. Not just for you, but for me too.' He looks at me with steely resolve.

The next morning, I walked into HEH with a plan. After Chen left, Tari and I had stayed up all night to pour over Winnie's journals and establish a basic itinerary. Tari would speak with her manager tonight about taking extended leave, and I would get HEH to organise for me to continue working remotely for the duration of our trip.

Sasha meets me at the bottom of the elevator with a latte in hand.

'Is it true!?' She stares at me wide-eyed.

'Is what true?' I frown across at her as we enter the elevator.

'That HEH is going to be handed over to that guy on the news claiming to be Winnie's son?' She chews her lip anxiously.

'No, HEH is not going anywhere. I promise you I will fight this to the bitter end if I have to.' I give her a half-hearted smile. 'You do make a good point, though; we should have contacted the staff yesterday to let them know what was going on.'

'It was only on the news last night; it isn't unreasonable for the staff to have to wait until this morning to hear from you.' She pats my arm.

'Can you do me a favour and get Abbie and Chen in my office as soon as they are in the building? We should get ahead of this as soon as we can.'

Not an hour later, Chen and Abbie stood in my office.

'Okay, when is the press conference set for?' I look between them.

'We thought lunchtime today?' Abbie looks down at her iPad. I nod, looking across at Chen.

'I think we need to record something and send it to the staff, so they know what is going on and where we stand. It also has to be politically neutral enough that if it gets out that it doesn't do us more harm.'

He nods in agreeance.

'I am happy for you to make the address to the staff.' He smiles across at me.

'No, it should be you. Again, in case it is leaked to the media.' I smile at him reassuringly. 'Abbie, are you happy to take a look and put something together with the team?' She nods and heads out the door.

'You didn't mention to her that you are leaving again?' Chen observes, watching Abbie disappear.

'Let's deal with one crisis at a time, shall we? I won't be leaving for a few days yet; Tari has to get herself sorted too.' I walk back to Winnie's desk and look at the news headlines on my laptop.

'Do you truly believe you will have success finding this woman?' He scratches his chin, eyeing me curiously.

'I have to try. I can't let this guy spend the next three months dragging HEH through the media mud.'

'What if he isn't lying? What if his mother told him Winnie was his father?' He scowls at me.

'Then we have to wait until the court demand a paternity test.' I turn to stare at him. 'Why are you trying to make this so difficult?'

'I'm trying to be realistic! What are you going to do if he wins this battle?' Chen throws his hands in the air.

'I will stand before HEH in apology and then go back to the life I had planned for myself, before, all of this.' I look around the room before coming back to watch Chen.

'Back to Ryan.' Chen's statement wasn't a question.

'I don't know.' I shake my head.

Sasha's appearance at the doorway draws our attention back to the present.

'I'm sorry to interrupt, but there is a bit of a situation downstairs.' Her face is apprehensive.

'Sasha?' I frown before following her and Chen from the room.

The scene in reception on the ground floor was beyond anything I had ever witnessed. There were people everywhere milling around inside and across the entire driveway. News vans, reporters and journalists took up every square metre available.

'Mr Chen!' Shouted a nearby man, shoving his recorder in our faces. 'What do you have to say to the allegations made by Mr Evans?'

'Why have you delayed responding to the allegations?'

'Mr Chen?'

The cacophony of voices shouting in our direction was rivalled only by the crush of bodies imposing upon us.

'Ladies and Gentlemen! Please! Exit the space, and I will take your questions in an orderly manner!' Chen hollers to the room. A sudden quiet settles across the room before groups of people begin shuffling out the door to find a spot in front of the podium the PR team set up.

'Chen,' I hiss, 'Are you sure about this?'

He says nothing but winks down at me. I follow in his wake as he ushers straggling journalists out the door.

He steps confidently up to the podium and smiles down at the crowd.

'Thank you for your time. HEH decided to delay officially responding to the accusations due to the ongoing legal situation at hand. I am willing to answer what I can here for you today.' He smiles, taking in the group.

I look up in awe, watching him answer questions with a sense of ease and comfort.

After 10 minutes of answering questions, Chen had the crowd in hand. The general sense of the group left me feeling as though they were reassured and comforted by his words.

'I thank you for your time. As you can imagine, we have some rather pressing business to attend to. Thank you for your time .' Chen smiles his panty-dropping smile down at the crowd, bowing briefly before waving broadly and stepping down from the podium.

I shake my head as he joins me, smirk and all.

'I told you so,' he chuckles down at me.

'Wait, so you're telling me this guy is trying to take everything from you? Jia! What are you going to do?' Linah throws a shady look across the top of her martini glass at Jia.

'I've done everything I can. Now we have to wait

for the courts to hear the case and we pray it gets tossed out.' She huffs, shrugging from her spot on the lounger.

I'd invited the ladies for dinner at the penthouse; I couldn't recall the last time I had all three of them over. It also gave Gladys the night off from cooking.

'Ava, are you okay? That is a lot to take in,' Margot hollers from the elevator where she thanked my doorman for bringing up our dumplings delivery. I jump up to help her with the multiple of bags; she smiles at me appreciatively.

'Well, Jia doesn't support my plan of 'attack' shall we say, but I have an idea,' I chuckle wryly. The others join us at the kitchen island as we perch ourselves on high chairs and dig into the boxes.

'Don't leave us hanging! Tell us this plan. If Jia disapproves, then I'm sure I will support it!' Margot winks across at me as she dunks a BBQ pork bun into chilli sauce.

'Well! Tari and I found an old journal of Winnie's, where he mentioned meeting three different women in Europe about 30 years ago! We decided, even though it might be a wild goose chase...to track them down and see if they know this man.' I stop and look at Margot and Linah's faces. Margot breaks out a huge grin, chewing hastily around her pork bun. Linah's chopsticks freeze mid-air reaching for a prawn wonton.

'What if you can't find them, or they refuse to talk to you?' Linah frowns, focussing again on her wontons.

'Then we go for a quick holiday and come back. We then resign ourselves to Jia's plan of 'wait and see'.' I shrug, shoving a whole vegetable gyoza into my mouth, the soy sauce dripping down my chin.

'I have argued myself hoarse, but Ava won't listen to logic.' Jia shakes her head, pouring herself a glass of wine.

'I say go for it! Maybe you'll meet the love of your life on this whimsical trip!' Margot sighs, a dreamy, faraway look dawning on her face.

'Ugh,' Jia makes a choking sound, throwing her napkin at Margot.

'I like the sound of that! I could use the distraction,' I laugh, contemplatively dipping a wonton in chilli sauce.

'How are things going in that 'department'?' Linah cocks her head to the side and peers at me.

'You mean since Ryan walked out on me and I impulsively slept with Chen? Oh, just grand.' I roll my eyes, mashing the wonton into my mouth.

I stop when I realise what I've admitted to. I look around at the three frozen faces before me.

'You what!?' Linah squeals, causing her dumpling to fall from her chopsticks onto her plate with a loud squelch.

'I knew it!' Jia points at me, accusatorially with her chopsticks.

'Ugh. I know. I was so angry and hurt by what happened with Ryan, and the opportunity arose with Chen. So I took it? I know he's supposed to be 'engaged' to Mei, but they don't even like each other!' I wail, dropping my head onto my arms on the table. 'Am I a terrible person?' I mumble into my arms.

'Oh honey, of course not!' Linah leans over and pats my hand. 'He's not married; you didn't do anything wrong.' I feel her withering stare toward Margot, daring her to disagree. I lift my head and smile at her weakly, picking my chopsticks back up. Jia leans over and pours me a large glass of wine.

'So, are you going to tell us the dirty details?' She wiggles her eyebrows at me suggestively. I can't help but laugh.

'It was great, but I realised afterwards that what I really missed was Ryan.' I shrug before taking a gulp of wine.

'Is there no chance of a reconciliation there?' Linah opens a new box of steamed BBQ pork buns.

'I don't think so. He was staying with Seal and Xi the night he moved out of my chalet. They would have told him we were leaving, but he didn't message me or anything.' I shrug again. 'He was so angry about me coming back to Singapore, and about the money.'

'This is why I can't tell Riley about my real work. I just don't know that he would understand.' Margot sighs, spearing a wonton with her chopstick. I see Linah nodding in agreement.

'Chip is an amazing husband, but he spends a few weeks every few months back in the USA at the Ranch. If he knew what I was really doing, I don't think he'd be comfortable leaving me here alone as often.'

I frown deeply, putting down my chopsticks.

'I don't understand how you can do it? I don't mean that to sound disrespectful, but I could never have felt like I was honest with Ryan if I kept HEH a secret from him. What do you tell them when they ask how your day was?' I pick up my wine and take a long sip. I watch with curiosity as Margot and Linah's faces change, more hesitant, more reserved, almost guarded.

'Why are you asking? We don't challenge the way you operate in your relationships?' Margot huffs, bordering on aggressive.

'I'm just trying to understand,' I offer, realising I've stepped in something much bigger than I'd initially recognised.

'For me, it was just easier that way. Chip is a confident, caring, compassionate man. It is my own fault in a way, I downplayed what I did when I met him, and it spiralled from there. I feel like if he found out now, he'd feel like I lied to him.' Linah stops and stares at her food. 'Which I guess I have. For years now.'

'Men don't always understand why we are invisible. They just throw out suggestions like 'just stand up for yourself.' Riley is a typical British man. He doesn't understand talking about feelings, and if I told him about being hidden by my workplace, he would tell me to 'pull my socks up' and get out there.' Margot grumbles, reaching for the wine. 'Then we'd have a fight because he doesn't understand that it isn't that simple and the whole thing could have been avoided.' She looks up at me, steely resolve in her eyes. 'Tell me you didn't have those exact same conversations with Ryan?'

'You're right. We did have those same conversations. But I felt better for having them.' I shiver at the cold that seems to have settled over the room.

'And now you and Ryan aren't together.' Linah looks at me pointedly.

'I don't think trying to hide it from him would have helped the situation,' I mumble.

'Well, I have tried it both ways, and I'm still single.

So what does that tell us?' Jia states, picking up her wine glass. 'That it makes no fucking difference.' I smile across at her, silently thanking her for breaking the tension. She continues, 'In my experience, men are only useful for two things; holding your purse while you a go to the bathroom and sex.'

The four of us burst out laughing.

The evening continued in the same manner as it had begun, with laughter and cocktails, my apparent faux pas forgiven for now. After they left, I couldn't help but wonder if perhaps these women were more comfortable being invisible, and that was why they didn't fight harder to be seen. Deep down I know I was being incredibly judgemental, but I couldn't stop the thoughts streaming through my head.

If you can't be yourself with someone, are they really the right person for you? Can you truly be honest if you are hiding such a big part of your life? If Chip and Riley learned about Linah and Margot's real experiences, and they chose not to stay, wouldn't it mean that they weren't right for each other?

Or are the ladies onto something? Are we better off to hide reality to keep the fantasy alive, as long as it doesn't rock the boat? My mind wanders to Mei and Chen, and the pickle they find themselves in.

No, I don't think so. Not for me anyway.

5

A week later and Tari and I sat snuggled together under a blanket on the Screaming Eagle watching movies and sipping cocktails, making our way to London. We decided we would start there, because why not? - before flying to Paris and searching for our first mystery woman.

'I can't get over how incredible this jet is. And it's yours! It is so big I feel like we haven't even seen Seal or Xi since we boarded!' Tari giggles, shoving a handful of popcorn in her face.

'It is so strange, isn't it? I know I've been living this life for months now and yet it still feels surreal.' I sip my black Russian. I feel Tari watching me and turn to face her. 'What?'

'We haven't talked about the 'Chen thing', and I was wondering what's happening there?' She peers at me curiously.

'What do you mean? We slept together and had a great night, but I realised I couldn't overlook all the other strange shit going on around us.' I shake my head.

'You're gonna give the man whiplash,' she chuckles sardonically.

'What do you mean?'

'You kept him at arms length, well kind of, and suddenly you sleep with him?'

'Is that so terrible?' I feel the guilt unfurling in my stomach.

'Of course not! You can sleep with whomever you want without having to explain it to anyone!'

'But...?'

She shoves more popcorn in her face.

'Tari! Why are you asking me about this?' I frown at her.

'Because,' she garbles, 'I don't want you to get hurt. Was it good?' Her eyes twinkle at me.

'Yes,' I whisper.

'Did you want to do it again?'

'Yes.'

'So what's stopping you? Other than the part about him being engaged and your employee and all.' She rolls her eyes.

'Tari, he was so rude to you. He didn't believe me about Tony, and he cares more about his family's feelings than his own...'

'But you still slept with him, so was there something more to it than that?'

I sip my cocktail contemplatively.

'Can't we chalk it up to bad judgement and I was horny?' I smile at her sheepishly. She laughs loudly, leaning over to pick up her drink.

'Of course! I just don't want you to get hurt. Things with Ryan didn't end all that long ago, and the two of you had quite a whirlwind few months together.'

'This is true. But the chemistry with Chen was there from day one. I guess I just wanted to know...you know?'

'Do you think he will go through with the marriage thing with Mei?' She eyes me, watching my reaction closely.

'Honestly? Yes, I think he will. And I suspect he will regret it. I feel for them both.'

'If there weren't a Mei, would you...?' Tari trails off.

'Chen asked the same thing. I don't know. I'm not sure if we are compatible as people with our different views of the world,' I shrug thoughtfully.

'Well, if it helps, I don't hate the guy even if he is a part-time asshole.' She nudges me with her shoulder.

'Thanks, Tari. You're a good friend,' I giggle.

'I'm sorry I haven't figured anything out with Winnie's diary yet,' she whispers across to me. I turn to look at her, seeing the sadness in her eyes. I frown, curious at the sudden change in mood.

'You have nothing to apologise for. Winnie might have thought he left us 'clues' but what he left us was a wild goose chase. The truth is we may never know what really happened to Winnie.' I sigh heavily, sipping my cocktail.

'Will that be enough for you? Will you be able to let it go?'

'Honestly? I don't know, but we can't beat ourselves up because we can't piece together an 'old man's riddle'.' I pat her arm gently. 'Winnie will understand that we tried our best and if that's as far as we get then that's all we can do. In the meantime we have a more pressing issue threatening HEH. We'll get back to fighting for Winnie's justice when we resolve the current crisis!'

We turned back to finish watching the movie and snoozed through the remainder of the flight.

London was a dreary city. Grey skies, grey buildings. The people didn't seem particularly festive either.

'Why would anyone wanna live here?' Tari whispers to me as she shakes out her umbrella. We'd decided to grab lunch in a pub on our second day in the city, in an attempt to escape the near-constant downpour. We were making our way toward the tables as we began peeling off layers of clothing in the dark, stuffy space.

Plonking ourselves down in a booth, we placed orders with the waitress and piled our shod clothing beside us on the benches.

'London can be quite pretty in the summer, but this constant rain gets old quickly,' I whisper across the table to Tari.

'Everything smells like damp,' She scrunches up her nose in distaste. Looking around the room, I notice that everything is built from dark timber, giving the space an oppressive feeling. The waitress comes back carrying two large pints of dark ale. I sip the warm liquid noticing just how much it tastes like vegemite from back home. There were very few other people in the pub, 11.30 probably too early for most Londoners for lunch.

'Okay,' sighs Tari, digging the map of France from her satchel. She places our beers to the side and unfolds the map across the table.

'We fly to Paris tomorrow, and according to

Winnie's journal, the village was somewhere near 'Chambord, Loir-et-Cher'.' She digs out another notebook with photocopied pages of Winnie's journal. 'From what I gather, Chambord is a castle in the French countryside.'

I dig out my phone and google 'Chambord'. Dozens of photographs of the liquor appear on the screen.

'Her name was Aurélie and she was the daughter of le Prêtre,' Tari reads aloud from her notes. 'What is that? 'le Prêtre'?' She frowns across at me.

I open google translate and type it in as best as I can guess.

'Uh? The Priest.' I read, looking up into Tari's scandalised face.

'Tell me that is a joke.'

I turn my phone to face her, the text prominent on the screen.

'Oh my, Winnie what have you done?' Tari crosses herself and looks up at the ceiling.

'I didn't realise you were religious?' I frown at her.

'I'm not, but Winnie,' she barely whispers, 'deflowered the daughter of a priest!'

'Who said she was a virgin?' I whisper back, barely containing the giggle fighting to burst forth. 'Never mind her maidenhood, does he state which town it was in?'

'No, this is where I lost the trail a little,' She looks up at me sheepishly.

'You mean we flew all the way here, and we don't yet know exactly where these women were at the time?' I sigh, sipping my beer. 'Are we completely insane? Maybe Chen was right.'

'No, I am certain we will find all three of these

women Ava, I promise you.' She reaches across the table and grabs my hand.

'Okay, does he mention landmarks or anything at all? Maybe read back the pages he wrote about the time he spent with her.' I shrug, watching the waitress with curiosity. 'Do you think she has our orders and can't find us?' I frown. Tari looks up and follows my gaze.

'We are two of about six customers; surely she can't be that slow.' She rolls her eyes.

I look down at the map as Tari begins to read.

'After visiting the Chateau de Chambord, I mistakenly drove my motorcar in the direction of Paris for a short while before the weather overcame me. I came upon a small village where a chapel stood in the centre of town -its tall steeple the highest point for miles around. I circled the high stone wall on foot in the frightful weather until a gate opened ahead of me. Soaked to the bone, I approached a gent cloaked in black. I attempted to converse in broken French, asking the man 'Un abri ce soir?' Shelter tonight? He waved me inside the compound.'

'I can't imagine doing that,' I sigh in awe. 'To just turn up at some random person's place and ask them to let you in. Winnie didn't know this guy wasn't a serial killer.' I shake my head.

'I guess they didn't care much for serial killers 30 years ago. Men still don't seem to fear for their safety these days either.' Tari shrugs, eyeing the waitress taking her third turn of the room with two large plates. Tari eventually catches her eye and waves her over.

'Oh, there you are!' She smiles down at us, placing mind-bogglingly large plates in front of us.

'Next time we can share an order,' Tari whispers across at me after the waitress departs. I look down at the typical English pub meal in front of me. Chicken pot pie covered in pastry, buttery roast potatoes and boiled vegetables.

I stick my knife into the top of the pie to release the steam and allow the insides to cool.

'Okay, so Winnie said he got lost and essentially backtracked toward Paris by mistake, 'for a short while' before coming across a village,' I state, stabbing a potato. Tari nods, slicing up her crumbed chicken steak.

I drag out my laptop and connect to the Wi-Fi, opening up maps onto the screen. 'Didn't you read to me on the plane that he drove south from Orleans but stayed south of the river?' I look across at Tari as I shove potato in my mouth. She nods, chewing hastily.

'Okay, well based on where Chambord is located, if we stayed 'inland' and drove directly back toward Paris, the first town you come across is 'Thoury'.' I trace along the map on the table before turning to type 'Thoury, France' into google maps and before me appear pictures of a lake and tiny town.

'Hm, that doesn't look promising. Perhaps we aren't the greatest detectives?' I frown, digging around in my chicken pie, flaky crust disintegrating everywhere. Tari reaches across and shifts the laptop slightly to click the pointer and drop the 'street view' man onto a roadway in the middle of town.

'Winnie does mention something about Aurélie taking him to the lake. I think that might be where it happened.' She winks across at me. I promptly choke on my chicken. Spluttering everywhere, I grab my beer and chug it.

'Winnie wrote the specifics in his journal??' I gasp.

'Yup, seems that way. He didn't want to forget a single detail!' She cackles across at me. I can't help but notice that our failure to use hushed tones indoors, is drawing attention from other patrons.

Tari clicks forward and backward through the town on the street view, looking for landmarks.

'Wait! Look!' She exclaims, pointing at the screen. There before us sat a tall spired church with stone walls.

'But how do we know it is this one? Doesn't every tiny French town have a church with a steeple?' I frown, peering at the screen.

'Okay, um, later on, he talks about the time he spent in the town with her and says something about the 'Mairie abutting the church with a sapling pollarded willow in the garden.'

'What on earth is a pollarded willow?' I cock an eyebrow and google it on my phone. 'Oh! It's the whomping willow from Harry Potter!' I exclaim, showing Tari my phone.

'Aha! This is the town - look Ava!' She points at the screen to a grey spiny tree eerily similar to the one that haunted so many childhoods.

'Then what is the Mairie?' I type it into my phone. 'Oh, the Village hall. It would make sense for it to be built beside the town church.' I smile across at Tari, stabbing a potato enthusiastically.

The front door of the pub opens and two men enter, laden heavily with shopping bags.

'Ah, good of you to join us.' Tari rolls her eyes across at Seal and Xi. We shuffle our food over to make room for them to sit. Seal sighs as he sits beside me and commences eating the chips from Tari's plate. Tari hands Xi a spare fork beside her.

'I miss Singapore already,' he sniffles.

'In other news,' I interrupt his whining, 'we think we found the town where Aurélie lived!'

'That is excellent news Miss Ava,' Xi smiles across at me. 'Have we found anywhere to stay the night tomorrow?'

'Well, I was thinking, because Winnie spoke so fondly of the Château de Chambord that we could stay in a cottage there. We are booked for three nights.' I turn my laptop to show them the photographs of the estate with views from the windows of the grounds and castle.

The Château de Chambord was the castle of my childhood dreams.

Rolling green gardens extended as far as the eye could see. The Chateau itself was a massive structure of light sandstone and spires. I spent the entire day having visions of running through the halls barefoot in a flowy ballgown.

After several hours of ogling the halls and sitting rooms within the Chateau, the four of us sat down at a restaurant within the grounds for a late lunch.

'I am still struggling with jetlag!' Tari huffed, throwing herself down in the chair beside me.

'I hear you.' I chuckle, cracking open a can of lemonade. 'Why don't we finish the afternoon here and head back to the villa for an early dinner and relax by the fire?'

Seal and Xi join us at the table, carrying cutlery and glasses of water. Tari and I both thank them as they sit down.

'So, what's the plan for tomorrow? Do we even know if this woman still lives around here?' Seal leans back in his seat, crossing his arms over his chest.

'We tried to find out who the priest was 30 years ago to see if we could get a surname for this woman, but we had no luck.' Tari shrugged. 'We figured we could ask someone when we get there and see if they have a written record somewhere in the church.'

A member of the waitstaff came past with Tari's burger and Xi's noodle salad. Tari looked at the burger, and politely indicated to the waiter.

'Uh, I'm sorry, is there bacon on this?'

The waiter looked at her, confused as his English wasn't great.

'Excusez-moi, y a-t-il du bacon dans ce plat?' Seal piped up, smiling across at the waiter. The waiter politely picks up the plate and returns to the kitchen with a slight bow.

The three of us turn to stare at Seal.

'Since when are you bilingual?' Tari eyes Seal accusatorially.

'Multilingual thank you very much. See, I'm not just a pretty face.' Seal rolls his eyes and sips his water.

'What other languages do you speak?' I raise an eyebrow, astonished.

'Aside from English and French, I also speak Cantonese, Mandarin and German.'

'That's very impressive.' I nudge him across the table.

'How are you single?' Tari frowns at him, sipping her soda.

'That is the million-dollar question, isn't it?' He winks back at her.

The next morning we set out to find Aurélie in the nearby town of Thoury. The weather was bleak, rain coming down in sheets as we peered out the windows at the passing farmland.

'What are we going to do when we find her?' Seal turns from the front passenger seat to stare at Tari and me.

'Introduce ourselves and ask if she remembers Winnie?' I hold up my phone with a photograph of Winnie from when he was younger.

'Isn't that a bit rude?' Seal frowns.

'We don't mean it badly. I guess she might find it rude? At least you can help us with the language barriers,' I smile back at him.

We follow the signs for the town until we come across the beginnings of a village. As we slowly make our way into the centre of town, we spot the spire of the church. The church and surrounding grounds appeared just as Winnie had described them. A tall stone wall surrounded the commune, creating an enclosed little fortress. Soaking rain left the roof tiles black as pitch.

The gravel crunched on the drive as the four of us piled out, underneath an assortment of umbrellas. We quietly made our way into the church and peered around, placing our dripping umbrellas by the door. Tari and I walked along the pews, noting a distinct absence of people.

'Where is everyone?' Tari frowned, looking across at me.

'I suppose because it is the middle of the week, everyone is still at work?' I look around, taking in the high ceilings and sandy stone walls.

I stop and turn when I hear Seal's voice conversing in French. The priest animatedly shakes his hand, deep in conversation. We watch as the priest nods enthusiastically, turning toward a door in the rear of the church. He stops and turns to beckon Seal follow him. Seal turns to wave at us; Tari and I immediately in hot pursuit.

We enter a small office space filled with dusty books and a small timber desk. The priest waves Seal behind the desk and points to an old photograph mounted on the wall.

'Wow,' Tari gasps, 'She looks just as Winnie described her!' She digs around in her bag and pulls out her notebook. 'Aurélie is a woman of 30 years, her long raven hair like a river of silk. Her eyes were ensnaring, all-seeing. I am beguiled.' The four of us stand there in awe, taking in the photograph of the woman before us.

'It has to be her. Seal, can he tell us where to find her?' I turn to catch Seal's eye.

'Où pouvons-nous la trouver?' Seal queries the priest. He hangs his head and beckons us to follow him once more.

'That doesn't look good,' Tari whispers in my ear as we follow the procession. We exit the church into the yard, the priest walking through the light drizzle toward the graveyard. He comes to a stop before a speckled grey headstone. Patting Seal gently on the shoulder; he slowly returns to the church.

'She died?' I frown, squatting down in front of the stone, the rain soaking my clothes and dripping from my hair. Seal leans down beside me, the frustration evident on his face.

'How else do we discover if Mr Evan's is her son?'

Xi asks no one in particular.

'He can't be,' I whisper, my fingers reaching gingerly toward the stone. 'She died the same year Winnie met her.' Tari leans over beside us, gasping softly.

'Does it say what happened?' Tari looks at Seal.

'Just that she was lost in a tragic accident, unwed and a spinster,' he states, reading the inscription on the stone.

'Well, Winnie and Aurélie, your little tryst shall remain a secret,' I smile fondly down at the headstone. 'Do you guys mind if we take a detour on the way back to the cottage? I wouldn't mind driving past the lake Winnie talks about, where he and Aurélie met up in secret.'

Sitting in the living room of the cottage before the roaring stone fireplace, sipping red wine from the Bordeaux region; the four of us planned the next leg of our journey in search of mystery woman number two.

'Where are we off to next?' Seal smiles across at us from his place closest to the fire.

'Barcelona!' Tari shouts excitedly.

'I like Barcelona,' Seal nods, 'a beautiful seaside city, full of intricate architecture.'

'What should we plan to see there?' I turn to Seal, propping my feet up underneath me, my cold toes relishing the warmth.

'Barcelona is covered in buildings designed by Antoni Gaudí; I'd recommend taking the opportunity to visit and view the highlights; the Sagrada Familia is a must.' Seal digs out his phone and swipes through photographs.

'Where should we stay? Somewhere in the centre of town?' Tari frowns down at her map.

'I thought we could try something a little more luxurious?' I smile across at her, turning my laptop to show her the W Hotel. The gigantic glass and steel building rose as if formed of the sands of Barcelona. Like a surfboard with one straight side, the luxury hotel stood on the shoreline of the beach staring out toward the ocean.

'It looks like something out of an Iron Man movie!' Tari claps her hands and laughs.

'I think we can find a way to make ourselves comfortable there,' Xi nods in quiet appreciation.

'Should we discuss what we know about mystery woman number two?' Seal cocks an eyebrow as he leans across to pour a glass from the whiskey decanter.

'Isabel Sanchez,' Tari states, flipping through her notebook. 'I met Isabel on the steps of the Sagrada Familia; she took my breath away. She was a fount of knowledge of Gaudi's work and life story. After spending a day walking the city together, Isabel invited me back to her village for dinner at La Colònia Güell, Barcelona. Her family owned a restaurant on the land adjacent to Gaudi's Crypt. The next morning she took me to see the village 'crypt', designed by Gaudi himself.'

'How does he keep meeting these women? They just seem to spring up out of nowhere,' Seal shakes his head, leaning back into the sofa.

'I think it was very free-spirited of Winnie to follow his heart,' Xi smiles fondly. Tari and I exchange a look.

I'm not entirely sure it was his heart he was following.

'How many days are we booked in Barcelona?' Tari turns to peer at me, 'I'd love to get in some sightseeing. Maybe we could drop by Madrid too?'

'Drop by Madrid?' I laugh heartily, 'Why don't we see how long it takes to track down Isabel first?'

A knock at the door has Seal and Tari running to collect our pizza delivery.

'Miss Ava?' Xi leans across quietly.

'Hmm?' I turn to face him.

'Would there be any chance we could make a detour before we head home?' He looks at me sheepishly.

'Where would you like to go?' I smile at him warmly.

'I've always dreamed of sitting at a craps table in Monaco.'

'Perhaps a night out on the town is what we'll need? Did you bring a tuxedo?' I grin at him.

'Always be prepared.' He winks back at me.

Seal and Tari return with four large pizza boxes.

'Who's hungry??' Tari hollers. Xi catches my eye as he passes me a plate; I recognise the twinkle of excitement.

6

The Spanish coast twinkled at us as the sun reflected off the water, the shore reaching far beyond what I could see. With temperatures sitting in the low twenties, it was perfect jacket and boot weather. Tari and I had great fun matching scarves and hats to accessorise.

The city itself was vibrant and colourful. Everywhere we turned there was something new to see or a delicious scent luring you toward them. We started to understand what Seal was saying about the architecture. Around every corner stood an incredible piece of history or a building so beautifully crafted, it might as well have been art.

We spent two days pottering around the city and frolicking along the beach before finally deciding it was time to track down Isabel Sanchez.

'I've come to a realisation,' Seal huffs from his seat, scratching his chin.

'That ham and bacon goes on everything? Because

we already knew that.' I state as I take another huge bite of my Jamon sandwich. The four of us had found a beautiful cafe with gourmet sandwiches and salads, just downstairs from our hotel for lunch on the second day.

'Sanchez is about the second most popular Spanish surname from 30 years ago. Isabel is also up there in the rankings of popularity.' He runs his hands through his hair. 'It might be harder for us to find her than we are anticipating.'

Tari and I exchange a look as Tari sips her lemonade.

'I thought we could just drive out to the town, see if her family restaurant still stood and see if they could tell us where to find her?' I shrug, picking an anchovy out of my sandwich and placing it on Seal's plate.

'What if it isn't that easy? What if the restaurant is gone or her whole family were wiped out by something? We got lucky with Aurelie.' Seal grumbles, piling the anchovy onto a chip and munching away.

'Seal, would you prefer to stay in the city tomorrow while we go hunting for Isabel?' I smile across at him, stealing a chip from his plate.

'You wouldn't mind?' He frowns back.

'Of course not, no one knows who we are here; besides, Xi will be with us.' Xi gives me a thumbs up from across the table. It seems like such an out of place gesture coming from him, but I find myself grinning back.

I look down into my lap and realise I've dribbled sauce everywhere.

Pure class, Ava.

'Ugh, okay I need to go back to the hotel and clean up. I'll meet you two at the spa at 3 pm.' I smile across at Tari and Seal. Xi had opted to spend the afternoon in the hotel's gym and sauna.

Back at the hotel, I dig out a clean pair of shorts and drag them on. I plonk down on the bed and drag out my laptop to check my emails. There were a couple of updates from Sasha and the usual copies into the daily goings-on from Chen. I open one from Jia and chuckle the whole way through it. It seems she had been on a rather disappointing date and needed to express her frustration to a single gal pal. I flip through the other email accounts to double-check I haven't missed anything and spot an email caught in my junk folder last week.

My heart jumps into my throat.

To: ava.elias@outlook.com

Hi Ava,

I called Seal yesterday, and he said he was half asleep because you were all in Europe. I saw on the news about the paternity challenge, that sucks. I just wanted to let you know that I gave the keys to Carcassonne back to the housekeeper. I'm moving back to Melbourne because the season has finished up. I've cleared out my stuff so, yeah. Thanks for letting me stay there and eat your food. It saved me a fair bit of hassle and I've saved some money too.

Anyways, catch ya.

-Ryan

I stare at the screen.

What am I meant to say to that? Do I reply? Why didn't Seal tell me Ryan had called?

I stand up and walk to the minibar. Digging out a bottle of orange juice, I sip it as I make my way to the window and stare out across Barcelona. I watch the waves far below, rolling like cotton balls upon the shore. Out to sea, I spot a few large vessels being guided in and out of the docks by smaller pilot boats. They glide across the ocean, appearing effortless at this distance. I know that not to be the case on board as the large ships face the waves breaking beneath them.

I should ask the team to get me on one of our ships for a few days. I haven't had much to do with the 'away from port' aspect of the job. Winnie spent half his time at the docks, at the coalface.

I pace back and forth before the window, contemplating what to do about Ryan. He was so angry the last time I saw him. I can't shake the vision of him bitterly packing his bag and driving away.

So much has changed since then, hasn't it?

I stomp back to my laptop and mash out a reply.
To: ryan.murphy@hotmail.com
Dear Ryan,
I appreciate you letting me know. I hope the season ended well for you. I am glad to hear you found Carcassonne comfortable and have saved some money. Yes, we are in Europe trying to track down the mother of our Plaintiff. I don't want to face the

reality that will ensue if we are unsuccessful in fending off the suit. Everything Winnie worked for, in the hands of strangers. Anyway, I shouldn't be burdening you with my woes.

Stay safe, love Ava x

I hit send before I chicken out, only to realise I wrote 'love Ava' as the sign off.

Eh, screw it. I will probably always love him, I can't help it if he doesn't want to be with me.

Although, he was mostly concerned about waiting around for me while I galivant around Singapore with Chen. And Chen and I did sleep together. But that wasn't until after Ryan broke up with me.

Oh god, this is such a mess.

I shut the laptop and find my fluffy slippers before heading to the lift.

Who needs men! I have an afternoon of pampering to get to!

The next morning Xi, Tari and I pile into our hire car for the drive to the town of La Colònia Güell in search of Isabel Sanchez.

'Any idea what Seal was up to today?' Tari turns to peer at me from her seat riding shotgun.

'No idea, probably some nerdy thing he's too embarrassed to admit,' I shrug, digging around my handbag for my lip balm.

'Nerdy? Really?' Tari scoffs, turning back toward the windscreen.

'I hope Isabel's family own a tapas place; I'm going to be hungry by the time we get there,' I declare, my stomach groaning up at me.

'We only ate an hour ago,' Tari laughs jovially. 'Are we going to visit Gaudi's Crypt while we are out here today?'

'I think it will be hard for us to miss. According to the map, it is across the street from the restaurant. I hope we find a more pleasant history for Isabel than we did for Aurelie.'

'Poor woman. How terrible to die so young? At least we know she died having experienced young love,' Tari chuckles.

'How long have you been married, Xi?' I ask conversationally, looking at the back of Xi's head in the driver's seat.

'15 years Miss Ava,' he states proudly.

'Where did you meet your wife?' Tari asks while reaching around to offer me a packet of gummy worms.

'We studied together at university. She was a chemistry major, and I studied international relations,' Xi looked out the window as he changed lanes, following the GPS.

'I didn't realise you were interested in politics,' I frown at the back of his head and grab a handful of sugary goodness from Tari.

'It was a passion, but not something I could sustain to make a living off. I took over my father's business and began driving a few weeks after graduation.' I could almost detect a twinge of sadness in his tone.

'I don't know that my girlfriend and I will make it to 15 years. She is so much hard work,' Tari chimes in, chewing grotesquely.

'Nothing worth keeping is easy,' Xi admonishes.

Tari sits back contemplatively, mulling over Xi's comment. I too found myself considering it.

Perhaps Xi is right, maybe anything worth having comes at a cost.

Driving down the narrow lanes, I realise the village is exactly what I had imagined. Square stone buildings covered in beige and brown stucco cement lined the streets, their balconies projecting out over the footpaths. Some had billowing sheets and laundry hanging from them; others had large flower pots, whose contents were mostly brown and recovering from the cold winter. I send a silent thank you to the technology gods as Xi followed the GPS through the winding laneways.

'Okay, so we checked out google maps and it looks like there are two restaurants on the same 'block' as the crypt.' Tari turns the paper map this way and that, trying to find the spots we circled.

'Why don't we just park at the crypt and walk back?' I suggest, recalling that everything seemed within walking distance on the map.

'Good idea Miss Ava, I will drive there directly,' Xi acknowledges and proceeds toward the tourist site.

Even from the car park of the Crypt, the large stone structure was clearly visible. A strange mishmash of stained-glass windows, coloured mosaic tiles and jagged stone, rose out from the ground.

'It looks like a spider,' Tari observes, the long spindly front supports sticking out like legs.

'I was going to say pizza oven, but spider works too,' I laugh. 'Gaudi designed this originally as a Church, but they named it 'the crypt' after they ceased work on it.'

'Do you think he was on drugs?' Tari frowns at the building, tilting her head this way and that.

'Maybe! Wasn't everyone who was influential from that time?' I laugh, zipping up my coat as a cold wind blew in. 'Let's go see if we can find the Sanchez family restaurant!'

Of the two restaurants we had noted, one was very clearly closed down. The door and windows had been boarded up, a thick layer of dust on the front stoop.

'I guess that leaves us with one option?' I frown down at the map as we turn the direction of the second restaurant.

We wander down the lanes, observing the concrete facades of the buildings, some with stone doorways, others covered in intricately carved clay tiles.

We come to a stop in front of a pale yellow single-storey building, its front door propped open by a large rusty milk pale.

'Here goes nothing!' I step toward the door before stopping and turning to Xi and Tari, 'Perhaps it's best if we don't crowd them? Do you mind waiting out here?'

I duck through the doorway into a dimly lit dining space. I don't immediately spot anyone, realising that it is probably too early for most people in this area to be eating lunch.

'Hola?' I call out, taking in the space. Circular

ANNA WINSON

timber tables sit scattered around the room, hand-
drawn menus sitting proudly astride the tabletops. A
woman appears, her greying hair pulled up in a bun
on her crown, tendrils breaking loose and falling
down her shoulder blades.

'Hola, Mi nombre es Ava. Habla inglés?' I silently
thank google translate for getting me this far.

'A little,' the lady replies, her wide eyes taking me
in. 'Lunch?'

'Uh, yes, please. But first, do you know Isabel
Sanchez?' I smile at her, hoping she understands.

'Isabel?' She frowns at me. Not an encouraging
sign.

'Sanchez restaurant?' I try again raising my arms in
question, hoping this makes sense.

'Isabel es mi hermana, uh - Isabel is my sister.' She
continues to frown at me. I feel a broad smile break
across my face.

Please don't let her be dead, please don't let her be
dead.

'Does she live nearby?' I ask, trying to keep calm.
The lady shakes her head in confusion. I pull out my
phone and open google translate.

'Um, Ella vive cerca?' I try, frowning at my awful
pronunciation. The lady turns and walks out of the
room. For the first time since I met Winnie, I
suddenly question the accuracy of google translate. I
stand there awkwardly, uncertain as to what to do
next.

Suddenly, her head pops back through the door,
and she beckons me to follow her.

I carefully tread my way through a narrow hallway

and up a very precarious flight of timber stairs to another landing. I hear the lady ahead of me calling out in Spanish, but she speaks so quickly I cannot catch a word.

'Isabel,' she stops and points through another doorway. I thank her and watch her disappear back down the corridor.

I gaze around the room, which seems even dimmer than the one we'd just exited.

'Hola?' I ask the room.

'My sister tells me you are Ava, looking for Isabel Sanchez?' I hear a quiet voice to my left. Turning in that direction, I spot a woman in a tall, rocking chair. Her dark grey hair flows wildly down from her head, tucked behind her ears to reveal a stunning angular face.

'I am Ava. I have travelled a long way to find you.' I smile across at her as I approach.

'Please sit.' She waves me gently into an embellished chair beside her. 'What can I do for you?' Her hazel eyes catching what little light there is in the room.

'I am sorry to come here uninvited, but I have a personal question, if I may?' I open my phone to the picture of Mr Evans. 'Do you know this man?' I hand her the phone, watching her reaction closely.

'I do not, I am sorry.' She shakes her head gently and hands me back the phone. I flip through a couple of photos and find an older one of Winnie from when he was younger.

'What about this man?' I hand her back the phone and see her face darken.

Oh shit. That was unexpected.

'Why did you come here?' She stares down at the

phone, her tone harsh and sharp.

'Mr Huynh passed away last year. I am trying to track down the mother of the man in the first photograph.' My explanation suddenly sounds exceptionally hollow.

'Why?' She doesn't look up.

'Mr Huynh left me in charge of his company in Singapore, and that man is claiming that Winnie is his father,' I whisper.

'And you came here to ask me if that man is my son? To ask if Mr Huynh and I had relations.' She practically spits the last word.

'I can see now; it was grossly inappropriate of me to have presumed.'

'How did you find me?'

'Winnie kept journals of his travels and adventures. He mentioned meeting a beautiful woman who taught him about Gaudi and fed him at her family restaurant in this village.'

She looks up at me, her face aglow in the light from my phone. I see her features soften as she looks back at Winnie's photograph, her fingers barely caressing the screen.

'We met on the steps of the Sagrada Familia. The queues were not as long as they are today, but we stood beside one another for 20 minutes when the wind caught my hat. He was such a gentleman; he left the line to chase it across the street.' She smiles fondly across at me.

'When he returned, the couple behind us argued that he had left the queue. I took his hand and explained that we were together. I had never felt such a jolt when touching another person before, nor have I since.' I hear the sadness in her voice.

'I immediately fell in love. We spent time in Barcelona, I showed him my University, and when the time came to part ways, I invited him to meet my family. He joined us here for dinner. The moment my father laid eyes on him, I knew he would never allow us to be together.' I feel my heart breaking for her, and this young couple who were never given the chance to explore their affection.

'My father took me aside and told me he forbade it. My sister told me he was so loud it was lucky Mr Huynh didn't speak Spanish for he would have blushed at my father's language. They could hear him from the dining room. Even though he didn't speak Spanish, he knew my father objected; I could see it in his face when we returned to the table.' I instinctually lean across to pat her arm. She looks at me in surprise, before laying an aged hand over mine and squeezing it affectionately.

'That night, I drove him back to his hotel in the city. I knew I would have to return before dawn or my father would come looking for me. We bade one another farewell, and I never saw him again. We did exchange letters and postcards on occasion during our travels. I was saddened to hear of his passing.' She hangs her head and looks down at our hands.

'Did you eventually meet a handsome young man your father approved of?' I smile encouragingly at her.

'I did, very soon after I met Winnie. Marco and I married and had five children. We lost two over the years, and Marco passed three years ago. He was much older than I was. I have spent much of the last few years looking after grandbabies and taking over the restaurant with my sister after we lost my parents.'

She smiles across at me.

'I am sorry for my lack of hospitality, my dear. I am but an old woman these days, with nothing but her memories from a lifetime ago.'

'You have nothing to apologise for. I came in here, barged into your home and interrogated you for my own selfish reasons. I cannot thank you enough for telling me your story.' I squeeze her arm, taking my phone as she hands it back.

'Would you like something to eat?' She smiles at me, waving one hand toward the door.

'I would be honoured. If I may, I'd like to introduce you to my travelling companions?'

'Of course, please.'

Downstairs I met an anxious Tari and Xi at the door.

'Oh thank god, we thought you'd been murdered in there!' Tari throws her arms around me.

'Isabel invited us to join her for lunch.' I smile at them both, waving them inside.

'Is he her kid, tell us quickly!' Tari hisses as we walk in the door, I turn and shake my head at them.

'Thank god,' Tari whispers underneath her breath.

Completely satiated after consuming more food than I'd care to admit, we bid Isabel farewell and drove back toward Barcelona in the early afternoon.

'What a lovely woman! And I must say, those chorizo meatballs...I will spend my life trying to replicate them,' I laugh, shaking my head.

'Did she study at a Western University? Her English was great, she hardly had an accent,' Tari observes from the front seat.

'I think she said she studied in Barcelona but I think she studied English as part of her Major,' I frown, trying to recall.

'It was very kind of her to invite us into her home and share her stories with us,' Xi adds from the driver's seat. We fall into a comfortable silence as we watch the countryside morph into the outskirts of the city once again.

'Ryan emailed me,' I state to no one in particular, staring out the window.

'Uh, what did he say?' Tari hesitates. I can imagine her cocking her eyebrow sardonically.

'That he gave the keys to Carcassonne back and returned to Melbourne.' I try to keep my voice nonchalant.

'Ah,' is all Tari says.

'Are you okay Miss Ava?' Xi turns slightly to look at me in the rear-view mirror.

'I miss him. How could I not? But he made his decision, and I can't force him to wait for me.' I sigh, feeling the weight of reality hit me.

He will meet someone new if he hasn't already. He will move on, and he will leave me behind. Is this how he felt? Like I was leaving him behind?

The thought unsettles me. I push it aside.

'I have an obligation to HEH. To look after the people Winnie left in my care,' I hesitate, only to realise neither Tari nor Xi have commented, 'don't I?'

'My girlfriend always says it is a 'matter of priorities'. She seems to think money grows on trees and complains when I take extra shifts instead of spending the time with her.' I can almost hear Tari's eye-rolling.

'So if I really cared about Ryan I would have prioritised him over HEH?' I frown harder.

'Oh, I'm not necessarily saying it applies to your relationship. I also think Ryan was childish by throwing a tantrum over you trying to look after your company. He seemed happy to enjoy the perks of dating a wealthy woman, but not so much the work that being wealthy took.' I see Tari shrug in front of me before turning in her seat to face me. 'I don't know that there was a win-win option for the two of you. Besides, isn't that exactly why the other Invisible women don't tell their husbands what they really do?'

'You make a fair point. And yes, Margot and Linah told me they didn't tell their spouses for different reasons but that does sort of cover it in a nutshell.' I chew my lip. 'There's no way I could have hidden HEH from Ryan. I had never even considered it.'

'Did you reply to him?'

'Yeah, just the usual pleasantries,' I sigh.

'I guess he hasn't responded?'

'Nope,' it comes out more like a huff.

'If the two of you are destined for each other, you will find a way back together,' Xi states confidently. I can't help but smile, Xi has surprised me a lot this trip.

'Thanks, Xi,' I shrug.

After returning to the hotel, we find Seal stretched out on a sun lounger beside the pool. I wrap my cardigan more tightly around me as the wind picks up across the deck.

'Seal, how on earth are you out here in boardies? It's cold!' I whine, watching with curiosity as a bartender walks across with a large cocktail on a tray. Seal takes it and tips him before sipping the colourful concoction.

'I am quite comfortable here thank you,' he smiles at our trio. 'How did you go with Isabel? Did you find her?'

The three of us sit down on the loungers and describe the events of the morning and the incredible lunch Isabel fed us.

'I guess that means we are on our way to Switzerland then?' Seal raises an eyebrow. The four of us look at one another, broad grins breaking out on our faces.

'Ah, Switzerland! The home of snow capped mountains and fancy chocolate,' Tari sighs. 'Why can't Singapore be famous for something fun and interesting like chocolate?'

'Don't start with that again! Australia is famous for being full of creatures that want to kill you and our passion for alcoholism. I'd take any of Singapore's famous icons in a heartbeat,' I scoff, waving the bartender over to order a warm Moscow mule.

'I'll be sad to leave Barcelona; I like it here.' Seal sips his cocktail and looks at the resort around us.

'I think I am going to enjoy Switzerland. The fresh air, tranquillity. I've heard the pace is much more relaxed in the smaller towns too,' Xi observes, stretching out on a lounger.

'We are searching for Elena Ottinger, who Winnie met in Engelberg. I know I'm still stuffed from lunch, but should we go get ready for dinner? I'm dying to try some genuine Spanish paella before we leave here!' Tari leans over and bumps me with her shoulder.

'Oh, me too! Full of seafood and chorizo!' I can

taste it already.

The restaurant we found sat on the marina. It had great reviews and sold several different types of paella, it was touted as 'the best Paella in Barcelona'. La Fonda del Port Olímpic was unassuming from the outside, but once we sat down and ordered our paella we were pleased with our choice.

'Ooh, look at that one!' Tari pats my arm enthusiastically, pointing in the direction of a waiter carrying a paella tray they size of my Jeep tyre.

The smells coming from the kitchen made our mouths water.

'Someone distract me before I crash tackle a waiter.' Tari turns back to the rest of us.

'Why don't we plan for Switzerland?' I suggest, sipping my red wine sangria.

'Great idea!' Tari digs around in her bag for her notebooks, while I drag out my laptop. 'Who's ready for story time?' Tari grins across at Seal.

'Dear Diary...' Seal chuckles, leaning back in his chair to flag the waiter down. 'If we are hosting story time we are going to need more sangria.'

I laugh and shake my head; I can no longer imagine my life without these incredible people in it.

Tari flips through the notebook and opens to a page copied from Winnie's diary.

'An unexpected result from my journey to Zurich was meeting Elena Ottinger. Elena worked for the export group with whom HEH tried building international relations. After the meeting sank like a lead balloon, I was rather frustrated and headed to the hotel bar to console myself. Elena followed me wishing to offer her apologies for her colleagues' behaviour. We got to talking, and she told me of the alpine village in which she grew up, Engelberg. It sounded idyllic, and after weeks of gruelling meetings, I felt it was time for a rest.'

'Of course he did, I can already tell Elena is beautiful. Even her name is beautiful,' Seal interrupts, pointing toward the notebook. 'Winnie, you sly dog.'

'Don't make this dirty! It's romantic!' Tari glowers across the table at Seal.

'My apologies, please continue!' Seal tries to placate Tari but not before turning to raise an eyebrow at me.

I'm just as surprised as you are mate, I wouldn't have picked Tari as the romantic type either.

'Elena mentioned she was returning home and invited me to join her and see what this country has to offer.' Tari stops and glares at Seal, daring him to comment. He raises his hands in defeat and gestures for her to continue. The waiter arrives carrying two more large jugs of sangria.

'Good lord Seal, we are going to be drunk before the meal arrives at this rate!' I laugh at him.

'Whenever you're ready?' Tari sulks from across the table, and I shrug at her sheepishly; we thank the waiter and Tari continues.

'Elena showed me the most beautiful parts of Engelberg. Her family operate the Gondola that ferries tourists up and down Mount Titlis. From what I can gather, it is rather a lucrative business.'

'So we need to find the headquarters of the people who run the Gondola,' Xi states, pouring himself a ruby glass from the jug.

'Okay, why don't we fly into Luzerne and take a helicopter down to Engelberg? It looks like we can probably make do on foot once we are in town?' I suggest clicking around the map on my laptop.

'Don't you want to hear the rest of his entry about Switzerland?' Tari looks like she is about to have a stroke.

'Does it help us find Elena, or does he continue to describe the food and scenery?' Seal levels with her, deadpan.

'Ugh fine,' Tari rolls her eyes and puts the notebook away.

'Perfect timing,' Xi pipes up, seeing a waiter making a beeline for our table. I feel my mouth water, watching the giant tray headed toward us.

The first paella we ordered was seafood; the second was seafood and meat. Giant prawns, mussels and chunks of crab stared up at us from the large rice bed. Everything was stained a glorious red colour, seeped in tomatoes and spices. I feel my stomach growl from beneath the table.

'This looks incredible!' Tari drags her phone out and begins snapping photos, occasionally repositioning glasses and plates to get a better shot.

After dinner we strolled barefoot along the beach back to our hotel. Back in my room, I fire up my laptop to check any important emails before I shower and crawl into bed. I feel my heart jump into my throat. One new email from Ryan Murphy.

What if he tells me he's seeing someone else? What if he asks me if anything happened with Chen? Realistically, the likelihood of that is low...right?

I stand before my laptop, staring blankly at the screen. I realise I am biting my lip, the anxiety rolling off me in waves.

I have to read it; there's no way I'm going to sleep tonight otherwise.

I open the email and take a deep breath.

To: ava.elias@outlook.com

Hey Ava,
I ran into your folks at the Fitzroy Gardens today. Seems they hadn't heard the news about us. They insisted on taking me to lunch to catch up. I didn't have it in me to tell them the truth, and they kept talking about that family trip to the USA we'd all talked about taking together.

Anyways, I just thought I'd tell ya in case your mum mentions it. I gotta say, it was kinda nice getting to hang out with your family again.

Catch ya

Oh my god, I still haven't told my family. Tari was right, I came to Europe to run away.

I look down at Ryan's email again, reading it through twice, three times.

How the hell do I reply to that?

I type out three different replies and delete them all. Each one was getting snarkier than the last. I decide my best course of action is to take a shower and come back to reply when I'm less frustrated. The shower didn't help nearly as much as I'd thought it would. I stand there under the steaming hot water, fuming at Ryan's email.

Of course he loves my family, he always has even when they'd come to visit in Dinner Plain way back in the beginning. Newsflash buddy, if you hadn't broken up with me, we'd still be together, and you'd get to see them all the time!

I'm so frustrated that I can't remember if I've shampooed my hair, so I wash it twice. After standing under the stream for far longer than environmentally considerate, I shut off the water and drag on my waffle robe.

I walk back over to my laptop and begin replying, chanting to myself, 'cool, calm, collected' although I felt anything but.

To: ryan.murphy@hotmail.com

Dear Ryan,

Thanks for the heads up. My apologies, I didn't have time to tell them before I left and I wanted to tell them in person. I'll clear it up the next time I'm back in Melbourne.

I hope you're keeping well.

-Ava

Well, that sounds okay, right? Here goes nothing.

I hit send and pace around the room a bit. After a

few minutes, I decide to brew myself a cup of tea and read a book before bed.

7

Tari held my hand for dear life as the helicopter soared through the Swiss alps.

'Ava! We're gonna die!' She screams into her cans.

'It can take a bit to get used to!' I call back, squeezing her hand between both of mine. I catch the look on Seal's face as he chuckles quietly.

From the air, Switzerland looked like every travel magazine I'd ever seen. Rolling green hills, snow capped mountains, deep blue green lakes.

The alpine village we were looking for stood out against the green landscape. Rectangular buildings stood in an array of colours at the base of the valley. A crisp blue creek ran through the centre of the town, cascading down from the mountains at higher elevation.

After landing, we spend quite some time reassuring Tari that we didn't die and will not die whenever we chopper back to the Screaming Eagle, parked at the airbase in Luzerne.

'But it is so dangerous! I read the news articles when all those helicopters crashed in the USA!'

I left Xi with Tari as Seal and I made our way on foot to our accommodation. The Ski Lodge Engelberg sat in the middle of town, a four-storey tall white building with dark trim.

'Not bad, but why did you pick this place again?' Seal turns to look at me quizzically.

'They have an outdoor hot tub and sauna sitting in the middle of a huge pasture with 180-degree views of the mountains!' I giggle, clapping my hands with glee. Even though it was technically autumn, the afternoon air was crisp and chilly. We step inside as Seal lets out a low whistle.

'Now this is my kind of place!' He steps further into the room and peers around. The entry, adjacent restaurant and bar had a distinctive speakeasy vibe— lots of dark leather, timber accents and old fashioned skis decorating the walls.

Once we had the paperwork signed, we discovered Xi and Tari had found their way to us.

'Look, Ava! Xi bought me a SWISS ARMY KNIFE! From Switzerland!' She waved the compact metal gadget in my face.

'Excellent! Give the woman having a minor breakdown a dangerous weapon,' I huff under my breath at Xi.

'Not to worry Miss Ava, she can't figure out how to get the blades out anyway.' He winks at me. I nod my thanks at him, knowing full well that thing must have cost him a mint.

We dined in the restaurant early that night, before heading to our respective rooms for some much-needed shut-eye. Before turning in, I grab my laptop from my bag and check my emails. I'd be lying if I didn't admit I was hoping to find something in my inbox from Ryan. I take a deep breath and open my inbox. Nothing. I double-check my junk mail. Still nothing.

Maybe this remote reconciliation I had going on in my head is exactly that, all in my head.

Feeling extremely deflated, I begrudgingly drag myself to bed and flip off the bedside lamp.

The next morning the four of us finished our breakfast and made our way toward the base of the gondola to Mount Titlis. You could cut the nervous tension with a knife. I think we were all very much aware that this was our last chance to find the mother of Mr Evans. None of us had been willing to voice what we would do if we did not find her in Elena Ottinger.

It was a beautiful bright blue sky day with a light breeze and very few people out at this time of the morning. We anxiously wandered through the cobblestone paths of Engelberg feeling the tension rise the nearer we came to the gondola.

I observed our unusual group as we each expressed our anxiety in peculiar ways. Seal continued to check his pockets in order; top left, top right, pant pocket left, right; Tari continued to feel for her new Swiss knife securely in her pocket; I felt the need to look at the time on my phone pulling it out of my pocket every 60 seconds. Xi appeared to be the only one who had his nerves under control. He calmly and confidently walked toward the gondola entry following the GPS on his phone.

The four of us stop at the entry to the gondola and look at one another. It would be the only recognition we each gave to our fear that we may be just moments away from saving HEH, or finding ourselves waiting for the court date in December to determine our fate.

Xi takes the lead and walks confidently through the glass doors toward the front counter. Within the room, I notice posters plastered on every wall of the beautiful mountain at which we stood the base. I take a deep breath and turn to follow Xi toward the counter where he orders four tickets up the mountain before politely asking the woman behind the counter if she knows of an Elena Ottinger. The woman tucks her silky blonde hair behind one ear and bats her eyelids up at Xi. I leave him to take directions from the woman on how to find Elena, turning to find Seal and Tari looking at the posters of the gondola on the wall.

'Ava!' Tari hisses. I walk across to her and wrap an arm around her shoulders.

'What's up?' I smile at her, feeling a smidge of relief.

'Did you know that the gondola thing is a GIANT FUCKING CABLE CAR?' She whispers accusatorially at me.

'Uh, how else did you think we'd get up the mountain?' I frown, confused by how angry she is.

'Can't we take the helicopter?!' She wails, clenching my arm hysterically.

'Yesterday I was quite certain you didn't like the helicopter?' I laugh at her, spotting Seal's raised eyebrows behind Tari.

'I'd take that over this any day!' She disentangles herself from me and strops across to throw herself down in a chair.

'Its okay, I can stay here with her,' Seal sighs kindly. I turn to look at him, to see him smiling down at Tari.

'She'll love it when we get to the top, I promise. Just let her cling to you instead of me this time, okay? I think her talons will leave a permanent scar,' I laugh and rub my forearm instinctively.

Xi returns to the group, tickets in hand.

'Okay. We have tickets and the lady at the counter told me that an Elena Ottinger works at the other end of the lifts. She gave me directions on where to find her.' He fist-pumps the air in triumph. I wonder to myself if I will ever see or hear this man do or say something that won't surprise me someday.

'Nope,' Tari crosses her arms over her chest and pouts like a child.

'I'd never take you for a whimp,' I jeer. It hits the spot.

'A whimp? Are you calling me a chicken?' She glowers from her chair.

'If it lays eggs and clucks...' I raise an eyebrow at her.

'Oh, I'll show you!' She jumps from the chair and storms across to the blessedly short queue for the gondola. Within 2 minutes, we were standing in a large rectangular cabin that looked much like a train or tram carriage floating in mid-air. The view of the mountains as we were carried up higher and higher, blew my mind. Towering, jagged peaks sprinkled with snow, met deep valleys of green grass and crystal blue lakes.

No wonder the Swiss alps are a poster child for Europe; this view takes your breath away.

After a couple of carriage changes; the gondola eventually docks at Mount Titlis. Across the mountain tops, we have an almost 360-degree view of the skyline. I turn to the others once we clear the exit and stand on the precipice of the small community that sits atop the mountain.

'Why don't you guys go find us somewhere to grab a coffee. I'm going to see if I can find Elena. Afterwards, we can go on the Cliff Walk and see the Ice Cave.' I shrug, taking a deep breath and praying to the gods that she can answer our questions. The others wish me luck before heading toward the Panorama restaurant. I take a deep breath and crack my neck anxiously.

I can do this—just one last one.

I can't bear to think about what I will do if she can't help me. I also can't bear the thought of having come all this way to return home empty-handed.

I turn toward the return of the gondola and find an attendant. A teenage boy stands wearing a 'Mount Titlis' safety vest in navy blue.

'Uh, Hello?' I start nervously, 'I am looking for Elena Ottinger?'

I see the boy look me up and down critically. He seems to mull it over before pointing toward a door to my left. I murmur my thanks and walk hesitantly toward the door. I say a silent prayer under my breath and knock on the timber frame.

'Ja?' comes the reply from the other side.

I gingerly turn the nob and open the door a crack.

'Was willst du?' The voice grumbles through the doorway.

'Uh, Hello?' I call out, peering through the gap. Suddenly the door is wrenched from my hand, and a tall blonde woman stands before me. She is utterly beguiling. She has long blonde corn silk hair, aged only by the slightest ashy tones. Her skin looks as though it wouldn't have aged a day since Winnie knew her. I realise looking up that she is much taller than I am, with a face of thunder.

'Hello?' I try again, attempting a smile, suddenly aware of how heavy her breathing is between us. She says nothing.

'I'm Ava; I'm a friend of Mr Huynh Li's?' I notice her face soften ever so slightly. I reach into my pocket and pull out my phone, finding the photo of Mr Evans from the TV. 'Do you possibly know Mr Marcus Evans?'

Her eyes lock onto the phone, and suddenly she is shoving me back through the doorframe. I trip and land on my ass just as the door slams in my face.

Ah, fuck. I guess that answers that question then.

In shock, I suspect, I slowly make my way to my feet and glare at the pimply teenager laughing his ass off at my embarrassment.

'Thanks for the help,' I mutter underneath my breath.

I make my way around the gondola shed and slowly walk toward the Panorama Cafe, stopping outside the doors to breathe in the mountain air on the veranda. Leaning against the railing, I squat down and drop my head into my hands.

How I have missed this icy mountain air, it brings

with it a wave of guilt afresh for Ryan and a deep homesickness. Sitting there peering through my fingers down the mountains, I feel a shadow pass over me.

'Why do you 'ave a picture of my son?' A heavily German-accented voice growls down at me. I peer up at the impossibly beautiful woman, her face, less angry than before.

'I was looking for his mother,' I state bluntly. I watch her face transform slowly into a quizzical scowl.

'Vhy?'

'He is suing me for something, and I wanted to know for certain if it was true.' I frown at myself, wondering if that sentence made any sense.

'Marcus iz suing you? Who are you?' She comes to sit on the veranda beside me. I kick my legs out from the squat and momentarily wonder how wet an ass I'm about to get.

'You're Marcus Evan's mother?' I look across at her. She nods mutely.

'I am trying to find out who his father is.' I stare at her blankly.

'Why iz he suing you, and what does hiz father have to do vith anything?' She frowns at me again. I dig out my phone once more and open the old picture of Winnie.

'Do you know this man?' I hand her the phone and pull my gloves out of my pocket. She stares at the image of Winnie, her eyes darting across to my face and back again numerous times.

'Marcus is claiming Mr Huynh,' I point to the photo, 'is his father.' I watch Elena's face closely, her eyes widen, and she looks away from me.

'Is there something you'd like to tell me?' I ask gently, leaning away to give her some space. A cold breeze whips up, lashing us both on the exposed platform.

'Marcus has always been angry; he never had a father.' She shudders, passing me back the phone. 'He died only weeks after Marcus was born. I gave him his father's surname so he could have a piece of him. Because I was pregnant, how do you say it? Not married?' She looks at me, lost for words.

'Out of wedlock?' I offer.

'Yes, it meant Marcus and I were left by ourselves. We were lucky my family had good money with the Gondola and were able to help us.' She lets out a heavy sigh.

'That must have been hard,' I offer.

'Marcus refused to believe me about his father, convinced he was out zhere somewhere. Why vould he think Vinnie was his father?' She frowns across at me.

'I was hoping you might be able to answer that? He appeared on television in Singapore after filing a suit against Winnie's company HEH for paternity rights. Did you hear about Winnie's passing?' I look across, seeing Elena's face crumple.

'I was very sad to hear; I found my old box of photographs and found one I 'ad taken of Winnie when ve met. Perhaps that is where Marcus got ze idea. Because I was upset about this man's death, and I knew him the same year I became pregnant to Marcus' father.'

'Would you mind if I asked you to tell me the story of how you and Winnie met?' I ask gently.

'We met in Zurich. The business deal he vas

arranging fell down. I invited him to come to Engelberg and meet my family. To get out of ze city.' She looks up at the sky and wraps her coat more tightly around herself.

'I like to take photographs, and we came up here, up the mountain. I showed him how to take good photos. He taught me about business; we talked about Asia. I had never been there, so he described ze food, ze people. We spent three days together, talking, taking photographs. When it was time for him to leave, I was very sad. I did not want him to go, and I took a photo of him to remember him by. I caught him by surprise, and my sister stood in the background. It is one of my most favourite photographs.' She smiles fondly at the memory. I smile across at her.

'I can understand why, from the glimpse of it I saw on the TV, it was a lovely photo.'

'I am so sorry Marcus is causing trouble. What you must think of me, for raising a son such as this?' She drops her face into her hands.

'I think nothing of the sort. But I would be very grateful if you would come with us to Singapore to help us fix this?'

She looks up and frowns at me, 'Us? Are you not here alone?'

I shake my head.

'I have three friends waiting inside the restaurant,' I shrug. She frowns at me.

'Then why are we zitting in the cold wet?'

I laugh hard, patting her on the arm.

'I have no idea. Would you like to meet them?'

8

Sitting around the fire pit, cherishing the towering snow-topped mountains, listening to the cowbells in the distance as the herds grazed in lush green pastures, the four of us celebrated finding Elena.

'Who would have thought this crazy plan would pay off?' Tari raises her glass, 'Here's to Winnie and his wild European adventure!'

We all raise our glasses in a chorus of 'to Winnie!'

'Elena seems lovely; I am so relieved she is willing to come back with us and help get her son's case kicked out,' I sigh, thanking the gods that my hunch was right.

'She seemed horrified; I don't know that she was aware of what her son was up to,' Seal observes, kicking his feet up to rest on the rim of the pit.

'Well enough talk of that, we've solved the mystery and now we can relax and enjoy being in Switzerland!' Tari hollers to the vast expanse surrounding us.

'I read in Winnie's diary about this famous Swiss

dessert, Zuger Kirschtorte,' she grins around at us.

'Ah, that is why you insisted we stop in the village on the way home,' Xi chuckles across at her.

'Exactly!' She leans over to her satchel and digs out four petite white boxes.

'What is it?' I frown, taking two boxes and passing one to Seal, lounging beside me.

'According to the internet - because of course I didn't understand a word the woman in the store said...' cake with layers of sponge, buttercream, and nut meringue.' And it looks delicious!' She beams at me. I open the little cardboard box to reveal a small round tart-looking cake under an avalanche of icing sugar.

'What did Winnie say about it?' I frown as I try and figure out how to eat the sweet treat.

'I thought you'd never ask!' She laughs, grabbing the excerpt notebook and flipping through the pages. She stops at a photocopy of Winnie's diary, pasted into her book.

'Elena and I talked for hours about food and culture in Switzerland. Interestingly, after farewelling Elena and beginning the journey back to Zurich, I came across a small village and decided to stop for lunch. On the menu was a delicacy Elena had mentioned; Zuger Kirschtorte. Knowing nothing about the pastry, I ordered one, intrigued by the name.'

I glance around at our group, watching the two men also struggle with the concept of how to eat this without wearing it. Tari continues to read as I take a significant bite and relish the sweet, nutty flavours.

Tari chuckles, and continues reading.

'It looked divine! If Tony hadn't stopped me, I

would have devoured the delicacy which I now realise is occasionally made with Hazelnut meal.'

I choke on the nutty pastry. 'Wait, are you telling me Tony was on this trip with him? You never mentioned him before?'

'Uh, yeah. Those two were inseparable. Tony went everywhere with Winnie. I guess Winnie didn't mention him much because he's basically part of the furniture,' Tari frowns at me, 'why are you having a meltdown?'

I turn to stare at Seal, feeling the blood drain from my face. I watch the cogs turning in his head. 'You don't really think he'd stoop to that do you?' Seal growls across at me.

'Honestly? I wouldn't put it past him?' I whisper.

'Would someone please explain?' Tari's head snaps back and forth between us like she's at a tennis match.

'Ava is suggesting that Mr Evan's sudden appearance was no accident and that Mr Tony contacted him and put him up to it.' Xi fills in the gaps, looking to me to confirm. I nod quietly.

'Do you really think he has that great a memory?' Tari frowns.

'Who knows? Maybe whilst Winnie was ill last year he took copies of these pages from the diaries? There could be any number of explanations, but I can't imagine that this guy woke up one morning and suddenly decided he wanted to contest the will of a man he had likely never heard of.' I anxiously twist Winnie's ring on my finger.

Fucking Tony!

'Even if that is the case, Elena is going to come back to Singapore with us next week and debunk the whole thing. We're saved!' Tari raises her glass, 'Here is a toast, to finally having something go right for HEH.'

I reluctantly agree to push the thought aside and enjoy the moment with my little family.

'To HEH.' We all clinked our glasses together.

'So, we have a week to fill. We are in Europe, what are we going to do?' Tari turns toward me, a twinkle evident in her eye.

'Well, I was thinking we deserve a night or two out after our weeks of detective work.' I turn to smile at Xi. 'Who wants to place a bet at the Casino Monte-Carlo in Monaco?'

By midnight we'd established the itinerary for our trip to the French coast and how to fill in the week as we waited for Elena. Halfway down the corridor to our rooms, I stop Tari as we say goodnight to the gents.

'What's up?' She nudges me with her elbow.

'I was just thinking about Winnie's diaries,' I whisper, eyeing the corridor behind us to check for eavesdroppers.

'What about them?'

'Winnie didn't really mention Tony in any of his diary entries about Europe, even though he was here the whole time. Right?'

'Right?' Tari cocks a quizzical eyebrow.

'So, what else might he have not mentioned that we've missed? You said all that really match up from his two diaries of those last few weeks are ramblings of how he was feeling?'

'And the plans he had to set you up at HEH,' Tari nods.

'What kind of symptoms did he describe? How long did he have them?'

'Do you want to play Dr House? Try to clue together his symptoms? Do you think Tony slowly swapped out medications he was on for ineffective placebos or something?'

I stop and stare at Tari, good lord this girl could be a crime writer with a brain like that.

'It hadn't occurred to me, but yes, maybe he was. I don't remember Winnie ever mentioning being on medication for anything though,' I frown, feeling suddenly weary.

'I'll take a look and let you know what I find.' She smiles at me sleepily before yawning widely. We bid each other goodnight and turn for our respective hallways.

I trundle back into my room, dragging off layers of clothing from the door to the bathroom before climbing into a steaming hot shower.

As has become my routine, I pull out my laptop as I prepare for bed and double check there aren't any pressing emails or news events.

I spot an email reply from Ryan and suddenly feel a bubbly giddy sensation in my stomach. I click the email and anxiously read his reply.

To: ava.elias@outlook.com
No worries, like I said, it was good to see them. Where abouts are you now?
-Ryan

I read and reread the two sentences over and over.

It isn't particularly conversational, but then again,

he didn't have to reply at all did he?

I drop my face into my hands in my lap. I am at a loss as to what this 'means'.

Does it mean anything? Is he just being polite? Does he want something?

I shut down those thoughts, knowing full well they lead down a dangerous path.

To: ryan.murphy@hotmail.com

We had some success today! We think we found what we were looking for in Engelberg, Switzerland. It is the most beautiful little town. You'd love it, it's an alpine ski town, just like Dinner Plain just more European! :P

xx

I sigh heavily, push my laptop aside and drag the duvet up.

The airstrip into Monaco was a little more 'exclusive' than we'd anticipated. Tari and I sat patiently sipping champagne while Seal and Xi spoke to the ground team with the pilot, where we'd been stopped by security.

'What? Do we need some kind of visa or passport or something to get in here?' Tari frowns at me, fiddling with the strawberry on the side of her champagne flute.

'I don't think so. Perhaps this is the 'royal' airstrip or something? Xi and I couldn't find anything about it on the internet, and the pilot wasn't particularly concerned about dropping us here,' I shrug, peering out the window. It didn't help much, where I was perched, I couldn't see past the wing protruding from the body of the plane.

'While we wait, I should answer your questions from yesterday about Winnie's diaries,' Tari shrugs, digging her notepad out of her satchel.

'Oh, yes please.' I nod, sipping my champagne.

'I wrote down all the 'medical-y' stuff he noted, but I have to tell you, looking at it again, it really does read like a whole lot of rambling,' Tari shakes her head, flipping through the pages.

'Something about being 'itchy', feeling 'fuzzy', he said he went to the doctors and they couldn't find anything wrong with him. He started feeling tired and said perhaps age was catching up with him. He talked a lot about age and his plans for you. After a few days he wrote that he feared he wouldn't get a chance to tell you what had happened. He said he was thankful he'd sent you 'the package' - I assume this refers to the box with his pen and the other diary?' She looks at me quizzically. I shrug, just as confused as she is.

'But why do the two journals 'go together'? I am sure he sent the journal to me in the box months before he started getting sick?'

'Maybe because he wrote in the first one a lot about his plans for you and the second one more about his declining health? If he was worried about Tony, maybe he was worried he'd die and Tony would never come and find you and try to cover up Winnie's wishes?'

'Did he write anything at all in the first half about being sick or health concerns of any kind?'

'No, nothing. His last entry he wrote in the book from the box was about the day you two met. He talked about being in the hospital and getting a lecture from the doctor. He added in there about his plans for you but nothing about health issues he'd had.'

The two of us sit there staring at one another completely confounded. Sighing exasperatedly, I down the remainder of my champagne.

I feel even more deflated, realising we are no closer to unravelling the mystery of Winnie's death than we were when I first returned to Singapore.

Maybe Ryan was right, maybe this is a wild goose chase and I am wasting time worrying about it. Does it really matter how Winnie died? Tony didn't 'win' after all.

I feel a shiver run down my spine. I can't shake the feeling that Tony sent that threat letter and if he did, it means he isn't done meddling yet.

We hear voices and footsteps coming up the stairs.

'We are cleared to stay for the week,' Xi smiles triumphantly down at us from the doorway. He steps aside to allow Seal past.

'Seems people can't afford to 'park' their planes here so they leave their planes on the airstrip. Luckily, HEH can afford it!' Seal chuckles.

I roll my eyes, wondering what kind of conniption the finance team are going to have when the bills from this trip start piling up.

The four of us disembark the plane and make our way to the BBSUV parked on the runway. After a short drive to the security booth, we have our passports stamped and drive into the main city.

The vista of the French coastline came into view; beautiful hillside properties reaching down into the crystal blue ocean. The marina at the bottom of the bay stood full of a mind-blowingly expensive yachts—some bigger than my chalet in Dinner Plain.

'Welcome to the world of the uber-wealthy,' I laugh as I dig my sunglasses from my handbag.

'In case you haven't noticed Ava, you are wealthy.' Tari punches me playfully on the arm.

'Oh no, this is next level Tari. You'll see.' I wink at her, only to remember I'm wearing sunglasses.

I had decided to surprise the team and book us into a once in a lifetime hotel. The Monte-Carlo hotel was the most ridiculously ostentatious building I'd ever laid eyes upon. I couldn't help but notice our group huddled in the entryway, adjusting our attire self consciously.

'You didn't tell us we needed tuxedos to check in to the hotel!' Tari whispers in my ear. I roll my eyes toward her and laugh nervously.

Approaching the counter, I am suddenly aware of many pairs of eyes on my back.

'Hello, I'm here to check in please,' I state politely to the man behind the counter. He puts down the piece of paper he is holding and takes a long look at me. After several heartbeats of scrutiny, he finally asks, 'Name?'

I breathe a sigh of relief.

'Elias, for Huynh Enterprises Holdings.' I dig my passport out of my purse. For some reason, these high-end hotels in Europe seem to insist on keeping a copy of your passport.

'Thank you, Miss Elias, we have your party booked into the Huynh Suite,' he smiles back at me.

'I beg your pardon?' I frown, did he say Huynh suite?

'The suite Mr Huynh would book whenever he

stayed with us, Miss. I also have the adjacent rooms booked for 'service staff.' He offers in a hushed tone, glancing toward Xi and Seal.

'Ah, thank you,' is all I can think to reply. I'm not sure how the guys would feel about being referred to as 'service staff'. They're more like family. I really should ask Sasha for a compendium of Winnie's favourite hotels and restaurants. It would make booking much more relaxed in future. I suddenly realise I could have requested Sasha to book all of this for us. I am so used to doing it myself that it hadn't even occurred to me.

Although - I know I said we were taking this trip in the interests of HEH, I realise now I definitely made it a priority for selfish reasons. And because it felt like a holiday, it didn't feel right to get Sasha to coordinate it. Besides, I've quite enjoyed playing travel agent.

I realise with a jolt that the man behind the counter is staring at me, holding my passport aloft to return to me. I reach across awkwardly to take it, feeling the eyes of my companions on my back.

'If you are ready, Miss?' I notice the bellhop standing to my left. I wave the others in through the door. As they join us, the young man takes our bags and places them on the trolley.

'This way,' he smiles broadly and pushes the trolley toward the elevators. Our group lingers in the entryway, taking in the vast space. Every surface covered in gold detailing, elaborate decorations, Venetian rugs and marble vases.

'This place is unbelievable,' Tari whispers across to me. I find myself speechless at the opulence surrounding us. The photos on the internet did not do this building justice. Almost every surface was either constructed of marble or covered in marble decorations. And if it wasn't covered in marble, it was plated in gold.

We followed the bellhop reluctantly down the corridor and into the elevator, the mirrored surface reflecting our awed faces.

The suite was even more ridiculous. Double french doors open into an ample living/dining space. The bedrooms each framed the area, their rooms and ensuites all hidden behind more rich cream and gold doors.

'Oh, wow,' Seal breathes. The four of us fan out into the space, each drawn to a different aspect of the room. I head directly for the balcony, opening the gargantuan door onto the terrace. The view that appeared before me was breathtaking. The huge marina bay sat nestled in the base of the mountain below, the bright blue sky reaching as far as the eye could see across the horizon. The sun reflected off the ocean below, the blue hues shimmering up at us.

'This is the most magical place I've ever seen,' Tari whispers as she joins me on the terrace. I turn to smile broadly at her.

'It's certainly something, isn't it?' I nudge her with my shoulder. The gents join us on the terrace as another attendant arrives with a cart of champagne and berries. He disappears just as promptly as he arrived after offloading his cart onto the table, crystal champagne flutes and all.

After a few hours settling into the luxury that was

our hotel rooms, I ushered the team out the door. I had one last surprise for them—dinner reservations in the casino.

Dressed in our best wares, Tari, Xi, Seal and I made our way to the casino across the street. Tari, in dress pants and a stunning long suit jacket; the white pinstripe ensemble made her glow. Seal and Xi were both dressed in tuxedos, bow ties and all. I decided on a black silk floor-length gown with gold detailing. The halter neck fell in a modest drop, conservative enough to avoid drawing too much attention.

We were seated in an intimate dining hall, surrounded by elegantly dressed couples and intricately decorated tables. A small bouquet sat in the centre of our table, surrounded by various tealight candles. The room held such ambience; it was hard to believe it sat in the heart of a casino.

'It feels like we're at a wedding reception,' Seal chuckled whilst adjusting his pocket square self consciously.

'I don't know about you, but I've never been to a wedding this fancy!' Tari giggled before proposing a toast, 'Here's to the dream team and saving HEH.' We raised our glasses and clinked them together, beaming smiles on our faces.

We really did it. We managed to find Elena, and in a matter of days, we will be back in Singapore, and this whole mess will be laid to rest.

The four of us hadn't made it far into our meal before a commotion across the room caught our attention. A woman shrieked as a man fell to his knees beside their table, clasping his throat.

'Choking?' Seal and Xi sated in unison as the four

of us stood. Making our way across to the table, the gents immediately set about clearing the space to attend to the man. We were relieved to find the man and woman, both aged somewhere in their late 50s spoke English.

'Sir, my name is Ava. We're here to help,' I pat him on the back as his wife assisted in loosening his tie. He appeared to be struggling to breathe; his face was swelling up. Even with his tie removed, his lips continued to inflate, and his face began to turn a horrifying shade of puce.

I turned to Seal and Xi, as Tari returned with a member of the waitstaff.

'The doctor has been called,' Tari announced, kneeling beside me.

'Does he have any allergies?' I ask his wife. She stands before me patting her hair anxiously, uncertain what to do with herself. She nods at me.

'Can you tell me what they are? Does he carry an EpiPen?' I begin to wonder if she is following what I'm asking.

'Yes, he is allergic to eggs. But we told the chef that,' she shakes her head and looks toward the waiter. She digs around in her purse before withdrawing a clear plastic tube with a blue lid on the end. I see Seal observing the meals and beverages on their table. I double-check the expiration date on the EpiPen before reading the instructions to check they haven't changed. I'm about to ask the waiter to call an ambulance when a low whistle causes my head to snap up. I lock eyes with Seal who is looking at the cocktails on the table.

'Is that a pisco sour?' Seal asks the woman. Her face turns ashen in horror.

'I didn't even think about it,' she whispers.

'Call an ambulance,' I state to anyone who will listen. I tell the man I'm going to administer the EpiPen. At this point, his breath is coming in short, shallow rasps. I line up the pen on the side of his upper thigh, feeling Seal hovering over me closely. I remove the safety cap off the button and press down until the pen clicks audibly. Seal counts out loud beside me.

'One, Two, Three seconds.'

It suddenly occurs to me that perhaps I should have let Seal take the lead on this. His SEAL training means he is basically a paramedic; his training would shit all over my first aid. I suppress the urge to giggle at the surreal situation in which we find ourselves. The group holds a collective breath for what feels like minutes as time slows down. All we can do now is hope his airways clear immediately; otherwise, we will need to commence CPR. I look up and lock eyes with Seal, both of us clearly thinking along the same lines. Seal begins to remove his jacket, preparing to take the first round of compressions when suddenly the man's breathing strengthens. We hear the sirens in the distance, blaring their way toward the casino. Suddenly several things happened at the same time; the doctor arrived on the scene, dragging his stethoscope out and checking the man's airways, the man's wife was overcome and dropped dramatically back into her chair. The gentleman began to take deeper breaths as the rasping subsided, and his face began to return to a healthier colour.

Feeling as though I was stuck in a time warp, or moving through jelly, I stood slowly and backed away from the scene. I watched from a distance as the doctor monitored the man's vitals; as the paramedics arrived and placed the man on monitors and a stretcher. I watched Xi and Seal walk the man's wife to the door with the paramedics. I hardly noticed Tari come to sit beside me, her jacket draped across my shoulders.

'Is that what it's like to work in emergency services, every day? No thank you, I think I'll stick to bartending,' she whispers, leaning against me.

That is what Ryan does every day—facing the fear of being unable to save the life of a stranger, multiple times a shift. Often in the face of danger himself.

A sudden wave of grief, loneliness and loss washes over me. I miss Ryan. And perhaps I realise now just how much I took for granted what he did every day, only to come home to me and put on a smile like he hadn't faced his own mortality over and over again in that 12-hour shift.

Xi and Seal return eventually, recommending we take our party home. It had been a long day after all.

Tari sits me down on the giant king-size bed with a steaming cup of tea.

'Are you going to be okay?' She raises an eyebrow at me in concern.

'I'm fine, I promise. I'll just take a bath and wash off the day.' I smile meekly up at her.

'No one would blame you for being in shock after that,' she sits down beside me on the edge of the bed, 'that isn't something people expect to deal with when they sit down for a fancy dinner.' We look at one another and laugh gently.

'This is true, but these things do happen. I promise I'm okay. Why don't you go and finish drinks with the boys? I'll be alright.'

'If you're sure.'

'I am.' I hug her fiercely, trying not to spill my tea all over her beautiful suit.

'You look smashing tonight, by the way.' I wink at her saucily.

'Aw thanks babe, but you're not my type,' she almost cackles, 'I think you're right. You're fine.' She blows me a kiss from the doorway and leaves me in peace.

After draining my teacup, I slowly make my way to the ensuite and run a bath in the gigantic jacuzzi tub.

While I watch the bubbles foam up before me, I dig out my phone and check my emails—nothing new from Ryan. I feel my heart sink and realise abruptly that more than anything in the world, I just need to tell someone what happened today. I begin mashing out an email to Ryan, not paying much attention to what I type. By the time I hit send, the message basically states that I just had a man collapse before me from anaphylaxis and although he is in the hospital now, I don't know what to do with myself or how I am supposed to be feeling.

Realising that Ryan isn't likely to reply to that garbled mess, I indelicately drag my dress over my head, remove my underwear and throw myself into the tub. I pick up handfuls of bubbles and blow them into the air. Tufts of foamy soap float around me in the water as the jets swirl a current beneath the surface. I'm about to reach for a jar of expensive-looking exfoliant when my phone begins to vibrate. I roll my eyes, assuming it is just Tari checking up on me. My hand freezes mid-air when I see the name on the caller ID. Ryan Murphy.

Is he calling about my email? How did he get it that quickly?

'Hello?' I hit speaker and lay back in the tub.

'Ava?' Ryan's concerned voice immediately melts my heart. I begin to choke up, feeling my throat constrict and my eyes welling.

'Hi,' is all I can manage.

'Are you okay?'

'I guess so.' Hot fat tears begin to pour down my face. I feel stupid for being so emotional.

'That must have been pretty scary to have to help someone in that situation.' His voice is warm and reassuring. I can hear in the background that he's shuffling around.

'Is that what it's like for you e..every dday?' I whimper.

'Sometimes. It depends on the day and the other call-outs I've had that day.'

'I'm sorry Ryan,' I sniffle, 'you always hid it so well, I never realised how much you might have been hurting.'

'You don't owe me an apology Ava, if anything I should apologise for hiding it from you. Do you want to tell me what happened? Sometimes debriefing can help after a trauma.'

I went through the event, detail by detail, surprised by what I remembered. Ryan listened attentively, asking questions here and there, sounding like the true professional I know him to be.

'Do you feel better?' Ryan sighs down the line, the audible sound of crackling plastic behind him.

'I do, thank you. What are you doing right now?'

'Restocking the ambulance. We just got back from an MVA, and we're out of a lot of supplies.' I can hear the weariness in his voice.

'MVA is a motor vehicle accident, right?'

'Yes.'

'And you're restocking, so it was pretty bad, huh?'

'It was,' he sighs.

'Do you want to tell me about it?' I feel a sudden homesickness, a yearning to be near him, to ensconce him in my love like never before.

'We will have to go write it up shortly; I just wanted to check on you before I'm out of mobile phone service,' Ryan's voice shakes a little.

'Oh, Ryan, I wish I could hug you right now. I'm so sorry. Here I am freaking about an EpiPen, and you've witnessed something truly traumatic.' I feel the tears begin to burn tracks down my cheeks once again. I hear a voice calling out in the background on Ryan's end.

'I...I've got to go, Ava, we're starting the debrief.'

'Oh, okay.' I feel my heart sink.

'Safe travels,' he sighs. I can't help but wonder if he's as reluctant to hang up as I am.

'Thanks, Ryan,' I manage to whisper. The line goes dead.

I sit there staring at my phone on the side of the bath feeling even more bereft than I did before he called. At least now I'm not freaking out about tonight; instead I'm mourning a lost relationship all over again. I sob quietly in the tub until the water turns cold. I drag myself out, wrap a bathrobe around me and collapse into bed.

9

I walk down a familiar corridor, the scent of disinfectant and sanitiser wafting through the air. I peer through a window in a swinging door and see Winnie lying propped up in a hospital bed. There is a doctor lecturing him on his cholesterol levels, asking about his medical care in Singapore. I take another step forward; a woman with glossy amber hair sits beside the bed, paperwork in her hands. It is me.

I awake with a jolt, feeling the dream slip away. My dreams these days are often like smoke; it takes just a moment before I can't remember what I was dreaming about when I wake.

Luckily I'd fallen asleep in my own recliner on the Screaming Eagle. It meant that I was much less likely to have woken anyone else up. I peer around quietly in the dimmed cabin. The others all appeared to be snoozing; their soft breath sounds drifting toward me. I spot Elena in the recliner opposite me, her arm propped up under her head as she sleeps.

I feel relief wash over me, knowing we are finally on our way to clearing HEH of the paternity suit.

Elena had spent a few hours before we all went to sleep on a Skype call with our PR team, composing a speech and media release for when we land.

Arriving at the airport, we were hastily swept through the security checks; our luggage scanned before being directed back to the airfield where the helicopter was waiting.

'Why aren't we driving? Taking the helicopter seems a little pretentious, doesn't it?' I chuckle as I place my cans over my ears.

'Abbie thought it might be best to get everyone cleaned up at HEH and in front of the media ASAP,' Seal smirks back. I watch humorously as Tari clings to Xi for dear life. Elena grins ear to ear in the luxurious cream leather seat opposite me.

The flight to Huynh Enterprises Holdings took a matter of minutes as the city skyline appeared below us. I watched Elena's face as she awed at the sight.

'Have you seen Singapore from the sky before Elena?' I smile, realising I hadn't either.

'No! Zis is magnificent!' She beams. The tall buildings of the financial district come into view as our pilot expertly brings us down to land on the HEH helipad. I watch as alternating rings of light glow below us, the large 'H' in bright red.

Disembarking after the rotors powered down, the five of us make our way to the standard elevator entry. I spot Tari peering curiously at the smaller entryway on the other side of the platform.

'I'll show you later,' I shout at her over the wind. She smiles broadly at me and drags her jacket collar up around her ears.

As we descend into the building, the peace inside

the elevator feels almost eerie compared to the screaming winds on the helipad.

'It's good to meet you in person. I'm Abbie, head of PR here at Huynh Enterprises Holdings,' Abbie holds out her hand in welcome to Elena. The two women exchange a firm handshake. Abbie then turns to extend her hand to Tari.

'Tari, pleased to meet you.'

'We will start by getting the team ready for the press conference where you will be introduced by our CEO Mr Samuel Chen before commencing your address,' Abbie flips through items on the iPad before her. 'Ava, I need you to come with me while we get Elena ready.'

I smile back at her and nod my acquiescence.

We leave Elena in the safe hands of the PR team with Xi, as Tari, Seal, and I follow Abbie back into the elevator toward my office.

'I thought you might want to clean up and catch up with Chen before the press conference,' she smiles at me.

'I appreciate that Abbie. I've been looking for an excuse to use my ensuite too,' I chuckle, already excited at the prospect of a hot shower.

'We'll have hair and makeup in there to tidy you up when you're ready. They should be finished with Chen shortly.' Abbie looks back at her iPad.

I hear a snigger from Tari's direction and try to hide my smirk.

'What does 'Mr Perfect' need hair and makeup for?' Tari cackles the second we are left alone in my office. I head to the fridge and grab a bottle of mineral water for each of us.

'It's just a formality,' I laugh, handing the bottle over.

'Can he get any more high maintenance?' She exclaims as she uncaps the water, propping herself against the doorframe as I walk into the ensuite. I suppress the urge to roll my eyes.

'Ava!' I hear Jia's voice calling from the office doorway.

'In here!' I call back as I grab extra towels from the cupboard in the ensuite.

'You are a miracle-worker!' Jia appears in the doorway, high-fiving Tari as she enters. I walk back across to her, embracing her in a warm hug around my armfuls of towels.

'It was certainly a team effort,' I beam at her, smiling past her to wink at Tari.

'We may be able to get the case thrown out if the Judge believes her statement. Abbie knows I need her to sit down and make an official statement before she speaks publicly. Then we can submit it to the courts before close of business today.' I feel the nervous excitement rolling off her.

'I'm going to take a quick shower and get changed. As soon as Abbie is done with Elena in PR, I am sure she will be delivered promptly to your door!' I laugh. I notice Jia looking around the room, taking in the elaborate decor.

'Can you believe what great taste Winnie had?' I chuckle. Jia and Tari left me to tidy up, making themselves comfortable on the couches in my office.

I relished the steaming shower and afterwards, dressed in one of my spare suits. Having resolved against washing my hair and dripping everywhere, I decide the stylists can negotiate it into an updo of some kind. As I wander out to join the girls, I grab my hair and tie it in a messy bun on top of my head.

'What's the gossip?' I ask nosily as I plonk myself down beside Jia on the lounger.

'We were just talking about Chen,' Jia admits guiltily.

'Why?' I ask, relaxing back into the chair.

'He hasn't been the same since you departed for Europe. Sulking around like a lost puppy.' Jia eyes me curiously, watching for my reaction.

'That doesn't sound like him.' I shrug.

'I think he's sad because he's fallen for you and now you won't have him,' Tari pipes up, a cheeky grin on her face. I roll my eyes and sigh dramatically.

'He's not in love with me. I'm sure he's just frustrated about his situation.'

'Well, you can believe what you want, but he certainly seemed lost without you.' Jia nudges me with her shoulder.

'I spoke to Ryan.' I probably should have prefaced that hand grenade before lobbing it.

Oh well, too late to shout DUCK now!

'What?!' Both ladies squeal.

'I am even more confused now than I was before.' I sip my mineral water contemplatively.

'You can't make a statement like that and not back it up! How did this happen?' Jia frowns at me.

'It was after the guy in the casino, wasn't it?' Tari points a finger at me, 'you called Ryan because you saved a man's life.'

'What?' Jia looks between us in frustration – 'This is clearly a conversation that requires cocktails and a MUCH more detailed explanation.'

I'm about to reply when the door slides open behind us. I see from Tari's face that it isn't Seal.

'Oh joy, Asian Justin Beiber is here.'

That answers that question.

'A pleasure to see you as always, Tarini. Aren't the jokes getting a little old?' Chen's silky voice carries over the back of the chair. I watch Tari's face scrunch up.

'Aren't you getting a little old for that hair cut?' She flips her head sarcastically, pretending to sweep her fringe across her face. I bite my bottom lip to stop myself from laughing.

'If you don't mind, the grownups need to have a discussion about serious matters.' I hear the steely change to Chen's tone.

'If I see any grownups, I'll let you know.' Tari isn't backing down. I stand up between them before they can carry on any further.

'Enough. Tari, do you want to stay for the press conference or would you prefer to get Xi to take you home?' I smile at her, knowing she'd rather pull out her own fingernails than watch Chen's announcement.

'You know I would, but I have to get home to bath my cat,' she chuckles, stepping toward me for a brief hug before making her way toward the door, giving Chen a wide berth and whispering; 'I don't have a cat.' She flips her imaginary fringe again.

Just as Tari reaches the door, Seal returns, stopping on the threshold as he spots our newest arrival. He rolls his eyes before sticking a finger in his ear like he's wearing an ear piece, raising his watch to his mouth, 'Yes Sargent, Seal en route,' he states sarcastically into his sleeve, while turning on his heel.

I watch him high five Tari as the two of them depart in fits of laughter.

'He's not wearing an earpiece is he?' Chen huffs, running an exasperated hand through his hair, 'why do your staff insist on belittling me?'

'I'm sure its partly because you can scarcely hide your elitism around them. But mostly because it's fun,' I shrug, turning to sit in the wingback chair Tari vacated.

'It is unprofessional,' he huffs again. I roll my eyes.

'Perhaps if you didn't treat them like staff, they would ease up.'

'That makes no sense; they are staff.'

'Therein lies your problem,' I state, deadpan. I see Jia watching us curiously; her grin barely concealed behind a glass of whiskey.

'If Mum and Dad are finished bickering, we need to talk about Elena,' Jia pipes in. Chen's head whips around to glare at her.

'A little early in the day for your alcoholism, isn't it Jia?' Chen sneers.

'What is your deal, Chen? You've been a bear with a sore paw since the moment Ava left!' Jia spits. I watch Chen's face contort with rage.

'Jia, will you give us a minute please?' I drop my head into my hands, 'and can you please ask Sasha to get me a coffee and a cinnamon scroll?'

Jia nods mutely before quietly making her way out the door.

'Why are you antagonising my people?' I tip my head to the side and peer at Chen.

'They started it,' he mutters. I shake my head in exasperation.

'I've had some...other things going on while you

were away,' he sighs, standing up to pace the room.

'Why didn't you just tell me that?'

'Because it is no body's business,' he growls. I watch him prowl around like a caged tiger.

'If you don't want people to know, that's your prerogative, but people won't know what you don't tell them.'

He stops and looks at me, confused.

'I suppose you are right. As always,' Chen groans.

'If you need to take some time away from HEH, I'll be here. I don't foresee needing to go anywhere again anytime soon.' I aim for reassuring. 'In the meantime, we need to get this lawsuit cleaned up.'

Abbie and the stylist team arrive and make quick work of my hair and makeup. We discuss Chen's opening for Elena's announcement and Abbie reassures us that Elena is prepared and confident in her statement. Elena, Jia and Seal join us shortly before we are to head downstairs to the podium outside HEH for the press conference.

'We got the statement to the Judge; he said he would review it in the coming days. We've been permitted to make a public statement,' Jia beams at me as our heels click-clack on the marble in the lobby. Exiting the building, Xi meets us at the side of the podium, having returned from dropping Tari home.

Reporters and news vans swamp the entire front yard of the HEH block. Photographers snap away as our group exit the front doors. I look around at our team, love and pride swelling in my chest.

I have so much respect for these people, this incredible team who surround me. Chen and Elena break away from the group, heading for the podium.

I stand there in awe, watching as Chen welcomes the media, smiling broadly and looking so at ease in the spotlight. I see his eyes come to rest briefly at the back of the crowd. Following his gaze, I spot Mei standing clear of the humdrum before her.

Before I know what is happening, I feel the world fall quietly into the background as my feet carry me toward Mei. She watches me approach, the same foggy look on her face as I am sure is on mine. I stop before her, the sounds of the world around us fading to nothing.

'Mei,' I state quietly. 'I am so sorry for everything. I'm sure you don't believe me, but I mean that sincerely. I honestly think if we'd perhaps met in another life, we could be quite good friends.'

She stares at me as though I've grown a second head.

'Friends?' She sputters.

'Yes. I know we have our differences but...'

'But what? You were not born into this world, Ava. You fell into it. Mr Huynh, may he rest in peace, had no idea what he was doing, leaving you in charge,' she sniffs, lifting her nose into the air like a poodle.

'What would you have done if you inherited your family company and found yourself in charge?'

I watch her eyes widen, wondering if perhaps I had misread the situation.

'I have an older brother, and my parents are both healthy. That is not a scenario I will ever need to consider. Besides, even if something were to happen, the responsibility of my family's affairs would fall to my husband.' Her face falls as she plays nervously with an intricate gold bangle on her wrist. For the first time I notice the beautiful cream pantsuit she wears, probably Chanel. Probably worth more than my Jeep.

My eyes are drawn back to Chen on the podium; Mei's soon-to-be betrothed.

'I'm always so jealous of how shiny his hair is,' I giggle, more to myself than to Mei. I feel her eyes on me, watching me with curiosity.

'What do you want from me?' Mei stares at me intently.

'I don't understand?' I frown, turning to face her. 'I don't want anything from you, but I feel like we should at least be civil to one another, like it or not, it seems our lives are intertwined for now.'

'Because you want the man who is soon to be my fiancé?' Mei cocks an eyebrow.

'Because he is my CEO. Besides, you gave us your blessing, what right do you have to be so salty toward me?' I whisper, hoping not to draw the attention of anyone standing nearby. 'For people who seem to have their lives unwillingly prescribed for them, the two of you are very quick to shut down anyone or anything different or unfamiliar.'

'Do you have many friends, Ava?' Her forlorn tone catches me off guard.

'A handful of very good ones, yes. I adore them.' I smile across at her. 'Why do you ask?'

'I don't have many friends. Not friends of my own that is, who I can be myself around.' She shrugs ever so slightly.

'You would be welcome to meet mine. They are kind-hearted and have a tendency to take in us lost souls.' I smile to myself, watching Elena approach the podium and make her announcement. She speaks concisely, clearly and her heavy accent makes me grin.

This incredibly beautiful woman flew around the world to be here for us. For me. For Winnie.

'Thank you for your time, und I 'ope zis offers clarity to all. I vill be 'aving a strong words vith my son ven I zee him.' Elena steps backward from the podium as Chen steps up to answer clarifying questions.

'Yes, Ms Ottinger is the biological mother of Mr Evans, and she has confirmed Mr Hyunh is not his biological father. HEH have offered to submit for a paternity test should Mr Evans wish to continue contesting Mr Huynh's Will.' Chen smiles his megawatt smile at the reporters. He points toward another journalist, taking her question.

'No, we do not currently have an update on the case, but we hope this new information will assist HEH in closing this chapter and moving forward as a stronger, more united entity.' He smiles, thanks the gathering and steps down from the podium.

I turn back toward Mei, only to find her staring at me.

'Do you love him?'

'I gave a big part of my heart away before I came to Singapore. I never really got it back after that,' I sigh, 'I know that probably sounds like an excuse, but that's the truth of it.'

'The two of you have chemistry,' she observes, watching Chen shaking hands and making small talk with the media. 'I can see it whenever you are near each other.'

'Yes.'

'He and I do not. It pains me to admit it, but he knows it as well as I do. We will never be interested in one another romantically.'

'Is there someone else?' The question is out of my mouth before I can stop myself.

'Chen knows he is not my type; let's just leave it at that.' Mei looks away uncomfortably.

'I am sorry, I didn't mean to pry.' I frown at myself, cursing my runaway mouth.

'I am thankful for your invitation to meet your friends; I imagine it must be nice to have people to talk to. To confide in.' I feel the sudden urge to hug her, offer some kindness or support, but settle for placing my hand on her arm and squeezing it gently.

'You know where to find me if you ever need someone to confide in.' I smile half-heartedly before dropping my hand. 'I had better go; we are going to take Elena to the hotel before the jetlag hits us.' I begin to step away when I hear Mei behind me.

'Thank you, Ava.'

I turn to smile back at her, 'anytime.'

'Wait, you invited her to meet us?' Margot exclaims, propping herself up against the bar at Spago.

It had been about a week since Elena's announcement, and Jia was quite confident we were going to have the case thrown out. In celebration, we all met at Spago for drinks, seeing as Tari was working the evening shift.

She smiles across the bar at me fondly before handing across a large glass filled with pink liquor.

'What is this?' I laugh, picking it up and peering at the contents.

'I named it 'call me a sex object,' she laughs heartily, her face lighting up. Jia and Margot sit on my other side, laughing raucously. I hesitantly sip the concoction.

'It's not going to bite you, Ava!' Linah chuckles, throwing a napkin in my lap. I relish the sweet syrup; it tastes of watermelon and berries.

'Delicious!' I announce, placing the glass down on the bar.

The girls erupt in a hoot of laughter. I look over to see Jia with a twinkle in her eye, and know she's up to something.

'You never finished telling us why you were talking to Ryan,' she winks across at me. I see Linah and Margot's jaws drop on either side of me.

'I knew you would bring that up! It was nothing really. When we were in Monaco, this guy collapsed in front of us, and we helped him out. I was a little shaken, so I emailed Ryan to let off some steam.' I pick back up my cocktail to sip it and hide behind the glass.

'What!? Why didn't we hear about this immediately!?' Margot wails, shoving me playfully.

'It isn't a big deal. Besides I haven't heard from him since. I think it meant more to me than it did to him.' I sip my drink self-consciously. I watch the others exchange looks.

'Ava, he called you, when you emailed him. Don't you think that means something?' Linah asks gently.

'I don't want to overthink it, so I'm just going to say no and leave it at that,' I state mulishly.

'Well, I for one would like to know when we are going to see this fancy ski chalet we keep hearing about,' Tari abruptly changes the subject. I shoot her a 'thank you' glance. She winks at me before busying herself wiping glasses with a crisp linen tea towel.

'I would love to have you all come and stay!

Especially in the wintertime, it is so beautiful.' I smile at the girls.

'I was born in the humidity, and I hate the cold. It is going to take a lot of convincing to get me there,' Linah pipes up before delicately nibbling on a potato wedge.

'Riley and I were just talking about a skiing vacation, would you consider renting us a chalet next season?' Margot grins at me.

'There's room for 12! We could all go and bring significant others,' I offer, looking around the group.

'We know Jia will want to invite Seal,' Linah teases. As our laughter dies down, I notice Tari shuffling uncomfortably from foot to foot. I catch her eye, and she gives me a slight head shake. I frown briefly and nod, letting it go.

Strange, I guess she'll tell me what that was about, in her own time.

'I have some news,' Margot offers hesitantly.

My mind immediately jumps to pregnancy. That is how every rom-com I've ever seen introduces a pregnancy into a plot line.

'Riley found the warehouse last week.' The five of us freeze.

'So I took Ava's advice,' she looks across at me, her big doe eyes gleaming. Tari stands frozen mid pour of a cocktail; her eyes lock onto mine.

Oh dear, this can go one of two ways. What advice was that? Lord, help me.

'He asked me why I had a warehouse and why I hadn't told him about it. He found the invoice for it when he was cleaning up at home.'

I feel the eyes of the whole group swivel to me. I send up a silent prayer that this story has a happy ending. These ladies didn't hesitate to make clear to me previously their thoughts on alternate endings to Ryan and my relationship, if only I had kept HEH a secret from him.

'I took him to the warehouse and showed him our hang out and then I took him upstairs to show him my studio. He was understandably confused; he didn't know why I kept it a secret from him for so long.' Margot begins to choke up, her voice catching. Jia and I immediately extend a hand each resting on her shoulder or leg in support.

'I explained to him about the executives switching the names on my work and hiding the truth about my designs. He was furious. He told me to quit then and there; that he'd help me set up my own label.' Margot sniffles as my eyes well up at the thought of Riley's love and support. She turns to me, grabbing my hands.

'Ava, I can't tell you how free I feel. He was a little upset in the beginning when he realised I'd been lying to him all these years, but after I explained it all, he understood I felt I had no choice.' I squeeze her hands, trying to hold back the tears.

'I'm so happy to hear that Margot, you deserve to have your husband love and support you in all your endeavours, just as you support his.' I lean over to hug her into a warm embrace. As we separate, she runs her fingers under her eyes, trying to tidy her running mascara.

'It is so strange, I come home from work now, and I can just tell him how my day was. I don't have to lie or sugar coat it. I feel like we are stronger than ever.' She hiccups a little, before grinning at us all. She raises her glass in a toast, 'to the Invisible Women!'

10

'Are you going to tell me what's going on?' I peer at Tari after the others have departed for the night.

She looks at me sheepishly, 'I had hoped you'd forget about that.'

I shrug a half-hearted apology, refusing to let it go.

'My girlfriend and I broke up. She was unhappy that I went to Europe and didn't invite her. So, she left me,' she sighs, wiping out a champagne glass.

'Tari, I'm so sorry. I had no idea. Are you okay?' I reach across the bar to pat her arm.

'I'm alright. We hadn't been together all that long, and I guess it wasn't much of a shock to me that we didn't 'make it'.'

'Do you want to come over this weekend and eat ice cream? I think I've managed to figure out how to get Disney + to work in the theatre room?'

'Thanks, Ava, but I have to work this weekend.' Tari pats my hand.

An arrival at the bar has Tari looking past me to the entry.

'Ava?'

I turn to see a familiar looking blush pink Chanel suit, designer heels and sleek black hair.

'Mei?' I frown, turning all the way around in my seat. 'How did you find me?'

'I called Sasha; she said you were heading here for dinner. I hope that's okay?' Mei slowly makes her way toward me at the bar, tucking a long silky strand of hair behind one ear. She places her Chanel clutch on the bar and sits up in a chair beside me. Tari eyes me pointedly, tipping her head toward Mei.

'Oh, uh Mei this is Tari, Tari this is Mei Yang.' I wave a hand between the two, realising even this bizarre situation called for some propriety.

'Pleasure, Miss Mei,' Tari holds out a hand, 'What can I get for you?'

Mei blushes ever so slightly before turning to me, 'What is it you're drinking?'

Tari and I burst out in fits of giggles, realising we are about to make Miss Chanel blush more.

'Call me a sex object,' I manage to compose myself enough to state, before bursting out in giggles once again. Tari leans over, resting her arms on the bar as she sucks in hysterical breaths.

'Oh,' is all Mei manages before giggling, herself.

After what feels like an age, Tari rights herself, wipes the tears from her face and begins shaking up two more cocktails. I manage to control myself, feeling giddy like a schoolgirl. I turn to Mei and ask her if she would like anything to eat.

'The kitchen is due to close, that's all.' I smile at her.

'You seem to know an awful lot about this bar,' she states, looking around curiously. You'd think by her inquisitive gaze that she'd never been atop the Marina Bay Sands building before.

'It's a pretty special place, I feel very safe and at ease up here.' I shrug, finishing the last of my cocktail.

'I can see why.'

I look up to see Mei staring at Tari's back as she expertly shakes up the cocktail whilst entertaining a couple at the other side of the bar. She turns around suddenly, a broad grin on her face. Sparkling green eyes come to rest on Mei, and suddenly I feel like I am intruding on a private moment.

I excuse myself and make my way to the bathrooms.

Well, that was unexpected.

I smile to myself as I wipe my hands and dig out my lipstick. I double-check my phone for messages and missed calls—nothing from Ryan. Childishly, I feel my heart sink.

Mei, Tari and I spend the next hour chatting and eating together. By the time Tari was ready to finish her shift, Mei was bidding us goodnight.

'Thank you for letting me interrupt your evening. It has been very pleasant to have girl-friends to talk to. I can't remember the last time I felt this relaxed.' Her smile never left her face, causing Tari and I to grin back like idiots.

'It was lovely to have you. You are welcome anytime.' As she stands up and collects her purse, Mei turns back to Tari.

'Perhaps I'll see you again too, Tari?' She smiles shyly and disappears.

I turn to see the biggest shit-eating grin on Tari's face. If that isn't the face of a woman developing a crush, I don't know what is.

'Did you know?' Tari hisses at me.

'No! She'd told me Chen wasn't her type, but I assumed she meant...'

'She doesn't date assholes?'

I roll my eyes and chuckle. Tari, always straight to the point.

'I think I like her, Ava,' Tari whispers.

'I think you do too.'

'Do you think she likes me?' I can hear the apprehension in her voice.

'Tari, I'm no judge of men. What makes you think I can judge women any better?'

'Because you are one!' Tari stares at me incredulously. I eyeball her back, needless to say, I didn't point out the obvious.

'I can't imagine why she wouldn't like you. Besides, she did spend the entire time she was here either talking to you or staring at you.' I grin at her.

'Come on missy, time for you to pack up. We'll take you home.' I pat her arm across the bar and collect my belongings.

I wake the next morning feeling lighter. Walking toward the fridge I pick up and flip through a pile of mail sitting on the kitchen counter.

In what feels like an act of groundhog day, I find an unusual looking envelope, missing a return address.

You have got to be fucking kidding me.

I hold the envelope away from me, imagining it full of anthrax or something deadly, and peel it open. After gingerly easing the page from its jacket, I unfold it—no powder in sight.

I'M COMING FOR YOU. NO ONE CAN SAVE YOU NOW.

I stand up and take the letter across to the fridge. Grabbing a novelty magnet Tari and I collected on our European adventure, I stick it up beside the other threat letters. They stand there boldly, like crude children's artwork from a kindergarten.

'Ah, a new edition of the 'Stalker Daily News' I see?' Seal enters the kitchen and takes a seat at the island bench. 'Oh, it isn't much more inventive than the last is it? That's disappointing. I hope he doesn't quit his day job.'

At this point, Gladys walks in and sees the new letter.

'Miss Ava, this is all too much. We must do something!' She opens the oven and removes a large tray covered in individual pots of Spanish eggs. She continues to shake her head as she butters toast and places the slices beside the bowls full of egg and tomato, chorizo and capsicum.

I open the fridge and remove the jug of orange juice, dragging a couple of glasses from the shelf.

'There isn't much we can do Gladys. We suspect it to be Tony, but there is no proof, and until he reappears again, we are at a stalemate.' Seal shrugs, pouring us each a big glass of juice.

'I can't believe you will let Miss Ava out in the world with that man out there.' Gladys shudders at the mention of Tony.

'We have not known Tony to be particularly violent in the past,' Seal seems to realise what he is saying halfway through, 'other than when he attacked Ava.' He frowns to himself and looks across at me just as Xi arrives for breakfast.

'Miss Ava got another letter and Mr Seal won't do anything about it.' Gladys all but points an accusatory finger at Seal. I see Xi's eyes track toward the fridge where the letter sat pinned.

'Doesn't get much more creative does he?' Xi observes, taking in the block magazine letters.

'It would seem not,' I garble around a mouth full of toast and tomatoey egg. The four of us sit there and scrutinise the fridge like an art installation at a museum.

We finish our breakfast in quiet contemplation as we each consider the implications of these threats.

'What's on the agenda today, Miss Ava?' Xi eventually breaks the silence.

'Just another day in the office, I hope,' I shrug, 'Jia is hoping to hear back from the Judge's chambers today about Elena's statement.'

'Does her statement carry that much weight?' Seal raises his eyebrows.

'I guess Jia is hoping it'll be enough for Mr Evans to drop his suit?' I shrug.

I excuse myself from the table and make my way to the wardrobe in the master suite. I switch on the stereo to play some inspiration music as I dress. Together, by Sia begins blaring through the surround sound speakers.

Ah, thank you, Sia!

I pick out a navy blue pantsuit and silk camisole top. Jigging around the bathroom as I apply some face, I wonder what Ryan is up to.

Would it be weird to call him and follow up on our emails? I've seen so many memes on the internet about how 'if a man wants you; they will make sure you know it'.

I sigh heavily into the mirror, pausing to scrutinise myself before applying my lipstick.

'What do you want, Ava?' I ask myself. I wish I knew. My first priority is getting HEH out of hot water. I'll think about myself after that is settled.

Making my way to the foyer, I meet Seal and Xi at the elevator door.

'Have a good day at work!' Gladys calls from the kitchen.

'You too!' The three of us holler back, grinning at one another.

Watching the city pass by out the window, my thoughts wander to Dinner Plain and the family I left behind there. Ivan, Danny, Ryan. The days spent on the slopes at the ski school, listening to the joyful giggles and squeals of the children. I miss kicking snow out of my boots on the porch of Arendelle, sinking into a bubble bath in the copper tub. Life was much more straightforward then. Here I sit in a BBSUV, with my very own private security and driver. I am wearing a pair of shoes worth more than my monthly mortgage repayment for the chalet.

'Feel like sharing the over-thinking going on back there?' Seal chuckles from the front seat, snapping me back to the present. I spot Xi shoot a frown in Seal's direction.

'I was just thinking about home. I miss the simplicity. Some days I don't know who I am in Singapore,' I sigh, twisting Winnie's ring on my finger.

'Have you heard from Ryan since Europe?'

I spot Xi lean across to cuff Seal up the side of the head; I fight to suppress the burgeoning giggle.

'No, I haven't,' I frown.

'You could always reach out to him?' Seal offers.

'You could always ask Jia to dinner,' I retort snidely.

I feel Seal's embarrassment from the front seat.

'I don't know what you are talking about,' he grumbles, pulling out his gun from under his arm, checking it. I can hear the mechanical clicks from my seat.

'I imagine she'd say yes.'

Silence, before; 'You do?' More metal clicks.

I wish I knew something about guns. Probably should put that on the 'to do' list.

'I'm not saying you should propose or anything, but I think she'd agree to dinner if you asked,' I smile to myself.

'She's a bit...'

'What?' I frown, cranky at his implied criticism.

'Out of my league.' It comes out as a sigh. I watch his back through the headrest as he re-holsters his gun under his left arm and buttons his jacket.

Xi brings the car to a stop outside HEH; I peer up at the monstrous building before me. My building. I shake my head, incredulous.

'Nothing is impossible, Seal.' I pat his shoulder across the seat.

I'm met at the front door by Sasha, a broad smile on her face.

'Good Morning!' She beams. I can't help but laugh.

'Why such a good mood for so early in the morning, Sasha?' I can't help but beam back, her smile is infectious.

'Jia is waiting for you, upstairs. I think she might have good news!'

I stare at her, open-mouthed. The two of us hastily make our way to the executive elevator, waiting anxiously as the floors melt away below us.

I race into my office, not stopping to put down my bags, dumping them unceremoniously beside me on the lounge. Jia looks up in greeting from the portfolio she peruses in her lap, latte in hand.

'Good Morning, Supreme Commander,' she chuckles, sipping the latte.

'Spit it out, Jia. Please tell me it is good news!' I sigh, my leg bouncing up and down anxiously in front of me.

'Mr Evan's lawyer contacted me this morning to advise that he has decided to withdraw his suit. HEH is no longer in danger,' she smiles across at me like the Cheshire cat. I jump up and air punch the ceiling.

'Jia! This is amazing!' I squeal. I dance around the space, kicking off my heels and enjoying a celebratory jig.

I stop only to catch my breath and ask Jia if she'd spoken to Elena.

'She will be joining us for lunch. Then she'd like a couple of days to see Singapore before returning home. I hope this is amenable to you?'

'Of course! Where are we taking her to lunch?'

The afternoon continued on a high as Chen hosted an announcement about the suit, and the media began spreading the news of HEH's resolution. Following the press conference, Chen promptly disappeared.

I took the elevator to his office, hoping to catch him, so we could debrief on what HEH would focus on now that the suit had been settled.

Strangely, I couldn't find him anywhere. I dig out my phone and try to call him. It goes straight to voicemail.

That's odd. I guess I'll catch him after the weekend.

I decide to leave him for the afternoon, texting Seal and Xi that we'd head home to get an early start to the weekend.

11

Monday rolled around far too quickly as the weekend became a blur behind me.

After sitting through several meetings for the morning, it occurs to me that I didn't hear back from Chen all weekend. I hadn't seen him so far this morning either. I frown down at my phone as Abbie's voice fades into the background. Contemplating sending Chen a message to ask him if he was okay, I realise Abbie has concluded the meeting, and the attendees are disbursing.

'Miss Ava, I was hoping to ask. Should we arrange something for Mr Chen?' I note her hesitant tone, uncertain what she is referring to.

'Uh?' I frown about to answer when her phone rings loudly between us. She apologises quietly before taking the call and leaving the room.

That was odd.

I head to the elevator noting uncomfortably, the curious stares following in my wake.

Why are people staring at me?

I exit the elevator, making a beeline for Sasha's desk to ask her if there is something wrong with my outfit.

I stop dead as I catch sight of Sasha. She sits quietly behind her desk perusing a magazine on her lunch break. With big glossy text splashed across the cover stood a photograph of Chen and Mei hand in hand, 'Wedding of the Century'. I feel the blood drain from my face.

Chen didn't tell me they were officially announcing the engagement. Come to think of it, Mei didn't either.

I feel dizzy. It dawns on me that perhaps I don't know Chen or Mei as well as I had thought I did. Deciding that I need a distraction, I turn toward the elevator and head to the restaurant in search of a cinnamon scroll and cream cheese icing.

The elevator feels like it is moving at a glacial pace. I fidget and pat my hair down in the mirrored interior. Staring critically at myself, I wonder if I should consider Botox someday. At some point these frown lines will be too obvious to hide. I start prodding and poking my face this way and that. The elevator comes to a stop at the restaurant floor, causing me to jump as the doors open. I blush as I make my way to the counter to order a coffee.

'And one cinnamon and cream cheese scroll, please,' I sigh swiping my staff card against the reader.

'Just the one Miss Ava?' Lou smiles across at me.

'And one to go,' I sigh even harder.

'Tough morning, Miss?'

'Just some unexpected news popped up. I wasn't entirely prepared for it.' I shrug, smiling back politely.

'How has your morning been?'

'Busy, Miss. It seems everyone is excited for Waffle Monday.' I turn to look around the room, only to realise it is bustling.

How did I miss how busy it is in here? Wait, Monday?

I feel my heart sink as I realise I will have to sit through dinner with Mei and the Invisible Women tonight. I've never felt uneasy at the prospect of our Monday night dinners before.

Was Mei planning on telling me about the announcement? I thought we were friends? Maybe friends is putting it too strongly? Perhaps she doesn't see our relationship the same way I do.

I start to wonder if Mei will take me aside at the dinner and explain what happened or why I wasn't told. Then I begin to think that perhaps it wasn't any of my business. What do I tell Tari? Maybe the reason neither Chen nor Mei told me was because they didn't think it concerned me.

Am I too, nosy? Am I too sensitive?

I realise Lou is staring at me, holding my two cinnamon scrolls mid-air.

'Sorry,' I blush, taking the scrolls.

'Would you prefer a decaf Miss Elias?' Lou offers, shrugging kindly.

I chuckle to myself, nodding at her as I move out of the queue. I decide to head for the executive bathroom to tidy myself up. Clearly, I am not hiding my feelings particularly well today.

Note to self, work on that.

I walk into the bathroom, thanking goodness the only other executive who is likely to walk into the women's bathroom is Jia, and she wouldn't mind me having a meltdown. I place the cinnamon scrolls down, deciding after a moment to take a large bite out of one. Cream cheese icing smears indelicately across my chin. I shrug at myself in the mirror and try not to think too harshly of the woman staring back. I chew slowly, observing my reflection. Today I have my hair pulled up into a chignon, the amber highlights catching in the luminous bathroom light. My emerald green dress wraps around me delicately, a soft silky hug. I take another bite of my pastry, my eyes never leaving the locked gaze in the mirror.

An unannounced arrival through the door has me jumping, a glob of cream cheese dripping onto my hand in my surprise. I shove the back of my hand in my mouth, sucking the frosting from my skin as I turn to look at the intruder. I jump with surprise as I see Chen staring at me, shaking with barely suppressed laughter.

'What is with you and those damn buns?' He bursts into chuckles, a broad grin on his face. I shrug back innocently.

'They make me feel better.' I frown, licking icing from my finger.

'Ah,' is all he says before perching on the edge of a settee. I turn to look at him, placing my morsel down and wiping my hands on a towel.

We both stare at one another, an awkward silence settling.

'Why do I feel like there is a huge space between us?' Chen scratches his chin, looking at me curiously. I frown across at him before sighing.

'A lot has changed in the past few months Chen,' I shrug, at a loss as to what else I can say. I realise suddenly mortified, that I forgot to wipe the cream cheese from my chin. Picking up the towel I turn to the mirror and wipe the sugary patch from my face. I catch Chen's eye in the mirror, watching him watching me closely.

'I suppose I should offer you the customary congratulations,' I try to smile at him in the reflection. I watch him hang his head, his hands finding his hair in agitation.

'I wanted to tell you myself,' I hear the anguish in his voice. 'Clearly, someone leaked it to the press without our consent.'

'You don't owe me an explanation, Chen. We both knew this would happen sooner or later. I just hope you are looking out for your best interests.'

'It was never going to be my decision to make Ava; you know that. You're talking about fighting a tradition that is centuries old.' I watch him in the reflection, as he stands slowly and paces toward me. I turn to lean back against the counter.

'I suppose your parents are elated at the 'news'?' I ask, aiming for chirpy.

'My parents are the ones who announced it to our family and friends. Mei and I were caught, somewhat unawares.' He runs a hand through his hair, his fringe falling back into place across his face.

That explains why neither of them told me before the public found out. They didn't know, themselves.

'I'm sorry, Chen. That's pretty poor form by your parents. They could have at least warned the two of you first.' I feel a wave of guilt for my selfishness wash over me. 'How is Mei handling it?'

'She's suitably unimpressed, but will never admit it to anyone. She can't afford to fall off the pedestal her parents have her precariously perched on.' Chen stops in front of me, his eyes searching my face.

'I can't even imagine how that feels. I always knew I was lucky with my family, but I never realised just what a blessing they are.' I shake my head at the situation Chen and Mei face. I have no concept of what it must be like to live with a family who have their own set of expectations for my life, my future.

'My father wants the wedding to take place as soon as possible,' Chen sighs, stuffing his hands into his pockets.

'Why the rush?' I frown, looking down and fiddling with my cinnamon scroll on the counter.

'My father has his reasons.'

'Has he shared them with you?'

'He doesn't need to.'

I bow my head, feeling a little chastised.

'I'm sorry. I suppose I will never understand how things work for your family.' Chen reaches a hand toward me, we both stand there watching it linger mid-air before he eventually drops it back to his side.

'I am not used to explaining 'the way things work' to outsiders. My whole life, I've been surrounded by people who see the world the same way I do. Suddenly you appear, and I begin to question everything I've ever known,' he whispers. 'You live with such passion and unrestricted freedom.'

I look up into his face, realising for the first time just how trapped he must feel in this life. 'Have you had a say in any aspect of your life?'

He shakes his head, staring down at his intertwined fingers.

'Chen, I'm so sorry. I never realised just how little control you had. Even coming to HEH wasn't your choice.'

A knock at the door causes us both to jump.

'Coffee, Miss Elias?' Comes a muffled voice.

'Thank you!' I call back.

I look up at Chen, feeling the tension between us.

'You are engaged now; you won't be able to come in here anymore. People will talk.' I shrug, shaking my head at the idea of gossip.

'Other than the engagement, I did have one other item to discuss with you,' Chen chuckles, reaching into his breast pocket to withdraw an envelope. He peers at my sugary fingers before seeming to decide to keep hold of it.

'Is it something we can discuss in my office?' I laugh, picking back up my scroll and continuing to nibble. Chen grins broadly at me.

'Now I know you aren't going to stab me with a pencil over the engagement announcement, sure.'

'Let's reconvene in an hour?' I smile back, picking up my spare scroll and heading for the door.

Back in my office, I sip my coffee as I check my emails. Sasha has done an excellent job colour coding the ones requiring my urgent attention. Teal, 'Ava's Colour'. My favourite. I spot an email from Chen this morning titled 'Melbourne Port Authority'. I'm about to click on it when I hear Chen arrive at the door.

'I was just about to open the email about the Port of Melbourne. Is that what you wanted to see me about?' I turn and smile up at him. He sighs heavily and sits on the edge of the wingback chair.

'We need to send someone out there to negotiate access to the port.' He runs a hand through his fringe; his hair pulled back in a bun this afternoon.

'Why has access changed?' I frown, peering at the

map on my laptop screen.

'Something political, as far as I can gather,' Chen sighs.

'Political political or environmental political?'

Chen looks up to smirk at me, 'You're a quick study, Miss Elias.'

'If it's environmental, we need to do everything we can to make sure we are reducing our impact. If it is political, then we need to tread carefully.'

'Having a fellow kinsman negotiate alongside our team might help ease the deal through.' I look up to see Chen eyeing me with curiosity.

'Do you mean me? You want me, an unknown, unnamed representative of HEH to engage in a face to face negotiation?' I feel the heat begin to rise in my face.

Am I ready for this level of responsibility in the public arena?

'You've already been negotiating with these people via written negotiation and sat in on plenty of Skype meetings. Why wouldn't this be the next logical step?'

'When are the team heading across?' I hadn't thought I'd be returning to Australia again so soon. I was starting to get used to being back in Singapore after our trip to Europe.

'Next week,' Chen eyes me hesitantly.

'Is there any particular reason you don't want to go?' I frown at him curiously.

'I have business to attend to here,' he states bluntly.

Okay then.

'I'll pack my bags. How many are going? It's probably cheaper to take the Screaming Eagle than book commercially.' I shrug.

'That is the other reason I suggested you go. The team aren't comfortable flying privately without the 'owner of the jet' present.'

'Why?' I frown at him.

'Call it superstition,' he sighs.

'Are you okay?' I stand and wander around the lounges. Chen's eyes lock with mine, a sea of mixed emotions.

'You mean besides the fact that I'm now publicly engaged to Mei?' His tone implies that I know more than I'm letting on.

Does Chen know that Mei isn't interested in men? Does he know that I suspect it too?

'I mean, is there anything else going on that you want to talk about?' I sit down hesitantly, contemplating helping myself to the whiskey trolley.

Hm, might be a tad too early in the morning for that.

I watch the cogs turning in Chen's mind, wondering what could possibly be so bad. I've never seen him like this before.

'I...' Chen starts just as Sasha enters the room, carrying what looks like a bag full of Mexican food for our lunch.

'Oh, I'm sorry. I didn't realise you had company. I'll come back,' she bobs a polite apology and retreats out the door.

'I should be going. I'll have Sasha sent the details of the meetings. Perhaps you can see your family while you are at home?' Chen adds, wistfully.

'Ah, sure. I'll do that,' I stutter, confused.

'Good...good. Well, I'd better leave you to it,' Chen mumbles awkwardly as he retreats out the doorway.

I watch Sasha as Chen passes her. She stands, Mexican in hand, frowning at Chen's retreating figure before turning to me.

'Uh? Okay?' She raises her eyebrows at me questioningly.

'Who knows with that one!' I chuckle, 'What did you find us for lunch?' I smile broadly at her as she brings in my favourite burritos and nachos.

'Apparently, I am to assist in the negotiations in Melbourne next week. Do you know who is booked to attend? I should meet with the team this week to catch up to speed.'

'Already ahead of you!' Sasha laughs as she collects mineral water from the fridge. 'It's already in the schedule, including departure times for the Jet and transfers into Melbourne on the Helicopter.'

'What would I do without you Sasha?' I smile at her, feeling eternally grateful that Winnie found her. 'Now, why don't you fill me in on what I've missed in your life since I was away!'

'Are you sure you don't need me to stay?' Seal asks for the 10th time since we began driving to Margot's warehouse for dinner.

'Seal, if you want to stay and see Jia, just ask. You don't have to pretend it is for my sake!' I laugh, shaking my head.

'I don't know what you're talking about,' he huffs gruffly. I can see from the back seat as he slumps down and crosses his arms across his chest.

He looks like a toddler throwing a tantrum. I suppress the urge to laugh at him further.

Arriving at the warehouse, I thank Xi and Seal,

knowing the after-hours driver will be back later tonight to collect me. Walking into the warehouse tonight, it felt different. Something had changed; and from the doorway, I couldn't for the life of me put my finger on what.

I spot Jia at her usual post behind the bar, slicing wedges of pineapple to go in frothy Pina Coladas.

Linah is sitting on the couches, chatting. I can't identify her companion from behind but based on the silky long black hair; I assume it is Mei. I can't spot Margot's long blonde ringlets anywhere. I make my way to the bar and offer to assist Jia.

'Thanks! I'm almost done here!' Jia blows me an air kiss from across the bench.

'Where's Margot?' I frown, peering around the space. 'Is she up in the studio?'

'Riley is here,' Jia whispers across to me. My eyes widen in shock.

'Riley, her husband?' I'm speechless. 'That's huge!'

'Crazy, isn't it! She tells him about everything, and now they are stronger than ever. I've never seen her this happy!' Jia grins at me.

'I'm so glad to hear it! I can't wait to meet him!'

'Linah hasn't said anything, but I think she might be struggling a bit with it,' Jia drops her voice lower. 'I think she's wondering if she should tell Chip.'

I look across at Linah's profile from where she sits on the lounge. She appears to be smiling, deep in conversation with Mei.

'Don't Chip and Riley get on quite well?' I frown, realising the imposition this places both Linah and Riley in. Jia nods gravely.

'Oh, bummer. Have Margot and Linah talked about it?' I frown. Jia shakes her head, while aggressively adding the pineapple wedges to the rims of the cocktail glasses.

'Is this my fault?' I whisper, eyeing Jia guiltily. Her head snaps up, eyeing me fiercely.

'No. All you did was help remind us that we have no reason to hide. Whatever happens with Linah's relationship has nothing to do with you, or any of us.' I nod, sagely.

Deciding I need to lighten my mood and the conversation, I giggle.

'You know who was asking about joining us?' I watch Jia's eyes twinkle.

'Who?'

'Seal.'

'Really? Interesting. What did he say?'

'Nothing too pointed, he just kept asking if I was okay to stay here without him and offering to join us if I would feel more comfortable.'

'Why didn't you let him come in?' Jia pouts at me.

'I didn't know if you'd want me to. I'll make sure to invite him next time. You do realise you could always invite him yourself, too? Come to think of it, the next time Tari is off work on a Monday, I'll invite her too.'

'How much you have changed our worlds, Ava Elias. Suddenly our Invisible Women of three are fighting our way back into the light, and gaining supporters as we go.' She smiles broadly at me, passing across a cocktail. I hold my glass up in a toast.

'To the fight,' I chuckle, clinking my glass against Jia's.

Movement at the top of the stairs has all four of us turning to watch Margot and Riley descend into the main space. I've never seen Margot beaming so proudly in the short time I've known her. I watch as she and Riley walk hand in hand toward our group. Riley's dark chocolate skin a beautiful contrast to Margot's porcelain white fingers clutched in his hand. I make my way toward them, ensconcing Margot in a warm hug before turning to Riley.

'Riley, this is Ava. Ava, this is my husband, Riley.' Margot beams proudly.

'It is a pleasure to meet you,' Riley's strong Oxford accent rolling romantically off his tongue.

'You too!' I laugh, embracing him. I am suddenly self-conscious of my twangy Australian accent beside this posh English gent. Margot introduces Riley to Mei and Jia. Linah and Riley hug warmly, exchanging pleasantries about Chip who's absence did not go unnoticed.

Leaving the trio to catch up, I notice Mei trying to catch my eye. I follow her further away from the group, propping ourselves up at the bar.

'Congratulations?' I scrunch my nose at the hollowness of the sentiment. Mei offers me a halfhearted smile, raising her glass to clink against mine.

'Cheers.' She upends the glass and chugs the contents.

'I'm so sorry, Mei. I don't know what else I can say?'

'It's okay, Ava. You don't have to say anything. Chen and I made this bed, and now we have to lie in it.' She swirls her cocktail twizzle stick around in the foam at the bottom of her glass.

'I'll bet it's going to be one hell of a party?' I nudge her with my shoulder, trying to raise her spirits.

'My mother is already booking meetings with dress

designers. She said it has to be bigger than a royal wedding, because the Chen's and the Yang's deserve the royal treatment.' She rolls her eyes, embarrassed.

'I think every mother wants her daughter to feel like a princess on her big day.' I chuckle, sipping my cocktail.

'Even if she is marrying someone she doesn't love?'

I turn to see Mei's fallen face. My heart breaks for her.

'Oh, Mei!' I stand up and ensconce her in a tight hug. At a loss of what else I can say to console her, I just stand there until I feel her relax in my arms.

What kind of a world do we live in, in this century, where two people still feel compelled to marry one another for the sake of their families' expectations.

We break apart as the door buzzer goes, signifying the arrival of dinner. I gently wipe a tear from Mei's cheek.

'Do you know what we are eating tonight?' I ask her, trying to get her mind off Chen.

'I think I heard something about food from the hawker centre?' Mei offers.

'Excellent, I'm starving!' I smile at her as we make our way toward the dining table.

'Did I hear you are going to Melbourne next week?' Mei asks conversationally as we sit down.

'Melbourne?' Linah cocks an eyebrow in my direction, no doubt thinking about Ryan. I roll my eyes in response.

'We have some business at the Dock to take care of. Chen suggested it would be a good opportunity for me to show my face, that's all.' I reach across to assist Linah in unpacking the food.

'Are you going to see anyone while you're there?' Margot asks, attempting to sound disinterested.

'I haven't heard from Ryan since Europe. Can we please let this go? I just don't think the 'Ava and Ryan' love story has any further chapters, okay?' I sigh, cradling a large container of piping hot chilli crab. I look up to see Riley watching me closely.

'I hope you do not mind; Margot may have filled me in,' he shrugs embarrassed.

'I don't mind in the slightest, but I am afraid you've joined at the end of the broadcast. I'd much prefer we talk about you!' I chuckle, passing him a pair of chopsticks. I am rewarded with a bright white smile.

'Where to start! My parents immigrated to London from Nigeria before I was born...' Riley transforms into a storyteller, producing elaborate tales of his childhood, growing up in London.

Partway through the dinner I notice Margot and Riley whispering to one another, Margot's face betraying her distaste at the conversation. I watch as she grabs Riley's arm in horror as he turns to Mei.

'So Mei, are you going to open a tender for the opportunity to design your wedding dress?' He smiles broadly at Mei across Margot.

The entire table quietens, all eyes on Riley. I watch Mei's mouth open and close at a loss for a reply.

'Riley, I told you not to suggest something so ludicrous!' Margot snaps, standing promptly before stalking from the table. Riley continues to eye Mei, undeterred.

'I saw the dress she made for Ava; you can't deny

the quality and design of Margot's designs.'

'I...I don't know what to say, Riley. My family expect that I wear a well-known designer,' Mei stutters. I can't help but feel for Mei, now that I understand a little more about what she is up against. I excuse myself quietly and follow in Margot's wake.

I find her sitting on the floor behind a sofa upstairs in her studio.

'There's no denying his love for you, Margot,' I chuckle, kicking off my heels and sitting beside her on the floor.

'I am so embarrassed; I can't believe he just did that.' Margot buries her face in her hands.

'Mei understands, and besides, I'm sure she would have asked you if she thought she had any say in the matter.' I nudge her with my shoulder.

'You think so?'

I wrap one arm around her shoulders, 'I don't doubt it.'

'I could strangle him, Ava! He makes me so mad sometimes!' Margot whines.

'I have no smart retort to that one, honey. I guess that's what happens when we love people; they do things that make us crazy.'

'Are you going to give it another go with Ryan?' I hear the hesitation in her voice.

'He's the one who walked away, Margot. I don't think I have much say in the matter anymore.' I shrug, looking up at the ceiling trying to stop my eyes from welling up.

'But you do love him still? More than Chen?' Margot pulls back to look me in the face.

'Chen knows I do not love him.'

'And he's marrying Mei.'

'Yes, there's that too,' I sniff quietly.

'Did you know?' Margot frowns at me questioningly.

'Chen told me this morning.'

'After it went public?'

'Yup.'

'Ah,' is all she manages to say. We sit there in quiet contemplation listening to the muffled chatter from downstairs.

'Well this is kinda fucked up, isn't it?' Margot whispers, giggling quietly. I nod enthusiastically, giggling back. It isn't long before we are laughing hysterically and rolling around on the floor. Tears streaming down our faces, hoarse from laughter, we lie there in one another's' arms.

'I'm so glad I met you, Margot,' I sigh.

'Me too, Ava.'

12

'Are we all clear on the plan for the meeting?' Mr Goh, our head of Transport, asks the table. We all nod our heads, murmuring agreement.

Our group sat huddled around a table inside Rockpool, the exquisite seafood restaurant within the Crown Hotel precinct.

The flight across from Singapore on the Screaming Eagle was a hoot with these gents. We played poker and sipped whiskey for hours before falling asleep in our respective recliners. We spent today holed up in a conference room at Crown, mapping out the plan for the meeting at Port Melbourne tomorrow.

As best I could keep up, it would appear the Port of Melbourne Authorities were trying to convince HEH to ship to the Williamstown Newport Foreshore rather than directly into the Port of Melbourne. The reasoning behind this was yet to be made clear by the Victorians. It was clear, however, to HEH that changing the docking location of our vessels would cost us a fortune in additional storage and transport charges. It had been decided that if necessary, we would negotiate an increase in payment for continued access to the Port of Melbourne.

'Another cocktail, Miss?' The waiter smiles kindly at me as he retrieves my empty glass. I feel the eyes of the table on me, aware of how eager the gents are to get into the Casino.

'The cheque, if you please,' I smile back politely. I feel the immediate wash of relief from the gathering.

After wishing the men luck for the evening, I retire to my suite. Digging out the in-room amenities folder, I flip through the pages until I come across the spa menu. Eyeing the opening and closing hours, I realise I am too late to book in a massage for the morning. Sighing heavily, I shut the book and dig out my laptop. I stare blankly at the email inbox, tempted to let Ryan know I am in Melbourne. I feel the loneliness creep slowly into my consciousness, the dark realisation dawning on me that Ryan was somewhere nearby, and yet out of my reach.

What would I even say to him? I suppose I could call him.

I push the thought aside, heading determinedly to the bathroom to run a bubble bath.

The next morning after we gathered together for breakfast, the HEH crew piled into a BBSUV and drove 10 minutes to the Port of Melbourne. Following closely behind was Xi and Seal in their own car. The building in which the meeting was held left little to the imagination. It was boxy, glass and egotistically decorated. Once the meeting commenced, I worked extremely hard to control my facial expressions as I witnessed the masculine pissing contest unfold before me.

The conversation got off on the wrong foot from the start, whereby Xi and Seal were ordered to remain outside as the meeting was for 'executives only'. I eyed our retreating hosts backs begrudgingly when I caught Xi's expression, a warning not to lose my temper. I watched their surprised faces as I filed into the room alongside my male counterparts.

After settling into the meeting room, my male companions were offered coffee. I was offered tea or lemon water.

'Coffee, black,' I replied deadpan, 'thank you.' I could feel the eyes of my male associates on me. I had to request not once, but twice for a copy of the 'packet' of documents supplied to my colleagues. Mr Goh resolved the issue by giving me his own to flip through.

Our host commenced his lecture on the reason for our visit before proceeding to pass Mr Goh a monogrammed sheet of paper with the increased fees for HEH's use of the port. I leaned over slightly to see the eight-figure sum. Knowing full well this was more than double our current fees; it took all I had not to spit my coffee.

'May I ask the reason for such a significant increase?' I ask, watching our hosts eyes boggle.

I am not here to be seen and not heard.

He turns to look at Mr Goh, as if to confirm the need to answer the question.

'If you please?' I add, my eyes not leaving the pompously suited man before me. His purple cravat wobbling as he swallows nervously.

Who even wears cravats these days? Maybe he has a tracheotomy scar? Perhaps he's just a douche.

'Uh, we have certain costs to cover...Miss..,' he stutters.

'Elias, Ava.' I reply sternly, 'Would you mind elaborating on these costs?'

'I, uh,' he stutters again, his eyes imploring Mr Goh to intervene.

'Are these costs being passed on to all stakeholders who make use of your port?' I enquire with an air of disinterest. 'I only ask because I spot our friends who own the Jazan sailing under the flag of Liberia, currently in port.' Beside me, I feel Mr Goh smother his surprise that I recognised the ship. I watch our host's face grow a deep shade of puce.

'Mr Stevens, let us be honest about your motivations here. I would hate to think you heard HEH is inheriting a female CEO and saw an opportunity to make some easy money.' I pause to allow him a chance to object. He sits mutely, staring at me in horror.

'If there is a genuine reason for these increases, I must be frank with you, Mr Stevens; we can ship to Sydney and transport our goods to Victoria for less money than this.' I level him with my most dispassionate stare. 'You have a choice; either we can assist you in covering the 'running costs', or you can say goodbye to our contract. Think carefully, for we will not be duped. Make no mistake, Mr Stevens; HEH having a female CEO makes no difference to our bottom line and we will not negotiate with philanderers.'

I watch his mouth open and close, once, twice, three times.

'Miss Elias, I must apologise, perhaps there has been a mistake,' he swallows deeply, reaching up nervously to adjust his cravat.

'Might I suggest you revisit your numbers and give Mr Goh a call this afternoon?' I prompt, reaching for my handbag.

'Ah, yes. We will do just that.'

'Excellent, a pleasure doing business with you.' I stand and offer my hand. A sweaty palm meets my grip, shaking hesitantly.

Back in the car, it took a minute for the group to find their voice.

'Well, Miss Elias. I must say, that was a phenomenon I am pleased to have witnessed,' Mr Goh stares at me in awe.

'Even Mr Huynh was a little scared of those guys. They play dirty,' piped up one of the associates.

'Bullies don't scare me. And I'll be damned if I let some ass wipe of a man come in and threaten HEH operations,' I adjust my sunglasses, trying to contain the beaming smile threatening to break out. 'I must admit, it felt pretty good,' I smirk. The gents erupt into laughter, and we drive back to the Crown in high spirits.

I released the team of duties for the afternoon and having established that Xi and Seal had far more 'interesting' things to do with their evening than have dinner with 'their boss' as we often do back home, I booked myself a table at a restaurant in the Crown building. I roll my eyes at the thought of the conversation with the boys this afternoon.

Am I really that 'uncool' to hang out with?

After showering and getting dressed, I headed down to the restaurant strip. I was too early for my reservation yet and so I began to wander contemplatively past the elaborate designer jewellery cases embedded in the wall along one hallway. Who buys this stuff?

I peer more closely at a bracelet with a jaguar-shaped head stuck to the side of it with bright green emeralds for eyes. My eyes boggle at the price tag of $55,000.

It's so damn ugly. Do people buy it simply to say they own something that expensive? I meander across to the next window, appreciating the much more straightforward diamond drop earrings displayed there. I reach up instinctively to check Winnie's earrings are still securely in place. Dropping my hand down, I look down at my fingers and adjust Winnie's ring, the pink diamond glimmering back at me in the bright hall lights. With a heavy sigh, I decide it is time to take my tired ass to get a drink.

Walking into Gradi, I wait patiently as the hostess mills around with other customers. I smooth down the wrinkles in my silk T-shirt dress, watching the fabric shimmer this way and that. I'd opted to change into my flat boots for the evening having spent the day in heels.

'Do you have a reservation?' the hostess asks as she returns to her computer.

'Elias, Ava,' I reply, smiling across at her. She frowns down at her computer.

'Uh, how many are in your party?' She eyes me curiously.

'One.'

'Of course, right this way.'

Scanning across the restaurant, I observe the extensive tables full of friends and families dining with one another. I try not to replay in my head the judgemental look of the hostess when she realised I was eating alone. I smile to myself; the thought of the freedom to order whatever I please brings me joy.

A familiar silhouette catches my eye; broad shoulders, beach boy blonde hair. Strange, it doesn't look so familiar in a suit and collared shirt. The man steps around his date, lifts her napkin from the table and shakes it out to lay across her lap. I gawk at the sight before me. Ryan stands behind the chair of his date, her half-draped napkin frozen in mid-air as we lock eyes. I feel my heart begin to pound in my chest.

He's here...on a date...

'Miss?' The seating hostess breaks the tension.

'Sorry after you.' I turn to follow her through the restaurant, where she seats me only a handful of tables from Ryan's, directly in his line of sight.

Oh, joy.

'Your waiter will be with you shortly.' She smiles and promptly departs. I stare around the room trying to look anywhere but at Ryan. I feel my phone vibrate in my clutch. Checking the caller ID I see it is Chen.

Hm, probably not the most fabulous time to take that call.

I place my phone back in my purse and peruse the menu. I'd been to Gradi before and knew I loved the Margherita pizza and the goats cheese and beetroot salad.

Damn, that didn't take long.

I begin flipping through the wine list when Seal appears. I frown up at him as he seats himself without a word. He casually adjusts his navy suit, unbuttoning it as he settles into his chair.

'Uh, hi?' I stare across at him, 'Did I miss

something?'

'No. I just decided you might like the company.' He states deadpan, reaching for the menu. 'What are you ordering?'

'Pizza and salad.'

He rolls his eyes at me, noticing my discomfort for the first time.

'What's with the face?' He looks around us and before I have time to hiss at him, and spots Ryan over his shoulder. He turns back slowly before asking, 'Will you fire me if I talk to Ryan?'

I cock an eyebrow.

'Be my guest.' I turn to the newly arrived waiter, place my meal order and request an Old Fashioned cocktail.

Turning around, I see Ryan and Seal embraced in a friendly hug. Ryan's eyes catch mine over Seal's shoulder. Clapping each other on the back, they break apart, and Ryan introduces Seal to his date. The three of them laugh animatedly at some unheard comment.

After an infuriatingly long wait, Seal eventually returns to our table, a grin spanning from ear to ear.

'Did you order me a beer?' He smiles across at me.

'Oh, you mean when the waiter was here? And you were over there embracing Ryan?' I bat my eyelashes innocently.

'I'll take that as a 'no',' he chuckles, lifting his hand to flag down the waiter and order a drink.

'Do you want me to tell you?' Seal looks across at me hesitantly.

'That depends, am I going to need to order another drink?' I look down at my purse in my lap, fiddling with Winnie's ring out of habit.

'It's a 'first meeting'; he found her on Tinder.' He

shrugs nonchalantly.

'Oh, well. I suppose I knew he would move on at some point,' I whisper, twisting Winnie's ring faster on my finger.

'He asked if 'we' were staying in the hotel,' Seal eyes me curiously. The waiter arrives with our drinks, and I sip my Old Fashioned contemplatively.

Seal and I fall into easy conversation as we wait for our food to arrive.

'You didn't tell me what you ordered?' He smiles across at me. I open the menu and show him the pizza and salad.

'Sounds great, but we are going to need seconds or dessert,' he chuckles.

'How long have we known each other now? Surely you understand dessert is a given.' I roll my eyes and laugh at him.

A sudden kerfuffle behind Seal has us turning to watch Ryan's date stand up and storm from the restaurant. Seal stands instinctively and paces toward Ryan. A hushed conversation followed, including much arm waving and hands indicating toward my general direction. Seal slowly turns and walks back toward our table.

'Uh, can Ryan sit with us?' He stares at me. I roll my eyes, secretly pleased at this turn of events.

'Sure.'

As he sits down, Ryan eyes me warily, 'She said she couldn't eat anything here because she's a gluten-free vegan.'

'I'm sure that's not true. I think the pizza boxes are vegan,' I smile at him hesitantly.

'I think you dodged a bullet there bud; she looked way too high maintenance.' Seal clapped Ryan on the shoulder.

By the conclusion of our dinner, it had begun to feel like dinners from the past, where Seal, Xi, Ryan and I would while away the small hours debating all manner of topics from current affairs to ancient civilisations, nestled around the fire at Carcassonne. As our laughter died down, and we emptied our second bottle of wine, Ryan and my eyes met across the table.

'Do you want...' He eyes me shyly.

'Want?' I smile hesitantly.

'Want to share a dessert?' He frowns. I can't help but feel that was not what he intended to say.

'Sure.' I shrug.

After placing our order for tiramisu, Seal yawns dramatically, stretching his arms wide behind him.

'Well, as much as I have enjoyed our evening, I'm ready to turn in. Enjoy the rest of your night. Ava, I'll see you in the morning.' He stands slowly, shakes Ryan's hand and claps him on the shoulder. They exchange a lingering stare, before Seal nods toward me and disappears.

'Don't worry, I guess I'll get the cheque then!' I laugh at his retreating back. I turn around to see Ryan grinning at me. 'What?'

'I've missed you. I don't know if I'm not supposed to say that, but I have.' He shrugs, sipping his wine as the waiter returns with our dessert.

'I understand congratulations are in order?' He waves his spoon in my direction as we dig into the creamy espresso parfait.

'Oh?' I garble around a large spoonful.

'In your last email, you said you'd resolved the

paternity battle. I didn't get a chance to catch it on the news here.'

'That, yes. Thank you. It was a team effort.' I smirk back. 'I never thanked you for taking the time to talk to me that night, about the anaphylaxis patient.' I look down at the dessert in front of us, feeling suddenly nervous again.

'You don't need to thank me. It was the least I could do to be there for you in a time of need.' He smiles lovingly across at me. I feel my heart melting.

'Tell me, what did you enjoy most about Europe?' He cocks his head to the side like a puppy. I smile at the memories, the trip already feeling like such a long time ago.

'The architecture, the history. Oh, the people! Some of the people we met were incredible.' I sigh wistfully as I scoop more dessert. I notice Ryan has only puddled in his half. 'You didn't really want to order this, did you?' I smile fondly across at him.

'You always felt less guilty about ordering the whole thing if I agreed to 'share'.' He laughs, raising his hands in air quotes.

'You have a great memory.' I sigh realising I have indeed consumed the majority of the dessert.

'Would you like to go for a walk?' He asks hesitantly. I look up and see him watching me anxiously. I feel my heart skip a beat.

'I'd love to.' I beam across at him, wondering momentarily if this means as much to him as it does to me.

Ryan and I stroll along the boardwalk, watching other couples cycle, jog and canoodle around us. The warm evening air whirling gently across the river.

'You know your dad thanked me, that day I ran into them in the Gardens,' Ryan looks away from me, out across the river toward the city.

'He was always rooting for you.' I nod, pulling my cardigan off in the warm evening air.

'Clearly I don't deserve it. He said 'Thanks for being so good to my little vegemite.' I feel rather than hear Ryan clearing his throat.

'Ha, he has never stopped calling me that. I'll clear it up with them while I'm down here. I'm sorry I hadn't told them sooner, I just wasn't ready to break their hearts.' I look up at the pylons, realising it must be close to time for the light show.

'He was wrong,' Ryan's voice comes out husky and sad.

'What do you mean?' I stop and turn to face him, grabbing his arm.

'All you were trying to do was get justice for Winnie, and I didn't trust you enough to let you go.' He looks around us, anywhere but directly at me.

'Why didn't you trust me?' I frown, looking up into his face.

'I guess it wasn't so much you, I didn't trust...' He doesn't finish his sentence. I feel sick; I know he's referring to Chen.

'I saw the way he looked at you, and you're too kind to hurt people, Ava. Besides, he fits way better in your fancy new world of luxury condos and tuxedos.'

'Sure there was always some chemistry there Ryan, but did you honestly think I would cheat on you?' I implore him, feeling the tears welling, threatening to overflow.

'You said 'was'.' He frowns.

'What?' I step backward.

'You said there 'was always chemistry'. What changed? Did you realise what a giant asshole he is?' Ryan's eyes search my face. I look away, terrified he'll see the answer written there.

Shit. I didn't think I'd ever be in a situation where I'd have to tell Ryan what happened. I didn't think he'd ever speak to me again; he was so angry when he left. If I didn't believe we were absolutely over, with not even a snowflakes chance in hell of getting back together, I'd never have slept with Chen. But I can't lie to him.

'I was so upset when you left...' the tears start to fall, derailing me. Ryan's jaw drops open, his face contorting into a painful grimace.

'No Ava, tell me you didn't?' He barely whispers. His hands find his hair as he clutches his skull. 'I can't hear this. Are you telling me that I caused this? My worst nightmare come true, and I'm the one who pushed you into his arms?'

'I'm sorry,' I gasp, 'I didn't think...you'd ever speak to me again. And I was so hurt and angry.' I watch him turn in circles, his face breaking my heart all over again.

'Why? Was it to get back at me? Were you trying to hurt me?' He stills and watches my face anxiously.

'Of course not, I missed you, and I just needed to feel wanted again.' I hang my head, realising how stupid it sounds. I trudge over to a bench and plonk myself down. 'I didn't think you'd ever agree to see me again. You were so angry when you left.'

'But then you ran back to Singapore without a word.' Ryan comes to kneel in front of me. 'You didn't even give me a chance to cool off before you jumped on your jet and disappeared.'

I look up into his eyes, seeing the sincerity in the crystal blue depths.

'You were planning on coming back?' I frown, the tears slowly subsiding.

'And suddenly I get to Carcasonne and Seal tells me you're all shipping out the next morning, without so much as a goodbye.' He hangs his head and reaches for my hand, gently squeezing it. 'I figured I'd blown it and that you wouldn't forgive me for being such a selfish prick.' He reaches up and gently wipes the tears from my cheeks with his thumb.

'We messed this up big time, huh?' I snort. I realise with horror that I've blown a snot bubble.

'Oh god, please just let me die here.' I hang my head, only to find Ryan passing me a handkerchief.

'That was the least disgusting thing I've witnessed all day.' He smiles up at me as I blow my nose.

'Does that include your date's hair cheap extensions?' I peek up at him, gauging the tension.

'They looked like my sister's Barbies from when we were kids. All stringy and plastic-y.' I watch as a shiver runs down his spine, 'I prefer redheads anyway.'

He looks up at me, reaching up to run his fingers through my tresses whilst slowly releasing a breath he seemed to be holding.

'What would you say if I asked you to start again?'

I frown, unsure what he means.

'Start again. How?' I reach down to swat away a bug from his arm.

'We forgive each other for the past, put it behind us, and I ask you to have a drink with me.' He smiles hesitantly at me. I lean forward and press my forehead against his, breathing in his scent.

'I'd love to,' I whisper, wrapping my arms around his neck.

'I know a great place nearby,' He whispers as I pull back and place a feather-light kiss on his lips.

All around us, the river lights up; the tall pylons spewing fire metres into the sky. We stand up, wrap our arms around each other and watch the light show erupt before us.

'I would have paid money to be there and watch you take that guy down yesterday,' Ryan whispers, running his fingers gently through my hair. I smile, nuzzling into his chest.

'It felt pretty damn good; I have to say,' I chuckle, recalling the look on Mr Cravat's face. 'Who wears cravats these days anyway?'

'That guy from MasterChef?' Ryan offers. I laugh, loving the ease of our chatter.

'Hm, I don't think he was Matt Preston. But I'll double-check next time.'

I feel Ryan place a kiss in my hair as a knock at the door interrupts us.

'That'll be room service!' I squeal, jumping up to throw on my robe and race to the door.

'Hold up, Ava! Let me put some pants on!' Ryan hollers from the bed while scrambling around aimlessly. I turn and throw the other robe at him before throwing the door open. I come face to face with Seal and immediately blush crimson. I already know he can see past me from where he stands and very likely has a view of Ryan's perfectly tanned bottom.

'I'd know that ass anywhere!' Seal hollers before

barging through the door toward Ryan. I giggle as I close the door, hearing the distinct sound of a palm slapping flesh, behind me.

'Argh! Seal you horny bastard!' Ryan roars, tying the robe closed before turning and embracing Seal tightly. I lean against the wall, watching the two of them bantering with one another.

'I should have put money on it!' Seal states pointedly, eyeing me as he flops down onto the sofa.

'Money on what?' I bat my eyelashes innocently, feigning ignorance.

'Xi didn't believe the two of you would, ah, 'make up', quite so quickly.'

A knock at the door interrupts the awkward 'make up sex' conversation. I'm praying it is breakfast. I'm famished.

Seal sat down to the multitude of plates that had been unpacked, and began piling bacon and pancakes onto a plate.

'Oh, please. Help yourself,' I state sarcastically. Ryan sidles up behind me, wrapping his arms around my waist.

'Leave him be,' he whispers, 'look how happy he is.'

I can't help but smile, feeling the love bubble return. I turn and smile up at Ryan, sliding my hands up to grasp his hair.

'I was hoping we could have breakfast in bed,' I grin at him mischievously.

'Maybe we can have a post-breakfast shower?' He wiggles his eyebrows at me suggestively.

'Hm,' I pretend to contemplate, tilting my head to the side. 'I suppose that is an acceptable compromise.' I giggle, standing on my tippy toes to kiss him chastely before turning toward the table. He playfully smacks me on the bum, causing me to squeal.

'That's enough of your obscenities for the morning,' Seal chastises humorously.

'Someone clearly needs to get laid,' Ryan observes quietly as he piles pancakes onto his plate. Seal pulls his signature sunglasses down his nose to give Ryan the stink eye before pushing them back up.

'I don't understand this game you and Jia keep playing. It's the most excruciating foreplay to watch,' I state, pouring a mountain of syrup onto my pancakes.

'Who says we're interested in each other?' Seal grumbles, stabbing a slice of bacon.

Ryan and I exchange a look.

'Suit yourself,' I sigh, reaching across to kiss Ryan tenderly.

'Ugh,' Seal groans. 'Have you called Chen back yet?'

I feel Ryan freeze beside me. I silently curse Seal.

'We'll be back in Singapore tomorrow; he can wait.' I feel Ryan give my hand a quick squeeze.

Note to self, strangle Seal later.

I sip my orange juice contentedly as the boys continue their conversation from the night before. I finish my breakfast and excuse myself.

'Seal, I'll see you later. Wheels up at 2100.'

'Yes, Ma'am,' he salutes me playfully.

I make my way into the bathroom and turn on the faucet. Steaming hot water streams into the tub as I empty several floral-scented bottles into the swirling foam. I'm about to disrobe when I hear the door open behind me. I turn slowly to see Ryan leaning against the door jamb.

'Seal?' I raise my eyebrows.

'Went to annoy Xi for the morning,' Ryan chuckles, unfastening the knot at his waist.

'And what were your plans for the rest of the day?' I mule, exaggeratingly placing one foot in the tub.

'I thought I'd hit the gym. A place as fancy as this must have a good one.'

'Is that so?' I ask feigning curiosity, stepping my other foot into the bath. I turn to face Ryan, watching him slowly open his robe. It slides down his toned arms and pools on the floor at his feet. He steps forward, reaching for the sash on my robe, wrapping his fingers around the tie.

'I suppose the gym could wait,' he whispers, pulling the sash loose.

As Ryan's caressing hands begin to wander under my open robe, we are interrupted by yet another knock at the front door .

'Go away!' We yell in unison.

'I'm going to get pruney,' I whine playfully, holding my hands up in front of my face. I sit in the tub; contentedly lounging in Ryan's lap. He takes my hand, playfully biting each of the pads of my fingers.

'When will I see you again?' He breathes, almost as if to himself.

I sigh heavily, wishing I too knew the answer.

'I'll try to come back as soon as I can,' I offer, hoping it is enough.

'Okay,' Ryan kisses my open palm, 'you're probably right; we should get out. You'll liquify if we stay in here much longer.'

Wrapped in fluffy white towels, Ryan and I lay on the bed watching one another, entwined in each other's arms.

'What do we do now?' Ryan chuckles quietly.

The evening arrived in the blink of an eye, and suddenly I found myself standing in front of the hotel bidding Ryan farewell.

'Aren't you going to miss your flight?' Ryan asks, holding my hands tightly between us.

'I keep telling people; the plane waits for you when you own it!' I laugh, squeezing his hands back. We stand there, both as reluctant as the other to say goodbye. I reach up and brush his blonde fringe aside, watching the light play amongst the strands.

'If you want to come visit, just say the word. I'll send the plane back,' I offer. He leans forward and kisses me gently, his hands drop mine to wrap around my waist.

'That'll make for the worlds most expensive booty call!' Seal barges past, bumping into the pair of us. We break apart, grinning at one another.

'Safe travels, my friend,' Ryan offers a hand to Seal before embracing him tightly, 'look after this one.'

I feel my heart warm at his tenderness. I reach up and plant one last kiss on Ryan before our trio pack into a BBSUV. My colleagues, including Mr Goh, were making their way in a separate vehicle.

For the first time in a while, as I watch Ryan's figure shrink into the distance, I feel a slight pulse beating in the heart of my romantic life.

Singapore felt more humid and sweltering than ever before. An unusual anxiety was palpable in the city. I felt relieved to walk through the doors into the penthouse, the scent of Gladys' cooking lingering in the air.

Sticky from the flight and heat outside, I decide on a bath before I get stuck into my work. I couldn't help the guilty niggle I felt at having spent the flight watching a Mission Impossible movie marathon with the guys whilst playing poker. The realisation that I hadn't checked my emails or turned on my phone hadn't hit me until we were standing at the security conveyor belt having our possessions scanned.

Oops. Oh well, Singapore was still here when we landed and as far as I can tell the world hasn't caught fire. It can wait for another hour or so for me to take a bath.

Clean, perfumed and ensconced in my fluffy bathrobe; I reluctantly shuffle my way to the office to unpack my laptop. I reach for the TV remote unconsciously, flipping on the 24-hour news channel to catch up on the death and destruction happening around the world. A stiffly dressed newsreader appears behind a perspex desk.

'Following on from our lead story this morning, Mr Chen of Chen Industries has died overnight. We cross live to our reporter...' I don't hear the end of the headline. My ears begin to ring as the world around me sounds fuzzy and very far away.

Died? No, it can't be!

13

I stare dumbfounded at the television.

'Mr Chen Senior of Chen Industries has died suddenly. He was believed to have been 71. Our thoughts and prayers are with the Chen family in their time of mourning. A public vigil will be held outside Chen Industries headquarters on Friday.' A series of photos and videos of Chen Senior scrolled across the screen.

I step backward until my legs hit the sofa, sinking slowly onto it.

Chen's father died.

A thought suddenly occurs to me. Was that why he tried to call me? Was his father unwell? I dig my phone out of my pocket and call Sasha. She answers on the second ring.

'Welcome to Huynh Enterprises Holdings, Ava Elias' Office,' she doesn't sound her usual perky self.

'Sasha, it's Ava.' I frown down the phone.

'Ava? Oh, I didn't realise you were back yet! Thank goodness, things have been going a little sideways here,' she whispers down the phone.

'What do you mean sideways? I've only been gone a week.' I frown even harder.

'Well, Chen has been quite sullen, and Jia was telling him to 'get over it' except then yesterday we found out...'

'Yes, I saw the news. Did Chen not tell any of you about his father?'

'No, he had spent a fair amount of time away this past week. He was cancelling meetings etc. but he didn't tell any of us why.'

'Has anyone tried to contact him to offer condolences?'

'Jia tried to call him, and we sent a huge bouquet, but he won't talk to anyone,' she sighs down the phone. 'He might talk to you if he knew you were home?'

'Is he in today? I don't know what the norms are for grief and mourning in Asian cultures.' I shake my head.

'We haven't seen him, but if I do, I'll let him know you're back.'

'Thanks, Sasha, I'll try to give him a call. I'll see you after lunch.'

I hang up the phone and google 'Singaporean mourning customs' on my laptop. As I am scrolling through the pages of notes on funerals and grief, I dial Chen's number on my phone. It goes straight to voicemail, so I leave a message offering my condolences; explaining I had seen the news and was back in the country if he needed anything. After hanging up, I push my laptop onto the sofa and stare at the now blank TV. Poor Chen. It is awful to lose a parent so young. His dad will never meet his children or get to see him marry Mei. I stand and slowly make my way toward the kitchen where I find Gladys cooking away busily. She does not bat an eyelid at my choice of attire.

'Burgers and salad for an early lunch, Miss Ava?' She smiles up at me as she slices tomato on a mandolin.

'Thanks Gladys, that sounds perfect.' I smile back, opening the fridge to retrieve the jug of orange juice.

'I even picked up pineapple and beetroot when I was at the store.' I look across to see the tins on the bench and up at her enthusiastic smile.

'That was very thoughtful of you,' I beam across at her, feeling just a little bit lighter.

'I saw on the news about Mr Chen's father. Terrible. Just terrible,' she shakes her head.

'It is,' I sigh, sipping my juice, at a loss for what else to say. I dig out my phone and text Xi to let him know we will head into the office within the hour.

Not five minutes after sitting down at Winnie's desk in the office, Jia arrives carrying coffee and doughnuts. She wore her hair in a sleek ponytail and matched her turquoise dress to her snakeskin stilettos.

'Thank god you're back. It has been mayhem here without you.' She air kisses me and hands me a coffee before sitting down on the sofa.

'Jia, I was only gone a week,' I stare at her deadpan.

'Yes but so much has happened in that time,' she sniffs, tossing her ponytail over her shoulder.

'Okay, well fill me in. What else did I miss?' I lean across to open the doughnut box and eye the various flavours inside.

'You mean other than Chen's slow descent into oblivion and leaving us in the dark?'

'Yes, other than that.'

'Well, not much, I suppose. That was very perplexing, though. We had word from the docks in Melbourne, seems they liked you. They've agreed to the new terms and signed off on negotiations.' She eyes me curiously.

'That is great news!' I smile across at her, lifting a glazed chocolate delight from the box.

'Seriously though Ava, Chen went completely AWOL about a day after you left. No word why, just cleared his schedule and bailed on us all. He missed important meetings.' She sips her coffee.

'Did he contact you at all to let you know?' I frown to myself.

'No, we found out at the same time the rest of the world did, it would seem.' She rolls her eyes.

'I'm sorry you were stuck here to handle this Jia, but from where I stand it looks like you did a mighty job holding down the fort by yourself.' I smile across at her half-heartedly.

'Yes, well. You should probably go and check on him,' Jia states matter-of-factly. I choke on my doughnut.

'Why me?' I frown spluttering everywhere.

'Because Ava, if the space for CEO of Chen Industries is suddenly vacant, Samuel Chen will be expected to fill it. That is what happens in business here,' she stares at me as though explaining something to a small child. The lightbulb suddenly clicks on.

'If Chen has to take on CI because of his father's passing, I no longer have a beard.' I feel a churning in my stomach.

'Exactly. Now the only question you need to answer is, are you ready to be the CEO of HEH in the daylight?'

After arriving home that evening, I wearily greet Gladys in the kitchen. A large pot of something delicious brewing on the stove, its scent wafting down the corridor.

'Miss Ava, welcome home. You have a visitor,' Gladys smiles at me politely before handing me a bowl and a ladle. I stand there watching her retreating from the kitchen, incredibly confused.

'Are you not joining me for dinner?' I call out to the void.

'If there's food on offer.'

I turn to see Chen leaning against the refrigerator. He looks a mess. He wore traditional grieving clothes; his white linen shirt sat untucked over his white trousers; his hair thrown haphazardly into an untidy topknot.

'Chen,' I whisper, placing the ladle and bowl on the bench before turning to embrace him warmly. 'I am so, terribly sorry.'

I feel his face in my hair; his warmth enveloping me through his light shirt, his arms wrapped tightly around me.

'Can I do anything?' I whisper. I feel him shake his head silently. We stand there, embraced for what feels like an eternity. I feel his grief and devastation wash over me; it takes everything I have not to stand there and cry in his arms. I lean back and look up into his eyes. No longer the eyes of a man, but the deep misty eyes of a lost boy.

'Why don't I serve up some dinner?' I reach up

and cup his face with my hand. He leans his face into my hand and closes his eyes, nodding slowly. 'How hungry are you?' I ask, gently removing my hand and turning back to the kitchen.

We eat in silence, sitting in the fresh night air on the terrace while watching the city below.

'My mother is beside herself,' Chen whispers, the sound of his voice startling me. 'Not that she would ever admit it.'

'She lost her husband. It is understandable.' I look toward him, searching his face in the dim light. 'How are you holding up?'

'I've been better,' he sighs, reaching across to take my hand. I squeeze it before taking mine back. 'It seems my life is about to change rather dramatically, once again.'

'Chen...' I can't find the words.

'I'm not ready to leave HEH yet. To leave you.' He turns toward me, the heat of his gaze falling upon me.

'I don't think I can do this without you. I don't know how.' I feel the fear constricting me.

'You already have been, Ava. You just don't see it yet.' He smiles knowingly across at me. 'The only aspect of the job you haven't been doing is representing the company publicly.'

'You do it so well, with such ease and confidence.' I look down at the table.

'Ava, you travelled around the world to find a solution to our lawsuit. No one asked you to do that; you just did it because you knew it was right.' Chen smiles across at me. 'I have every faith that you can do the job with your eyes closed. That isn't why I'm hesitant to leave...'

'We can't do this , Chen,' I shake my head. 'You're

officially engaged to Mei.' I stand from my seat and collect our bowls from the table.

I haven't told him about Ryan, but his father just died. What the fuck do I do?

'Ava,' Chen implores me, 'please don't do this.'

'I know you are grieving Chen but I told you, I will not go there again.' I walk into the kitchen and place the dishes in the sink.

'But Mei gave us her blessing?' Chen stops short of begging.

'That was before, Chen.'

'Before what?' He frowns.

'Before everything! Everything has changed. Can't you see that?' I turn to find him standing so close I can smell his aftershave. 'Please, don't. Mei and I are in a good place now. I don't want to ruin how far we've come.' I place my hands on his chest and push him backward.

'You really don't want me?' Chen's face falls. I feel my heart breaking inside my chest.

'You know that isn't an option anymore,' I whisper.

'My father was the one pushing for my marriage to Mei,' he whispers, clutching my hands on his chest. He looks up at me, those same wide eyes.

'I can't hear this, Chen. You've made your choice; and now you need to respect mine.' I pull my hands away, feeling the tears welling. 'I think you should go.'

As the elevator doors close on him, I'm confident of only one thing; Chen's grief stricken face at that moment, will haunt me forever. I feel my legs give way beneath me as I slide down the wall to the floor.

Why am I so upset about this? Is it because I know

I'm lying to him? Would it be better if I just told him about Ryan?

The feeling of Ryan holding me beside the river in Melbourne hits me like a rhinoceros on a skateboard.

I miss him. I miss the way he laughs, his warm, gentle hand in mine. Tobogganing down the slopes together and snuggling in front of the fireplace to defrost. I can't wait to get back to him. We will find a way to make this work. He is the right choice.

I dig out my phone and stare at it through a blurry haze. Deciding now isn't the time to call Ryan, I stash it back in my pocket and peel myself off the floor.

This bitch needs a bubble bath.

The following morning, I am unable to fight the reality that Chen will be leaving HEH. The thought both terrifies and excites me at the same time. To live in this world in Singapore as the CEO in the daylight, without my beard is exhilarating. The idea of doing it without Chen now seems unimaginable. Laying in bed, I roll over to check my phone. The screen blinks awake in the early morning light; I squint at it as my eyes adjust. I flip through my emails, checking for anything urgent from overnight.

It seems nothing has caught fire, that is one saving grace I suppose. As I lay there the handset begins to vibrate; Ryan's glowing face appears on my caller ID.

'Good morning, handsome,' I croon, placing him on speakerphone and laying back in bed.

'Good morning, beautiful,' comes Ryan's silky reply, 'how are you?'

I momentarily wonder how much I should tell him. I don't know if he'll be happy Chen will likely be leaving HEH or sad that it will mean my return to

Australia is on hold.

'Ava?'

'Sorry, yes. I'm here. It is going okay. I don't know if the news has reached Australia yet but, uh. Chen's father passed away,' I mumble softly.

'Oh, uh. I'm sorry, Ava,' I can hear the indecision in his voice. 'What does that mean for you?'

'Chen is likely to move to CI to take up his place as Chairman of the Board. Which will leave HEH without a CEO, again,' I sigh, unsure how much further to elaborate.

'I suppose that means you won't be coming back just yet then?' Ryan's disappointment rings clearly down the phone.

'I'm so sorry, Ryan. I wish I had another alternative, but I don't know that I have any other choice. It is time I step up for HEH and prove to myself that I can do this.' I wish I felt more confident in my convictions.

'I have no doubt you will blow their socks off, Ava,' Ryan breathes, 'listen, I'm at the station. Can I call you after my shift?'

'Of course, be safe.'

'You too. Offer Chen my condolences, okay?'

The line goes dead. I roll over amongst my pillows and stare at my phone as the screen returns to the home buttons. Feeling my anxiety rising, I decide to raid Winnie's medicine cabinet to look for some valerian.

It's natural, so it isn't anything to feel guilty about. I tell myself. Perhaps I should consider going for a run or a swim or something....ha! Jumping up and dragging on my silk kimono, I watch the peach blossoms dance this way and that as the fabric shimmers. I meander to the bathroom, throwing open the cabinet doors in search of the herbal supplements. Row upon row of identical jars lay before me; each labelled with beautiful calligraphic script. After a few minutes of shuffling, I find the jar I am looking for. Dragging the lid off, I peer curiously at the brown tablets inside. I tip one into my hand, looking around for a drinking glass. Making my way back to my dresser, I pick up my water canteen, trying to twist the lid off one-handedly. Succeeding in uncapping the device, I turn to peer more closely at the tablet in my palm.

I wonder how old these are? Maybe I should buy new ones instead and toss these out, just in case?

I examine the tablet; realising it seems to be producing an oily residue. I frown down at it, leaning forward to smell the pill. Scrunching up my nose, I decide that it isn't wise to take it. It smells like stale nuts. Is this some strange Singaporean version of Valerian? Making my way back to the bathroom, I toss the tablet in the bin and check the rest of the container. The remaining pills also look oily and smell terrible. I recap the jar quickly and stow it back in the cupboard. Darn, I guess I'll be heading to the pharmacy after all. Washing my hands to remove the residue and smell, I roll my eyes at myself in the mirror. Can't anything ever be simple anymore?

HEH felt different that morning. It was as though the entire building was in mourning. I couldn't be sure if it were for Chen's loss, or our loss of Chen. Seal by my side, we made our way in quietly, greeting Sasha on the way into the office.

'It's like...' Seal looks at me as we cross the

threshold.

'Someone died?' Chen's voice echoes around the room. Seal and I exchange a glance before he turns on his heel and departs. I round the tall wingback chair to spot him laying on the sofa.

'Make yourself at home,' I tease, placing my handbag down and sitting on the edge of the coffee table before him.

'He's never going to like me is he?' Chen sighs, scrubbing his face with his hands.

'I wouldn't be holding my breath if I were you.'

I sit there quietly watching him, noticing the way his chest rises and falls with every breath. The way his brow furrows into a sharp crease when he concentrates. His hair falls loose, splaying silkily over the arm of the chair. His caramel voice interrupts my thoughts, 'have you had any more of those letters arrive?'

I frown across at him, and he turns to eye me speculatively. 'I take it from your silence, that's a 'yes'. You really ought to have someone look into it. If it is Tony, you need to be on the lookout, and if it isn't, then you need to find out who it is.' I shrug in reply, at a loss as to what else to offer. Chen rolls over, propping his head on his hand. 'I'm serious, Ava. It's dangerous. I don't want some psycho to try taking advantage of you the second I'm gone.' Neither of us had voiced plans for his departure before now. It made it feel too real. The idea of running HEH without him felt like riding a bike without training wheels.

'We will need to make plans to announce the changes at some point, Ava. My mother is beginning to doubt my commitment to CI.'

'But your father is barely... How can she expect you to jump and rejoice and move your belongings into CI so quickly?'

'This isn't about feelings, Ava. This is business. It is normal,' Chen sighs, running his free hand through his hair. 'CI just purchased a new factory in China, and my new board expect me to be present for the signing next month.'

'Next month!' I exclaim, feeling my jaw hit the floor, 'that's only a matter of weeks away.' Chen slowly unfurls himself from the couch, leaning forward to grasp my hands between us. 'It's not like I'm going anywhere, Ava, you can always call me if you need me.' I stare into his crystal blue eyes, caught up in a waft of his cologne.

'I still have so much left to learn,' I whisper. He squeezes my hand warmly, grinning across at me.

He lowers his voice, 'do you want to know the real secret?' I frown at him as he leans forward and whispers in my ear, 'do whatever you feel is right, and Jia will tell you if you shouldn't.' I feel myself break out in a broad grin, leaning back to laugh at Chen.

'Are you telling me to operate however I want to, and that my lawyer will interject if I'm about to do anything illegal?'

'Precisely. You will feel an immense sense of freedom,' Chen chuckles.

'Wow, it's a whole new world,' I laugh, shaking my head, 'who would have guessed, a Harvard scholar, telling me to ask for forgiveness, not permission.'

'You are in charge now, Ava. You need permission from no one.' I stare at Chen as his statement hits me. HEH is mine. Mine, alone. If I wanted to I could pack up shop, move back to Dinner Plain and never think of Singapore again. I could say 'not my problem' to the thousands of people HEH employs around the world, turn my back on everything Winnie built; if I felt like it. A small part of me longed to return to my simple life. To go back to working in the ski school in Wintertime and writing stories when I have time off in the summer. I could go back to helping other people balance their business's books and not worry about those of my own. Back to Ryan, where we could get married and have babies and settle into a simple, uncomplicated life. Wake up, feed children, school run, housework, writing, school pickup, dinner, bath time, bedtime. Sneak in sex between feeds and Ryan's shifts. No more death threats in the mail; no more need for Seal watching my back; no more invisible women or Christian Louboutins.

I stare into Chen's eyes, feeling the warmth of his hands, his minty breath on my face as we sit knee to knee, face to face. Or I could, if I wanted to...I could beg Chen not to marry Mei. He and I could become a powerhouse couple; royalty perched atop our respective thrones. We could travel the world, hand in hand, just like this. We would be surrounded by security 24/7, photographed and hounded every minute of our lives. And yet, here I sit feeling safe and warm in his presence. We could learn to love each other, learn to be more than just this chemistry that burns between us. It wouldn't be like that though would it? I can see us now, both on the Screaming Eagle (or whatever ruby encrusted private jet Chen's family own) both jumping from teleconference to teleconference on our laptops, taking phone calls and popping Advil for the permanent headaches we have.

Taking five minutes out of our day to facetime our children and their nannies in Singapore, until they are old enough to start school and get shipped off to boarding school in England. Chen and I under the strain of the responsibilities we bear to our respective companies, to our families and our nations, weighing heavily on us. Holding one hand across a Dom Perignon and caviar dinner, the other scrolling through urgent emails from other time zones around the world.

Great going, Ava. You've overthought yourself into a panic attack.

'I don't even like caviar,' I whisper to myself, feeling suddenly overwhelmed.

'Caviar? What? Ava, you're not making any sense?' Chen lifts me easily from the table and into his lap, crooning in my ear, patting my hair. I snuggle into his shoulder, wondering why I don't feel as guilty about the intimate contact as I probably should.

'You don't have to know where you're going, Ava. None of us do, we just figure it out as we go along. I...I still don't know what I'm going to do...' Chen's voice breaks. I wrap my arms around his neck as we sit embraced, nestled amongst one another. After an age, I lean back, brushing Chen's hair off his face.

'Some days,' I whisper, 'I wish there was a map I could follow. At least that way I'd know where I was meant to be going.' Chen reaches up, tucking a wayward ginger curl behind my ear, tugging gently on my earlobe.

'Now where's the adventure in that?'

14

Having spent the day sitting in meetings regarding Chen's 'offboarding' from HEH and the coordination of the 'roll-out' of my stepping into the CEO role, I decided it was time for a drink. It felt like an age since I'd seen Tari and I desperately needed to get away from HEH for a little while.

I fix my hair in the mirrored interior of the elevator, fidgeting irritated at the slow ascent. I find myself reflecting on Chen and my conversation this morning. Not just the conversation, I begrudgingly admit to myself. What is it about Chen that gets so under my skin? Even thinking about the way it felt, wrapped in his embrace, causes guilt to unfurl in my stomach. It isn't fair to Ryan. I shouldn't be thinking these things when I promised I'd try to get back to him. For some reason, I can't shake the vision of Ryan and me walking hand-in-hand through the snow with our little strawberry-blonde children. It is a heart-warming scene; hearing their squeals of joy as Ryan stands holding me in the Australian sunshine.

The elevator pings as it hits the rooftop. I clear my throat and step out toward the bar. I spot Tari from behind, her short black hair gelled up into a mohawk on top. I park myself at my usual corner, observing the colourful touristy couples smattered around the rooftop. A hot breeze blows across the tables, flapping menus erratically. It smells like rain, and I can feel the electricity of a thunderstorm brewing. As I wait for Tari to finish serving the couple opposite me, I dig out my phone and check the radar. A large red blob sits on the edge of the map, indicative of a downpour and strong electrical storm headed our way.

'I love this season,' a voice to my right states quietly. I look up startled, realising Mei sits perched on a high barstool on the corner beside me. She looks utterly glorious, wrapped in a silk dress and designer sandals. I've never seen her dressed in casual daywear before. She eyes me nervously, fiddling with an oversized diamond earring.

'There is something about the rain that seems to wash everything away: the sweat, the grime. Suddenly Singapore becomes a whole new city, full of endless possibility,' she sighs. I follow her gaze as she watches Tari laugh whilst entertaining the young couple opposite us. The silver cocktail shaker glints in the overhead lights as she expertly mixes an unknown concoction. We both watch in awe as she flamboyantly cracks the top off of the shaker and pours a pink candy cocktail from a height, into a small fluted glass on the counter.

'She's rather talented at that isn't she?' Mei observes whimsically.

'I've spent months watching her do this job, and

every night she pulls out something different. I could never do what she does,' I grin at her back, watching the couple before her applaud and offer her high fives across the counter. She whips out her crisp white tea towel, wipes down the bench and turns toward Mei's corner. She stops when she sees me, grinning broadly. She runs out from behind the counter and embraces me in a warm hug.

'I didn't know you were coming by tonight?' She states accusatorially.

'I honestly didn't know I was on my way here, until I was on my way here,' I offer shrugging honestly. I see her eyes dart toward Mei. 'But I won't stay long, big day ahead tomorrow,' I babble. She offers me a big shit-eating grin in reply. Returning to the other side of the bar, she asks for my order.

'Espresso Martini,' I offer. Tari stares at me, not moving an inch toward making the cocktail. She cocks an eyebrow at me, knowing my low tolerance for caffeine at this time of evening. I drop my purse down on the counter, rolling my eyes.

'Fine. Whiskey, neat.'

She nods her approval and turns toward the island of alcohol in the middle of the bar. I can't help but laugh as I pick up the dessert menu to peruse the options. I feel the nervous energy rolling off Mei beside me. She taps her heel against the metal bar on the high stool, drumming a comfortable rhythm. Is it my presence that is agitating her or is she nervous about being so close to Tari?

Tari interrupts my thoughts as she returns with my drink.

'I feel like I haven't seen you in ages?' She frowns across at me as she picks up a champagne flute to clean.

'Because we haven't,' I agree, sipping my whiskey appreciatively.

'How's Ryan?' She asks, cocking an eyebrow in my direction. I can't tell if she is intentionally trying to bait me in front of Mei.

'He's okay, understandably concerned about Mr Chen Senior's passing and what it means for me at HEH,' I shrug, trying to play it off. I give her the stink eye over my high ball tumbler. I know she's cranky I haven't caught her up in person on the goings-on in Melbourne. Based on her pout, I assume my brief text messages were insufficient.

'Do either of you believe in soulmates?' Mei's question catches Tari and I off guard. We swivel to stare at her, her focus trained on the glass of white wine in front of her.

'I, uh, don't know?' I answer hesitantly, 'I've never felt like I've met someone and recognised them as my soulmate so I don't know that I can answer that?' I feel Tari's eyes on me as she considers my answer. Mei continues fiddling with the stem on her glass.

'I believe in soulmates, but I don't necessarily know how early you know, that they are your soulmate?' Tari offers, 'for example - are you meant to feel love at first sight when you first lay eyes on her?' I laugh and shake my head as she looks to me for confirmation.

'Don't ask me, my friend. I feel like if I'd felt it, I'd know?' We both turn to look at Mei. She eyes us warily, slowly raising her wine to sip it contemplatively.

'Do you believe in it? In soulmates or love at first sight?' I tilt my head to the side, curious about her perspective. I'd never seen this side of Mei before, so raw, so honest.

'I think they do. Exist, I mean,' she states quietly, more to her wine glass than to Tari or myself. 'Do you think Ryan might be yours?' She looks up, her wide eyes ensnaring mine unsuspectingly.

'I, uh,' I mumble, 'I don't know. We haven't talked about the future much, more just trying to figure out how to get back to each other and make a plan from there?' Mei eyes me curiously, a small frown creasing her delicate face.

'That's not what I asked.'

I begin to feel the heat rising in my face and look down at my whiskey as a distraction. I trace the intricate carvings on the side of the tumbler.

'What about Chen?' My head snaps up to find Mei still watching me intently. Tari steps back a pace, as though she's about to duck for cover.

'I...don't think so?' I frown, unsure how to respond. I don't know if I believe that Chen and I are destined to be together. He's so angry at the world, and he doesn't always seem to understand that his perspective isn't the only one to exist. Admittedly, I have seen a different side to him lately. None of that matters though, because the woman sitting beside me is currently wearing a diamond engagement ring the size of Jupiter.

'You're wearing his engagement ring; it hardly seems right to be discussing it,' I whisper, noticing the ring on her hand for the first time. My hand reaches across, almost of its own accord, to pick up Mei's hand and peer at the ring up close.

'It could be yours! For the low price of...a lifetime of servitude,' Mei sighs heavily. I reach up to lay a hand on her shoulder, unsure how else to offer her comfort.

'It sounded like his dad was the one pushing the engagement, do you think now that he's....'

'Dead?' Mei shrugs.

'Can't you and Chen decide between yourselves what you want to do?' I see Tari turn in my periphery to serve another customer. Mei chuckles humourlessly before stating, 'I think our parents would rather us be dead than suffer the humiliation of having us break off the engagement.' I feel a shudder creep down my spine.

'I'm so sorry, Mei. I really am,' I squeeze her hand back, feeling at a loss for words.

'You know, you have a choice,' she whispers. I turn to look at her, confused. 'You don't have to pick Ryan or Chen, if you don't want to.' I watch her as her gaze falls once again on Tari's back.

'Chen may be the man I am going to marry, but he is not the person I choose,' she blushes as Tari turns to wink across at her. Clearly, there is something Tari hasn't filled me in on either. I watch them glow, looking at one another adoringly. 'I personally believe, when you know, you know.'

I have flashbacks of my conversation with Chen this morning, and seeing the possibility of two very different futures, down two incredibly different roads. Mei makes an excellent point though, maybe the road I am destined for doesn't include Ryan, or Chen?

We sit there entranced watching Tari's performances as she entertains other customers around the space. I feel Mei's eyes on me and turn to cock an eyebrow at her. 'Sorry, I don't mean to stare,' she blushes, embarrassed. 'I was just wondering, if you don't mind my asking; what would you be doing right now if you hadn't met Winnie?' I pick up a cocktail umbrella from the tumbler and twirl it this way and that, watching the colours merge into a rainbow.

'I suppose I'd just have continued living my life on the trajectory it was on? Writing for fun, working the winter seasons at the ski school, and helping local businesses throughout the summer.' I frown at the memory, realising my description doesn't sound particularly enthralling. 'I probably would have gone on more dates with Ryan, and I guess eventually might have got married and had a couple of kids?' I watch Mei peer at me with intense scrutiny.

'Do you want children?' She asks, observing me as she sips her cocktail. I wonder if she finds it odd to ask someone else these questions so freely, knowing she, herself is unable to make such decisions. I ponder her question for some time; my umbrella fiddling slowly escalates to gnawing the stick in agitation.

'I honestly don't know. Some days I like to think it would be fun, but then others, I see people with children, and it looks like a terrible life choice.' I shrug, wondering if I am too candid. 'At the moment, I am on the fence, but leaning more toward 'yes'? I guess?' I frown, uncertain if I've answered her question at all.

'You realise there is no right or wrong answer?' Mei giggles, reaching across to take my hand on the bar top. 'You can be unsure if you want children and still be a good parent.' I smile across at her, appreciating her support in that moment, more than she will ever know.

Arriving back at the penthouse, I decide I need a cup of tea. Hoping it will settle the two cocktails in my empty stomach, I drag a couple of tins from the shelf, pondering the beautiful Chinese characters on the front. I lift the lid on the first tin, the scent of jasmine and green tea wafting toward me. Replacing the lid, I turn to the second tin, wondering what delightful aroma is awaiting me. Opening the canister, I realise instantly that the contents do not smell appealing.

I feel Gladys' presence behind me, 'ah, that was Mr Huynh's favourite tea,' she sighs melancholy. I begin to wonder if Winnie was right in the head; this does not smell like something one should be consuming.

'I think it might have gone bad,' I wrinkle my nose, sniffing the contents again, 'it smells like stale nuts. That can't be right can it?'

'No, Miss. I think you are right. Would you mind terribly if I rinsed the contents and kept it out?' Gladys smiles at me sheepishly.

'Not at all, I'd be happy to keep it on display.' I pat her arm gently, wondering if perhaps it was time I have Winnie's perishables cleaned out of the house as my mind drifts to the valerian I'd found in Winnie's bathroom.

'Sleep well, Miss Ava,' Gladys smiles at me gently before departing the kitchen quietly.

Crawling into bed that night, I feel a wave of emotion wash over me. Reflecting on the conversations of the day, both with Chen and Mei, I begin wondering if there is something wrong with me.

I cannot help but feel I am forever changed since meeting Winnie and I don't know if I'd ever be able to return to the my life in Dinner Plain again, without always looking back. Not when I've lived these past months in this crazy, unexpected world. Lived a life I could never have imagined myself in, and yet suddenly, here I stand. Without giving myself a big head, I feel as though I've coped reasonably well with everything HEH and Singapore have thrown at me thus far. My real test is still to come, when Chen steps down from the helm publicly and I face the real world, unguarded, unbridled and exposed. Can I see myself giving up this life, giving up this whole new world I find myself in? I feel as though I am in the midst of an identity crisis. I can see myself in both worlds, living the life I had planned, quiet and contented; but I can also see myself living in this busy, cut throat, competitive, glamorous world of Asia.

Could I really be contented to return to Dinner Plain, shack up with Ryan and pop out a couple of kids or do I see myself living my life differently now? I find myself questioning; will I ever make the choices that lead to Ryan and me raising babies in the sunshine? Is that a life I want anymore?

15

The following week, HEH was buzzing. Chen and I had meetings, back to back all day to finalise details of his departure. His mother and Chen Industries hadn't given him much time to get his affairs in order before commencing with them. We spent tireless hours and late nights in the office going through the portfolios and ensuring there wasn't a single aspect of HEH that we hadn't discussed. Most of the high level discussions, I had already been included in. It was more the 'watercooler business' Chen needed to update me on. Bits and pieces of discussions and planning that hadn't been floated at a senior level, but raised in passing. One sticky afternoon, after hours of feeling trapped in Winnie's office, Chen and I decided to escape to the hawker centre for dumplings and juice. The heat of the afternoon was a relief from the blasting air-conditioning in the office. I roll shoulders and turn my face toward the sun as we clamber out of the BBSUV. I stretch my fingers, feeling the blood flow return to them, relishing the warmth.

'Is this what 'outside' looks like? I hardly remember it,' Chen chuckles as he joins me beside the car. I turn to watch him pull on his sunglasses, making him look like the Hollywood hunk he is in the magazines. He unbuttons his jacket suddenly, removing it and laying it out on the back seat. He catches me staring, tilting his head to the side like a puppy dog. 'What?'

'Nothing,' I smirk innocently, quietly enjoying the view as I put on my own sunglasses and turn toward the market.

Xi pulls the BBSUV into the front carpark of HEH just as my phone begins to ring. I pick it up and see Ryan's face appear on the caller ID. I smile across at Chen, before answering and stepping out of the car. I watch as Chen and Seal wander into the lobby, escaping the now sweltering humidity. Xi drives off to park the car in the basement garage.

'How is your day going?' I ask Ryan, peering at one of the beautiful floral shrub beside the entry.

'Not too bad, just about to start the shift. Was strangely cold today, some sort of Antarctic blast blew through the state.' I can hear Ryan shuffling around in his car, no doubt packing his bag before walking into the station.

'I wish we had an Antarctic blast her, it is bloody sweltering,' I sigh, hoping I don't end up with sweat patches on my dress.

'I've gotta run, I'll talk to you later?' Ryan's voice echoes down the phone, so full of love.

'Be safe,' I blow him a kiss and hang up the phone.

Walking inside I notice the lobby stands relatively

quiet for this time of the afternoon, giving me an opportunity to examine the space more closely. I realise for the first time, how the light shimmers through the tall windows, reflecting off the long pendant chandeliers. Here and there, the light hits the glass in such a way that rainbows dance across the floor. Peering at my shoes, I notice the stark contrast between my black patent stilettos and the crisp white marble. I stand there for what feels like the longest time, soaking in the sunlight, enjoying the peace of the space.

From somewhere near the door, I become aware of a presence as the glass slides open behind me. A light breeze brushes at the hem of my dress, causing the silk to dance playfully. A strong scent in the wind forces me to freeze.

They smell like a brewery! And at this time in the afternoon? I peer down at my watch, noting the early hour of the afternoon. Hm, probably should establish who that is and get HR to address drinking and workplace behaviour. I'm about to turn around when the world around me slows. I can't tell if my brain is processing everything faster or simply that the whole situation feels surreal. Somewhere in the distance, I hear a shout.

'Ava!' It sounds to me like Seal, but why would Seal be shouting at me? I was only sitting in the car with him two minutes ago. I turn in the direction of the call, only vaguely aware of my surroundings. Something hits me from behind, coming through the door. I lift my hands to catch myself as I tip, face first toward the stone. But the stone never comes, as an arm snakes around my waist, catching me upright.

'You'll pay for what you did to me,' I feel Tony's

breath on my shoulder and face, angled slightly due to my height in these heels. I gag at the fumes he's emitting; the man must be pickling on the inside.

'Tony?' I frown, my brain failing to comprehend the bizarre situation. I spot Seal standing frozen, arms outstretched like a line-backer. I watch as one hand drops to his waist, unsnapping the holster on his belt.

'Make another move, and you'll be needing a mop,' Tony sneers at him, 'where's your perfect haired paramedic when you need him?'

I can't help but frown. Why does Seal need a mop? It's at that moment my brain registers the remarkably shiny machete in Tony's free hand. Where on earth did he find that? I wouldn't even know where to look for one of those in Singapore, a camping shop maybe? Is camping a popular past time in Singapore?

Focus, Ava. Now is not the time.

'What do you want, Tony?' I breathe, locking eyes with Seal. His face betrays his apprehension; I can see the dread etched into his features, every muscle in his body wound tight.

Seal fears for my life. That is a concerning thought. If the man who is paid to keep you safe, looks like he's seen a ghost, it is probably a bad sign.

'I warned you. But you didn't listen,' he snarls. Icy dread creeps into my stomach.

'The letters?' I swallow, suddenly parched.

'I wanted you to know I was coming for you. You couldn't just leave well enough alone, could you?' Tony hisses, his breath singeing my nose hairs.

'What are you talking about?' I frown, turning my face away from his putrid stench.

'You, in your slut outfits, with your women friends. Not a single brain cell between you,' he rants,

218

'come in here and take what's mine!' At a loss as to a response, I stand there mute.

'What?' Tony shouts in my ear, 'no smart reply, no come back?' I realise by this time that a few people have heard the commotion in the lobby and begun creeping out to watch inquisitively, their curious faces morphing into masks of horror. I spot a familiar silhouette behind the garden to the executive elevator, and pray Chen doesn't escalate the situation somehow.

'Tony, I didn't-,' I start before Tony shakes me violently.

'Shut up! Shut up! Shut UP!' He shrieks, 'I gave my life to Winnie. He knew one day I would outlive him and then HEH would be all mine. But then, he met you.' The scent of unwashed bodies begins to mix with the fumes wafting around us, causing me to gag.

'You ruined everything! I had a plan. I had a good plan, that would have worked if you hadn't stuck your nose in!' Tony begins to cough violently; I lean as far away from him as I can reach. He yanks me back harshly, causing my teeth to clatter together.

'You ruined me. You left me with nothing! I sank every penny into that deal!'

'The deal where you intended to sell foundation land illegally?' I state in an undertone, careful not to raise my voice.

'I had to find another way when I realised Winnie was going to leave you everything. So I did what I had to do. His doctors would never know what really killed him,' his voice drips, ice-cold, cascading shivers down my spine. I feel my stomach drop and my throat constrict. Tony killed Winnie. He admits it.

'And then he manages to sign off his will in secret.

I was finally rid of him, free to begin living MY life, and I learn of his deceit,' I watch the machete in his hand begin to wave around uncontrollably. My eyes snap up to Seal, watching Tony's every move minutely. His holster remains unsnapped, his hand hovering painstakingly closely to it. I begin to feel the sweat trickling between my shoulder blades and an uncomfortable gurgling in my stomach. Now is really not a good time for stress tummy.

'And you have the audacity to come in here and fire me! ME! Zhang Wei Tony! I built this place with my own two HANDS!' His voice is gaining octaves as well as volume now. 'So I track down that bastard boy, and convince him to sue for Winnie's estate. Yet again I underestimated you; I should have burned those journals!' I see Chen's shadow fall across the floor, peering out behind the garden. I see first an arm, then a shoulder and finally his horror-stricken face. He steps forward; his open palms held up in front of him.

'Tony, why don't you put the knife down and we can talk about this?' Chen's presence instantly intensifies Tony's hostility. I feel him tense behind me, his arm around my waist constricting.

'Ah! YOU! I was counting on you when you started here! I thought you understood what was at stake!' Tony begins shouting at the top of his voice. I'm immediately confused by this statement. I watch Chen's eyes widen in horror as his gaze meets mine.

'What?' I breathe, almost to myself.

'Ava, I can explain,' Chen takes another step forward, his eyes imploring mine.

'Explain what? That you knew what Tony was up to this whole time?' I spit, feeling the tears brimming, 'tell me it isn't true?' My legs begin to tremble; my hands shake in front of me.

'How does it feel, Ava? To know the man you trusted, lied to you?' Tony hisses in my ear.

'Don't listen to him, Ava,' Chen continues to inch forward.

I feel the fear begin to recede as volcanic anger seeps in, causing my cheeks to flush. How dare these men come in here and treat me like some child they can toy with.

I'm vaguely aware of Seal's hand now resting on his holstered gun.

'What do you want, Tony?' I breathe, trying to contain the rage building inside, 'how do you want to see justice served?' I feel Tony begin to laugh, the vibrations of the movement reverberating through me. I breathe slowly, trying to calm my racing heart.

'Justice?' Tony spits, 'there is no justice for what you did to me. You left me with nothing. I was a KING! Now, look at what I've been reduced to!' I realise Chen has inched to within machete swiping distance.

'And now, this guy,' Tony swings the machete around to jab at Chen, 'is getting his own company!' Chen jumps back slightly, further out of range.

I can hear the sound of sirens approaching and can't help wondering if that was the smartest idea - tell the guy with the hostage that you're coming. Tony seems to realise his time is running short. I feel him looking around in agitation and noticing the audience we have amassed.

'Look how many people came to watch you die,' Tony sneers in my ear, raising the machete awkwardly across my body, toward my throat. I notice at this proximity; the weapon seems to be quite heavy in his teeny-tiny hand. I see Chen and Seal freeze in my periphery, Seal's gun half drawn. I find myself wondering what kind of marksman Seal is, kicking myself for not asking sooner. At this distance, a well-placed shot could probably hit Tony if he weren't cowering behind me. That begs the question however, could Seal get a round off before Tony has time to sever my carotid? The statistical likelihood of my surviving that is relatively low; I decide from my years of prestigious education at the 'Grey's Anatomy' Medical School.

'Tony, think about what you're doing,' Chen tries again, eyeing him over my shoulder. The flash of the police lights shimmer and dance around the walls as car after car screams into the parking lot.

'Think? Think! All I've been doing these past months is think! How and where to enact my revenge!' He roars drunkenly, his machete arm swaying slightly away from my body. Caught up in his dramatic display, Tony splays his arms out wide momentarily, as though addressing the audience, 'rather poetic, don't you agree?'

The second I feel his grip loosen I throw myself forward, praying his drunken reflexes are too slow to realise in time.

Reaching my arms out to protect my face, I hit the marble just as the ear splitting sound of a discharging gun echoes around the room. I feel rather than see Tony's body hit the floor, his weapon clanging loudly in the now eerily silent space. I watch as, more officers than I can count pour into the lobby, their weapons raised.

I turn my head toward Seal, watching as he slowly

lowers his gun to the ground before raising his arms above his head. I realise with horror that the police have witnessed Seal shooting Tony. Panic and hysteria rip through me as I watch an officer violently shove Seal to the ground, a knee in his back as he is handcuffed.

'SEAL!' I scream, terrified. I am suddenly aware of Chen's presence at my side, pulling me off the floor. I begin to claw at him, desperate to get to Seal, to explain that he was defending me. Tears stream down my face as I scream his name, over and over again. The officer arresting Seal finally lifts his knee from his back, grabbing him by the shoulder and dragging him to his feet.

'Chen, you have to do something! They can't arrest him!' I push myself away from him, trying desperately to fight my way past the throng of people now surrounding Tony. I manage to get to the lobby doors, watching the officers walk Seal to a car before shoving him through the door. A paramedic steps into the doorway, blocking my view.

'Miss, are you injured?' Her voice calm and steady as she takes in my dishevelled appearance. I look down at myself, only to realise I am smattered with blood down one side. Tony's blood. I turn slowly to watch as a team of people lift Tony onto a stretcher, a tourniquet wrapped around his lower leg.

'Miss?' The paramedic tries again, reaching a gentle hand toward me.

She follows my gaze as I whisper, 'Is he dead?'

'No, Miss. It looks like a flesh wound,' she frowns beside me, clearly curious.

Through the lobby door I spot Xi, standing uncomfortably. I dodge around the paramedic and launch myself at him.

'Miss Ava!' Xi embraces me tightly, 'thank the gods you are alright.'

'Xi, they took Seal! They saw him shoot Tony!' I can barely get the words out as my throat constricts.

'We need to follow the rules, which includes giving witness statements before we leave,' he smiles down at me, 'Seal will be fine.'

Several hours later, having been interviewed by three different officers, washed, changed and escaping via the back door, Xi and I made our way to the police station.

'I couldn't help but notice you were avoiding Mr Chen,' Xi observes quietly. I sigh heavily and deciding I don't give a damn, kick my bare feet up on the dash.

'I know I should give him a chance to defend himself against Tony's accusations, but right now I just need to make sure Seal is okay.' Xi nods contemplatively from the drivers seat.

'Mr Chen is a lot of things, Miss Ava, but a bad guy isn't one of them.'

The police station was cold and clinical, it reminded me of a hospital. Xi parked me in a chair opposite the front desk before making his way toward the perspex barrier. I don't know how long I sit there, staring into nothingness. I try my hardest to stop the same reel of images flashing through my head. Tony's crumpled body on the ground, Seal kneeling with his hands in the air, his body being shoved in the back of the police car. I shake my head, hoping it will dispel the visions. I feel my eyes droop and my head nod as I relax back into the plastic seat.

The sensation of swaying wakes me mid-dream. My eyes open with a start, foggily coming to the realisation I am being carried. My head rocks gently back and forth in time with Seal's footsteps. I reach my arms up and gently hug him around the neck. Relief washes through me.

'Ah, the princess awakens!' He chuckles, looking across at Xi. I realise with horror that he has a split lip and a shadow of a bruise blooming across his cheekbone.

'Seal! They hit you? That's police brutality!' I squirm until he stops and puts me down.

'Nah, one of the other guys in holding wanted my watch,' he winks at me, 'don't worry, I won.' I can't make out if he is being sarcastic but decide to let it go.

I sigh heavily, rubbing my face with both hands. 'Okay, who wants to tell me what happened to Tony?' The three of us walk back to the BBSUV, before slowly clambering in.

'He was taken to the local hospital, he is under police guard and will be charged in due course,' Xi says. He turns to eye me in the back seat. I nod in acknowledgement, uncertain what else to say.

'I'll have to answer some questions at his hearing, but as far as the cops were concerned, I was just doing my job,' Seal states from the front seat.

'Okay, good,' I reply absently, digging my phone out of my purse to realise I have hundreds of missed calls and text messages. 'Oh, man.'

'Ah, yes. It seems the whole world heard about what happened. Don't worry, Chen did a press conference. You're off the hook,' Seal laughs.

'Speaking of, Miss Ava, are you going to talk to Mr

Chen tonight?' Xi peers at me in the rear-view mirror. I pout petulantly and stare out the window.

'Yes.' I roll my eyes.

'You know Tony was just trying to mess with your head right, Ava?' Seal swivels around in his seat to look at me. The bruise on his cheekbone growing more prominent by the minute.

'You didn't see the look on Chen's face,' I offer to Xi's headrest, refusing to make direct eye contact with Seal.

'Ava, my face would have looked like that too if I'd just been accused of being an active participant in Tony's scheme!' Seal reaches an arm across to poke my knee playfully. 'Give the man some credit. I'll admit I'm not his biggest fan, but at least trust him on that.'

I stare out the window, watching the city lights passing by. Why do I find it so easy to believe Tony? Is it just the fact that when it comes to Tony, Chen always seemed to side with him? But isn't it true that I've seen a different side of Chen since I came back from Australia? I feel a puddle of guilt grow in my stomach.

Arriving back at the penthouse, rather than face reality, I decide on a bubble bath. I hug both Xi and Seal at the elevator before retreating upstairs to the master suite. I stop only to dump my phone and shoes on my bed before peeling off my clothes on the way to the bath. Reaching across the tub, I flip on the faucet and begin pouring scented oils into the water. I watch it foam and bubble like a cauldron as I light some candles and flip off the lights. I hear my phone ringing on my bed and decide to ignore it, pondering as I step into the tub, how many times it will have to ring before I get back out and turn it off. Oh well, that's future Ava's problem!

I lay back in the suds and close my eyes, allowing the lavender and patchouli to wash away the horrors of the day.

Not five minutes into my relaxation I hear Seal coming up the stairs, having a boisterous conversation on facetime.

'I swear to you, she's not dead!' Seal hollers, getting closer. I sink further down into the bubbles.

'I want to see her for myself!' I hear Ryan's angry voice echoing out the speaker. Uh, oh.

'Seal, I'm in the tub!' I call, kicking my feet up at the base of the bath.

'Did she say tub? You had better not go in there!' Ryan shouts at Seal. He stops on the threshold of the bathroom, 'Do you want to see her or not?' I look over to see Seal with his back to me, holding the phone up over his shoulder.

'Ava?' I see Ryan's face peering critically at the screen. I wave back at him, unable to keep the grin from my face. These two are quite a pair.

'Hi! Can I call you back in a bit?' I ask.

'Seal, put me down. I want to talk to Ava in private please,' Ryan orders. I see Seal's shoulders slump in defeat as he paces backwards into the bathroom.

'And close your eyes!' Ryan hollers from the screen. Seal shuts his eyes and holds his phone out to me. I lean over to dry my hands before taking it. 'Thank you, Seal,' I laugh.

'You'd better not get it wet,' he grumbles as he departs. I watch him go, biting my lip to avoid laughing at him again.

'I'm sorry I haven't called you back, things have

been nuts and I just needed a moment to myself,' I shrug at Ryan. I can see the anxiety in his face. He drags a hand through his hair, taking a deep breath.

'I'm glad you're okay,' is all he says. Hm.

'Ryan, is everything alright?' I frown.

'Now isn't the time,' he sighs heavily. I purse my lips, frowning harder.

'Isn't the time for what?'

'Alright, you asked for it. I don't think you should stay in Singapore. It is clearly unsafe.' I stare at him deadpan. 'I knew you wouldn't want to hear it.'

'Ryan, Singapore was never the issue. Tony was. And now he is in jail.' Where is he going with this?

'I think you should come back to Australia.'

Dear gods, give me strength.

'I am not coming back to Australia yet, I have work to do here. Chen will be transitioning to CI shortly and I need to be ready,' I keep my voice level.

'You're going to stay there!?' A vein begins to pulsate in Ryan's forehead.

'Yes.'

'Are you crazy?' Ryan's voice echoes with barely contained hysteria.

'I don't understand why we are even having this conversation. You had an ice addicted patient hit you with a crowbar last year!' I counter, trying to keep calm.

'What's that got to do with anything?' Ryan frowns.

'What about the time you had a patient cause a needle stick injury because he thought you were 'stealing his soul for your alien experiments'?' I stare at the phone, deadpan.

Ryan sighs heavily, 'What's your point, Ava?'

'I have never asked you to stop being a paramedic, just because what might happen to you scares me. Correction, because what does happen to you scares me.'

'It's one of the hazards of my job. You know that.'

'I do, but I don't understand how you can't see my point.' I shake my head, exasperated.

'Do you know how worried I've been? I've been beside myself, sick in the gut,' he whispers. I see the anguish return to his face.

'I'm right here, Ryan. I'm fine, I promise,' I try to smile reassuringly at him. I turn my head, hearing a commotion coming up the stairs.

'What is it?' Ryan watches my face closely.

'Thought I heard something,' I frown, wondering how I can mute Seal's microphone, so Ryan doesn't hear.

Damn Samsung! Where's the button??

I find the microphone/mute button two seconds too late.

'Ava! You have to listen to me; Tony was lying!' Chen's voice echoes around the bathroom.

'You can't go in there!' Gladys screeches from behind him. I see Ryan's face turn thunderous on the phone.

'Is that Chen?! In your apartment? Wait, IN YOUR BATHROOM?' I look up to lock eyes with Chen standing on the threshold. He freezes, hearing Ryan's voice.

Fuuuuuucccccckkkkk.

'He's shouting from the stairs. I think Gladys caught him,' I pray he doesn't see the look on my face in the candlelight.

'I'm not gonna lie, I'm glad to know that wanker

won't be hanging around HEH much longer,' Ryan states loudly, I imagine in the hopes that Chen overhears him. I see Chen recoil in my periphery.

'Ryan, I should probably go. Can I call you later?' I smile down at him, hoping he won't dwell on Chen's presence. He sighs down the phone, running his hand through his fringe again.

'Of course, I'll talk to you then.'

'Have a good night.' I hang up the phone and check it twice before turning to look at Chen.

'You really shouldn't be in here,' I admonish gently. I realise he is holding a bottle of whiskey and a platter of cheese and dried fruits.

'Sit facing away from the tub.' I point to the plush mat at the base of the bath. I'm rewarded with a sexy chuckle as Chen prowls toward the tub. I reach an arm up, holding out my hand for the whiskey. I yank the cork out and sip straight from the bottle.

'You'll be drunk in 10 minutes if you keep that up,' Chen cocks an eyebrow at me as he settles himself on the floor, leaning back against the black granite.

'How did we get here, Chen?' I ask melancholy before taking another swig. Chen reaches one long arm out before him, removing the cufflink and rolling the sleeve back to his forearm. I watch him, mesmerised as he tends to the other sleeve, his long elegant fingers making short work of the task. He looks up suddenly, catching me staring. His tongue darts out to lick his bottom lip.

Hm, Chen, whiskey and a bubble bath. I suddenly feel like this was not the best decision I've made today.

I watch anxiously as he slowly leans across the tub, extending one bare arm toward me. I don't know what I'll do if he touches me. He grasps the whisky bottle gently and pulls it from my grip, before leaning back against the tub to sip it contemplatively. He eyes me curiously as he lifts the cheese platter, which I perch on the edge of the bath. We quietly alternate sipping whiskey and nibbling cheese until my bathwater begins to cool.

I reach a hand over to pat Chen's hair, 'I'm going to have to get out.' He leans his head into my fingertips, closing his eyes, relishing the contact. 'Why don't you go and ask Gladys what's for dinner? I'll be down in a minute.' Chen slowly unfurls himself from the floor, reaching down to pocket his loose cufflinks. He makes his way to the door before turning back and watching me longingly. Moments later, he was gone.

I drag on a pair of shorts and a t-shirt before descending the stairs into the kitchen. I spot Gladys beside the stove, tossing spaghetti in a large pan.

'Do I smell garlic bread?' I grin at her, feeling the whiskey settle warmly in my stomach. Gladys turns to smile back, nodding her head. She's about to reply when we hear raised voices coming from the balcony. I turn to follow the trail of expletives out the glass doors, spotting Chen, Xi and Seal in a heated discussion near the barbeque.

'Uh, hello?' I call, frowning at the trio. All three men stop and stare at me, caught out.

'Miss Ava,' Xi turns toward me, excusing himself from the conversation before making his way inside. Seal begins to pace toward me, and I catch his arm on the way past.

'Why don't you give Jia a call and update her for

me?' I pat his arm absentmindedly. He nods stiffly and disappears. Chen stands with his back to me, staring out across the Singapore skyline. 'I love this view,' I sigh, walking up to lean against the glass balustrading beside him. The Singapore flyer stands tall in the distance, glimmering amongst the lights of the city.

'Why is it that I always seem to find you at the centre of an argument?' I lean sideways to nudge Chen with my shoulder.

'I didn't start this one,' he huffs, running his hands through his hair. I chuckle beside him, uncertain if I believe him. He stretches out quietly, stroking down my arm, until he reaches my fingertips, intertwining my fingers with his own. 'I uh, take it you haven't seen the press conference yet?'

I frown up at him, uncertain what he means. He catches my look and elaborates, 'the one at HEH, after you and Xi left to find Seal.' I shake my head slowly, uncertain where he is going with this. He nods quietly, but says nothing further.

We stand there, hand in hand, until Gladys calls for dinner. I turn to Chen, pulling my hand free, just as he ensconces me in a warm embrace. I feel his heart pounding beneath his crisp white shirt, and find myself wondering how he isn't sweating more, considering he's wearing sleeves and trousers. I feel him whisper into my hair, as he strokes my back. I lean back, staring into his stormy azure eyes, watching the turmoil within. Reaching up, I stroke his face, hoping to erase his tortured expression from my memory.

'Tell me you trust me,' he begs, 'tell me you didn't believe Tony today.' I reach up and stroke his hair, tucking an unruly strand behind one ear.

'I didn't know what to think at the time, and he caught me off guard. I know you weren't in on his plan; you even warned me to be more vigilant. I guess, I just never thought he'd have it in him.' I sigh, feeling a little silly. 'Is that why you were fighting with Seal and Xi? Because we didn't take his threat letters as seriously as you thought we should?'

'They put you in danger,' he growls. I shake my head laughing, my whiskey consumption catching up with me.

'Seal has barely left my side since the ball,' I grin up at him, 'I am under 24/7 supervision. What did you want them to do, hire a team of people? A human wall of bodyguards?' I begin to giggle. Chen rolls his eyes and stares down at me; an unfamiliar emotion etched into his face.

'I am no china doll, Chen. Although, I will be talking to Jia about hiring additional psychologists onto the staff. It seems our people at HEH have suffered an unusual amount of trauma this past year,' I raise a sardonic eyebrow up at him. 'Perhaps you'll find CI a much more mellow, with less drama?'

'My mother sits on the board of CI; there's bound to be drama,' he chuckles, squeezing me tightly, 'let's go eat.'

Throwing myself into bed that night, I feel utterly spent. Having spent the last hour essentially copy and pasting the same text message reply to the majority of my friends, family and colleagues who had tried to check I was okay. I roll over onto my back, holding my phone above me, aware of the risk that I will probably drop it onto my face at some point. I flip through my emails, checking anything I'd missed from the afternoon, when I find a link from Tari.

Odd. I frown at the email before tapping the link which opens in the YouTube app. I watch transfixed as a news anchor reports the headline of the attack at HEH.

'In breaking news, we cross live to our reporter on the ground, Wong, Nazira, who is standing in the grounds of Huynh Enterprises Holdings. Nazira, what can you tell us about the situation?' The camera pans around the front entry of HEH, swarming with police cars, reporters and camera crews.

'Thanks Ted, we are here in front of HEH headquarters where less than an hour ago Zhang Wei Tony, former General Counsel to HEH was taken via ambulance following a terrifying standoff.' Footage of an ambulance appears on the screen. I find myself wondering if they arrived at HEH fast enough to capture that or if they are using generic file footage. 'Details are still emerging of the events that unfolded here this afternoon. However, it would appear Zhang Wei Tony was shot by an unknown man, it is not yet known how or why these events came to pass. We are currently awaiting on CEO Samuel Chen to make a statement.' The reporter appears back on the screen, her bubble-gum pink blazer standing out brightly, referring to handwritten notes in front of her. 'It is understood shots were fired around 2 pm local time, the number of casualties has yet to be confirmed by law enforcement.' A commotion behind the woman has her turning to face the front doors of HEH. 'Here comes Mr Chen!' The reporter, her camera crew and the masses around them all crush forward toward the podium. The camera focusses on Chen as he makes his way up the steps, Abbie from PR following closely in his wake. He looks exhausted; his hair pulled back in a stern ponytail, his shirt sat open at the collar underneath his dark suit jacket. He seems to take a minute to compose himself before commencing his address.

'Afternoon ladies and gentlemen, members of the press. I stand before you, not as the CEO of HEH, but as a man whose house was attacked this today. Zhang Wei Tony arrived here this afternoon in an intoxicated state and began threatening members of staff with a weapon. We believe he may be psychologically unstable following his departure from HEH a few months ago. The chief of police has advised me that I can confirm, a weapon was discharged during this ordeal which has resulted in Mr Tony's hospitalisation with a minor injury. He is in a stable condition and under police watch.' Chen pauses to take a shuddering breath as the camera zooms in closer. For the first time since I've known him, I watch Chen struggle through the press conference. He looks visibly shaken, grasping on to the edges of the dais before him, as though it is the only thing holding him up. He clears his throat before proceeding, 'on behalf of HEH, I would like to thank the first responders for assisting us and ensuring the safety of our team.' He clears his throat again, reaching one hand up to pinch the bridge of his nose.

'This will be my final address as CEO of Huynh Enterprises Holdings, and I'd like to take this opportunity to thank my family, my fiancé and my successor, Miss Ava Elias, for their support throughout my short time here. It has been my greatest honour to serve you.' His voice breaks as he waves a final goodbye to the gathering before stepping down from the podium. The camera tracks his movement as he walks toward the lobby, pausing to run his hands through his hair, bend forward and rest his hands on his knees. Abbie from PR appears in the foreground, announcing the conclusion of the press conference. Through blurry eyes, I watch the reporter return to focus. I feel the tears creep down my face and into my hair, as I drop my phone onto my chest.

So that's it. Chen really is leaving us. There's no going back now. The sense of loss grows in my stomach, as I roll over and cry myself to sleep. □

16

The final night in Switzerland swirls up from a hazy fog. As though an outsider observing our group, I wander quietly toward Tari, Seal, Xi and myself. I see us laugh as Tari digs her notepad from her satchel. She is reading to us as we look sceptically at the pastry she bought us in town. I watch myself as I take a big bite of the dessert, my ginger locks glinting in the firelight. Tari continues to read from Winnie's excerpt, 'if Tony hadn't stopped me, I would have devoured the delicacy which I now realise is occasionally made with Hazelnut meal.' Hazelnut meal. Hazelnut....

Thunder cracks as I sit bolt upright in bed, the sheets wrapped in a knotted mess at my feet. I'm still wearing my t-shirt and shorts having fallen asleep in them. A pre-dawn storm rumbles overhead, electrifying the darkness surrounding me. Disentangling myself, I stagger into the bathroom, mashing the light switch on my way through.

Wrenching the doors on the mirrored cabinet open, I spot the valerian jar. My hands shaking, I lift the jar from the shelf, remove the lid, gingerly raise the contents to my nose and inhale, closing my eyes. Hazelnut.

Could it be that Tony spiked the valerian tablets with Hazelnut oil? The tea Gladys found, could he have poisoned it too? Just enough to cause Winnie's blood pressure to drop and airways to seize when taken in small extended doses?

I feel my heart grow heavy as the tears begin to well. Poor Winnie, being slowly murdered cruelly and painfully. I look down at his ring on my hand, glinting in the lightening strikes overhead. I feel my heart break for him all over again. I'm so very sorry, Winnie.

Several hours later, the skies clear and fresh sunlight streams in my window. I've watched every second of the sunrise, unable to sleep, unable to think, just staring. Shell shocked. Winnie was right; Tony was poisoning him. I know in my gut that I'm right. I don't need to hear it from Tony to know its the truth. I hear footsteps on the stairs, turning my head toward the entry to watch their arrival. Gladys peers around the corner quietly, smiling when she sees I'm awake.

'Ah, I hope I didn't wake you?' She frowns slightly. I shake my head, rolling over to kick my feet off the side of the bed.

'Not at all, I've been awake for a while,' I shrug before rubbing my face.

'There are some gentlemen here to ask you some questions about Tony, are you up to it this morning? I have french toast in the pan for you too.'

'Thanks Gladys, what would I do without you?'

I take a quick shower and head downstairs in denim shorts and a singlet. I am relieved to see Seal and Xi are both present, albeit sitting quietly at the other end of the kitchen counter eating their breakfast and eyeing the detectives warily. After introductions, they commence their questions; all fairly standard. How do I know Tony, did I suspect there was anything wrong with Tony, did I feel his attack was premeditated. I stifle a giggle as I point to the threat letters pinned to the fridge. The detectives look between one another with raised eyebrows. The letters are taken down from the fridge and placed in zip lock bags as evidence. I explain my theory about Winnie's death and the hazelnut oil and hand over the valerian container. Luckily, with all the stress last night, Gladys hadn't cleaned out the tea canister either. I watch Seal and Xi's faces as I explain to the detectives, what led me to believe Tony was poisoning Winnie. They exchange glances as I detail Winnie's final warning in his diary and Tony's statement at the ball about 'getting rid of me too.' The detectives were understandably confused as to why I hadn't come forward sooner. All I could tell them was the truth - that I had no idea if any of it was real or just a trail of breadcrumbs that led nowhere. Two hours and several cups of coffee later, they wrapped up their questioning and departed. I find myself with three pairs of eyes watching me, confusion plain on their faces.

'How did you figure it out?' Seal frowns, scratching his jaw.

'I had a dream which triggered it. Tony was well and truly aware of Winnie's allergies; they'd been working and travelling together for so long. It made sense that he'd poison the tea and the valerian, because the worse Winnie felt, the more he'd take. I knew something smelled off about them both, but couldn't quite put my finger on what it was.' I shrug before making my way to the fridge to withdraw the jug of orange juice. I turn back to see the three of them staring at me.

'What are you going to do now?' Xi asks, passing me a glass. I shrug again.

'I guess we go back to work?'

Walking into the executive floor the next morning, Sasha looked as though she was going to fall off her chair. Her head swivels back and forth between Seal and I; with her mouth hanging agape. I stride across to hug her fiercely.

'Thank heavens you're okay!' She screeches, hugging me back tightly. 'Is this really it? Is he out of our lives forever?' I lean back, looking her in the eye.

'I hope so, but he is a bit of a cockroach. I don't know if an apocalypse would fell that monster.' I shudder just thinking about him. From over my shoulder I hear Seal turning for the elevator, 'I'm going to check in with the team, I'll be back.'

I release Sasha and make my way into my office, swiping my card against the electronic lock on the way in. I stand there momentarily, taking in the room as the door slides quietly shut behind me. The sound of nearby breathing causes a shiver down my spine, as I creep further into the room. Rounding the couch, I spot a head of silky black hair splayed across an elaborately embroidered cushion. Chen must have come back to the office after he left the penthouse last night. I tiptoe to Winnie's desk to set up my laptop and send Sasha a text message asking her to lock my door and go to the kitchen to fetch coffees and bagels. I switch my phone to silent and sit down to commence scrolling through the hundreds of new emails in my inbox. After the first dozen I decide I need a new system, creating a rule for any messages containing the phrases, 'are you okay', 'gunman', 'hostage situation' and 'I saw on the news', straight into a separate folder in my inbox. After waiting a few minutes for the rule to run on the inbox, I find a much more manageable 50 emails remain unread. I sign off on the updated port approvals for Melbourne and Oman, silently patting myself on the back for my hand in negotiating them. I approve a budgetary diversion from fresh floral decorations throughout the HEH offices around the world to increased security for staffed premises. I also reply to the HR team with my feedback on the Psychologist CVs collated for the temporary hiring for trauma counselling at our building.

I see a shadow on the other side of the glass and kick off my heels to let Sasha in quietly. I give her a quick wink as she hands over the coffee and bagels, which smell divine. Creeping back to the couches, I place Chen's coffee and cream cheese bagel on the table in front of him, before settling myself into the wingback chair opposite him to enjoy my blueberry bagel with espresso whipped crème fraîche and plum jam. I've hardly taken my first bite when I hear Chen begin to stir. Crystal blue eyes dart around the room before landing on me, assessing me from my bare feet propped underneath me, my silk navy wrap dress and loose curls before coming to rest upon my face.

'Morning Goldilocks,' I chuckle, watching Chen right himself and reach for the coffee. He frowns and looks up at me, 'Goldilocks?'

'Surely you've heard the childhood tale of Goldilocks and the three bears?' I tilt my head, enjoying our relaxed moment of banter. He rolls his eyes rather aggressively before staring at me pointedly.

'I was only implying that you seem to find my vintage leather couch a most comfortable place to rest your head these days,' I quip before taking a large bite of my bagel. Chen places his coffee back on the table before scrubbing his face with his hands. 'If you'd like to take a shower, you're welcome to.' I point toward the ensuite, nonchalantly.

'Are you laughing at me, Miss Elias?' Chen cocks an eyebrow as he delicately lifts his bagel from its cardboard box. I shake my head, feigning innocence.

'Never!' I smirk. I watch him slowly devour the savoury treat, without dropping a crumb. He catches me staring, freezing mid sip of coffee.

'How do you do that?' I huff, wiping a blob of fallen jam from my bare knee. Chen frowns at me, prompting me to elaborate. 'How do you eat so, cleanly?' The grin that breaks out on his face could stop traffic. It makes me feel all warm and gooey inside.

'Practice?' He chuckles, the sexy sound resonating through me. I watch him stand and stride confidently into the bathroom without a backward glance. Damn, that man does inexplicable things to me. I snap out of my daydream of Chen removing his clothes in my ensuite and return to my emails, placing my coffee down on the pressed metal coaster. I am only a few emails in when I hear a shout from the bathroom. I feel my heart immediately leap into my throat as I launch myself toward the door.

'Ava?' Chen calls again as I go careening through the door.

'What is it? Are you okay?' I state breathlessly as I take in the scene. There's no blood, nothing broken, no flooding or damaged surfaces as far as I can see. My eyes come to rest on Chen's face, a deep frown developing on my own. Chen begins to laugh, a deep guttural sound, 'You should see your face!' I stop dead, realising he's still standing in the shower cubicle. The barely fogged up glass doing little to hide his sculpted body, naked as the day he was born.

'Ava? Can I have a towel please?' Chen continues to laugh as I feel the heat rise in my cheeks. I contemplate walking out and leaving him there to drip dry. Serves him right. Nearly gave me a damn heart attack. I step out the door of the ensuite and collect a towel from the wardrobe. Stepping back inside I toss the towel in Chen's direction, knowing he'll catch it from that distance.

'Don't be cranky, Ava. I didn't think you'd come running in like that!' Chen calls from the cubicle as I shut the door on him. I may not necessarily be in love with Chen, but my goodness, walking away from that bathroom feels like a hard task right now. Hard. I begin to giggle like a schoolgirl. Clearly the stresses of the past few days are beginning to catch up with me. I'm losing my mind. I trudge back to the sofa where Chen lay only minutes ago and throw myself down. Closing my eyes, I take a few deep breaths, trying to clear his the scent from my brain.

I hear the door to the ensuite open behind me and roll my eyes to the ceiling, determined not to let Chen see that he got to me.

'Who's the goldilocks now?' Chen snickers as he spots me lying on the lounge. I feel him walking toward me and possess half a mind to extend my arm and catch him in the nads as payback.

'Don't tell me you're going to report me to HR for indecent exposure? I really need a good reference right now,' he chuckles, feigning fear as he perches himself on the edge of the coffee table beside me. I turn my head to the side to glare at him. Come to think of it; we aren't dating or sleeping together, which means it was indecent exposure. Chen must see the cogs turning because his face immediately morphs into a mask of horror. 'You wouldn't?' I purse my lips, in mock consideration. I scratch my chin dramatically before bluntly stating, 'Too much paperwork.' I watch the relief wash through Chen. I suppose he too, is wondering where the line exists between us now. He sighs heavily before running his hands through his damp hair.

'Are you okay?' I sit up and watch him, frowning in consternation. He cocks an eyebrow at me as though I asked an insensitive question.

'We are just days from my extrication from HEH. Soon I will have no excuse to call you or pop by your office,' he looks at me sheepishly. I reach over and pat his hand, aiming for reassuring.

'I'm not going anywhere, Chen. I'll still be right here, if you ever need someone to talk to; a colleague or a friend,' I shrug.

'So   you're   not   going   back

to...Australia...permanently?' Chen's gaze drops to my hand on his, tracing my skin with his index finger. I frown back at him, uncertain where he could have picked up that idea.

'What are you talking about?'

Chen looks away embarrassed, a guilty expression passing over his face. 'When I walked in on your phone call with Ryan after the attack, I must admit, I assumed you might be planning on returning to him.'

I pull my hand back, immediately seeing red. 'If I were returning to Australia, it would not be solely for the purpose of chasing down a relationship.' I stand up, unexpected fury burning through me. Chen stares up at me as though he's been slapped.

'Ava, I didn't mean...'

'What? That you think that I'd make major business decisions based on who I'm currently fucking?!' I rage at him, 'How would you feel if I assumed you'd walk away from Chen Industries for me?' Chen stares at me, mute. 'Exactly! It's ludicrous! Why do you assume that I'd be so naive as to make such irresponsible decisions?' I stand there staring at Chen, feeling the fury burn. Secretly proud of myself for not immediately bursting into tears, I hold onto the rage, letting it fester inside me. Chen blinks up at me, as I stand mulishly before him, barefoot and radioactive.

'I almost did.'

It comes out barely a whisper, more like an exhalation. I feel the breath knocked out of me as the vision of Chen's tortured expression flashes back to me. It feels like a lifetime ago; sitting on the floor in the elevator bay of the penthouse; Chen drunkenly explaining he was giving up his birthright to CI. I slowly lean down, trying to catch my breath before finding myself sitting in the middle of the floor.

'Holy shit. I'm such a hypocrite,' I drop my head into my hands and feel hot, angry tears well up. I sense Chen come to kneel beside me, before pulling me into his arms, kissing my hair.

'You're not a hypocrite, Ava. You didn't ask me to give up CI for you, quite the contrary. You reminded me how hard I'd worked to get where I am today,' I feel him chuckle humourlessly around me, 'that being said, that night; one word from you and I'd have thrown it all to the wind, no questions asked,' he sighs heavily into my hair, 'I guess that's what happens when you love someone.'

His words hang in the air, pregnant with emotion and unrequited longing. 'I will never forgive myself for not listening to you about Tony from the beginning. I wrongly assumed that the people I had watching him were infallible. You have taught me so much about the world, about life, that I never knew; I never knew.' I feel him tense up around me, his breath coming in rigid, sharp rhythms. 'And then I saw you, standing in the lobby, realising too late, that you were in danger. If I could have traded places with you, I would have in a heartbeat knowing it meant saving you from Tony's threats and violence.' Chen's voice breaks, coming out a whisper, 'All I could think was, I can't lose you.' I lean back and wrap my arms around his neck. We sit there for the longest time, uncertain what to do next. Eventually, Chen sighs, 'I had best get to work,' he laughs quietly, 'I'd hate my boss to give me a bad reference.' He squeezes me tightly before standing and walking to the door. He turns to watch me as he waits for the glass door to slide open, his gaze kind and forlorn. I sit on the floor and watch him go, wondering what had got into me.

Why is it that Chen seems to help calm me down, and Ryan seems to be the one doubting me? Why does Chen seem to understand better, why I can't abandon HEH, safety be damned and yet Ryan is the one who works in dangerous situations all day?

I pick myself up off the floor and make my way into the ensuite. I frown at Chen's towel, neatly hung over the rail beside the shower. Why did I expect to find it dumped in the middle of the floor? I shrug to myself and go about tidying up my appearance before facing the remainder of the day.

Later that afternoon, I am sitting at Winnie's desk, trawling through profit and loss statements for the end of month reports. I catch myself wondering how Chen's meetings are going, thinking about grabbing a drink and inviting him to join me.

My phone suddenly begins to vibrate on my desk. I look down to see Ryan's face on my caller ID. We have a phone date planned for tomorrow, so his call is a little unexpected.

'Hi Ryan!' I answer cheerfully.

'Ava, how are you?' He sounds odd.

'I'm good, just busy with offboarding Chen. How has your day been?' I ask, fiddling with a bulldog clip on a stack of files.

'Do you need me to move to Singapore?' The question catches me off guard. I feel the air leave my lungs as my eyes begin to water.

'You would do that for me?' I whisper, the depth of my guilt blossoming.

'I have made the decision that I don't want to live

without you, so it makes sense for me to follow you. Wherever you go,' he murmurs.

'Ryan, I...I don't know what to say,' I feel the guilt constricting me like a South American reptile.

'Say you'll marry me, and we can start our lives together,' Ryan gushes.

'Marry you?' I frown to myself, hoping my tone isn't too incredulous, 'Ryan, we haven't talked about that far into the future yet. We've only been dating for a few months.' I begin to feel the panic creep up inside me.

'Don't you want to get married? Don't you want to have a big family?' Ryan's tone changes, it's sharper somehow, accusatory.

'I do want to get married, at least I think I do, but I just don't know that I'm ready for all that right now. Besides, how big is a 'big' family?' I'm babbling.

'You don't know if it's what you want, Ava, or you don't know if I'm what you want?' Ryan sounds plain angry now. I close my eyes and take deep breaths, trying to regain my composure. 'I don't want to be an old dad, Ava. I thought we were on the same page about our goals?'

'Can't we talk about this in person? I'll be back in Melbourne in a few weeks, can we discuss it then?' I hear deafening silence at the other end of the line. I pull my phone away from my ear to check if the call has dropped out. 'Ryan? Hello?'

'I don't know that I can do this again, Ava. This sitting around waiting for you to come home, waiting to keep living my life when it fits on your watch,' he all but spits it down the line.

'Ryan, where is this coming from? What are you saying?' I feel the hot fat tears begin to plop onto the desk in front of me. I know what he's saying. He's said it before. He isn't willing to wait for me. If I'm honest with myself, I know I can't blame him for that. I've always known Ryan would want a little wife to sit at home and wait for him with dinner on the table.

'I need some time to think, Ava. I'll call you in a couple of days, once I've got my head straight,' Ryan sighs heavily before hanging up. I sit there and stare at my phone in my hands.

'Why, Winnie?' I whisper to the space surrounding me, peering out toward the financial district from my desk, 'why do the two main men in my life drive me so crazy?'

Perhaps it is time to let Ryan go. Maybe Mei was right; maybe I'm not destined to end up with Ryan or Chen. I gaze down at my laptop, noticing the time.
Cocktail   hour,   I   grin   to   myself.

17

The decks surrounding Spago Bar are packed full of people. The sweltering heat has brought the crowds from inside the hotel to swarm the infinity pool on the rooftop. I approach the bar, spotting Tari serving a customer and stepping up to find a seat as I wait. I have a minor 'Sheldon Cooper moment' when I realise there is a petite blonde woman sitting in my regular seat at the bar. I fight desperately not to roll my eyes at her back and calmly make my way to the next vacant seat. I place an order with the tall, chiselled male bartender who serves me immediately, before turning to watch dusk settle across the shipping lanes. When I first started visiting Tari at Spago, I'd often sit and face the city, watching the lights twinkle far below. Lately, I've been watching the gargantuan ships creeping into the ports, their lights glowing off the water.

'Hey babe, if you haven't eaten, I recommend the arancini balls - crab and aioli!' Tari breaks my reverie as she bounds up in front of me. I offer her a smile and confirm an order for the fried balls of goodness.

'What's wrong? You have that look,' she peers more closely at me.

'What look?' I frown, pouting slightly.

'The 'all the men in my life are morons' look,' she chuckles, 'but then again, maybe that's just me projecting.' I can't help but laugh, I will never tire of Tari's energy.

'You're bang on the money actually,' I laugh out loud. Tari picks up her water bottle and waves her hand in front of me, promoting me to elaborate.

'Well, I had a marriage proposal and a declaration of undying love?' I smirk across at her as her mouth pops open. Admittedly, I may have been exaggerating just a little.

'No!' She squeals, clapping her hands in delight.

'I just want to run away and hide, Tari. It's all too much right now. Chen's leaving HEH, he and Mei are getting married and...' I eye her speculatively, 'and I think that both of those friendships might be getting murkier by the second...' I watch her closely as she blushes, looking anywhere but directly at me.

'You're sleeping together, aren't you?' I cock an eyebrow at her. She frowns at me in mock horror, protesting the accusation vehemently. I roll my eyes, knowing perfectly well that she is lying, and badly. 'I just don't know what to do, it is all such a mess. I feel like everywhere I turn, there is a saga waiting to unfold.' Tari leans forward on the bar, propping one elbow on the marble top.

'Well if you ask me, my vote is for lesbian. We are way more fun with much less drama,' she stops and stares at me before we both crack up into fits of laughter. 'Who am I kidding? We're also a cataclysm of crazy pants. I don't think there's a win-win situation,' she eyes me curiously before adding, 'so, who proposed and who declared undying love?' I can't help but laugh, I'm about to answer when another bartender calls upon Tari for assistance. I begin to ponder my life before I met Winnie. I can't help but feel a little guilty about feeling as though my situation with Ryan and Chen is a curse. When I was in Dinner Plain, I'd imagine what my life might look like if it were full of adventure and mystery. Excitement and exhilaration, joy and wonder. And yet here I am, wealthier than I know what to do with, and knee deep in drama. I have two men declaring their hands, but can't seem to find my goldilocks moment with either. Am I too picky? Should I overlook Chen's elitism and assholey tendencies? Should I forgive Ryan his possessiveness and impatience? Or do I cut them both loose and see what the world has in store for me? What's the worst that could happen? I suppose I could spend the rest of my life alone, unable to find someone to love me the way Chen and Ryan both seem to. I mean, I could do worse than Chen or Ryan, right? They are both strong, stable, independent (Chen's family aside), capable gents who I'm insanely attracted to. Any girl would be lucky to end up with either of these men. Ryan's trust issues and impatience are doing my head in, and as far as I can tell, Chen is still not an option because of Mei and his family. To cap it all off, now I also have to try and pretend to forget about Tari and Mei's secret relationship. I know Tari will elaborate when she's ready.

I watch her, fascinated as she laughs freely, assisting her colleague with a large order for a big table near the restaurant. I turn to stare out toward the water, eyeing the shipping lanes, smiling to myself. Who would have thought 12 months ago that I'd know where the invisible lines lay on the ocean, where our ships come in to port and have such a comprehensive understanding of what happens at the docks. Having spent time getting to know the teams at the docks here, I've come to understand why Winnie loved it so much. The life by the water is much more simple. Everything is dictated by rules and regulations, governed by safety measures and procedures. I'll bet no one on the docks have ever been told 'do whatever you like until your lawyer steps in'. As someone who likes order and planning, the idea of taking free reign over something as monumental as the operation of HEH seems utterly reckless. I sip my cocktail contemplatively as I watch Tari return to my corner of the bar. She straightens her vest and picks up a tea towel.

'Okay. Continue,' she chuckles. I explain to her about my interactions with Ryan and Chen, watching her face morph in to a mask of horror and bewilderment.

'He said what?' She rolls her eyes, after I tell her about Ryan. I nod sullenly, admitting reluctantly that this might be it for Ryan. 'Why is he behaving like that?'

'I suppose he's uncomfortable with Chen's presence and I've always had a feeling that he wanted a little wife at home, doting after him,' I shrug, sipping my cocktail.

'Well, I think Mei might be right. Perhaps it is time to focus on you, and HEH and let all the melodrama fall away?' Tari nudges my arm across the bar. I look up at her and smile sardonically.

'Oh, you think Mei is right do you?' I cock an eyebrow at her. She frowns back at me, realising what she's done.

'I mean, she and I might have had a brief talk about it, at some point,' she shrugs, embarrassed. I grin across at her, putting her out of her misery.

'It's okay, I can't pretend I'm surprised the two of you have discussed the train wreck that is my personal life. I'm not going to lie, if Mei just refused to marry Chen, it might make things easier for all of us.' I watch Tari stare me down, as she decides how to phrase her reply.

'I thought you said you weren't sure if you'd have Chen, even if Mei weren't in the picture?'

I sigh heavily, 'Yes, I did say that. I feel so selfish to be so indecisive about the whole situation.' 'Well, we won't solve it tonight. Let's talk about something else?' She pats my arm gently. I cock an eyebrow at her, sarcastically offering, 'oh, please take your pick! Should we rehash Tony's pending trial, Winnie's murder, the awkwardness with the Invisible Women after Riley's stoush with Margot?'

'How about I show you my new experimental cocktail?' Tari chuckles. I nod, realising that I am not going to resolve anything tonight anyway.

As Monday rolled around, my anxiety rose in anticipation for dinner with the invisible women. The way the last dinner ended I am not sure if anything was truly resolved between Margot and Mei. I understand Riley was simply trying to support Margot in her endeavours and I must admit it was beautiful to watch how passionate he was about her work. I also haven't had any opportunity to talk to Linah about her position and how uncomfortable she may be knowing Chip is now the only person in our circle who is unfamiliar with the truth that lies behind the invisible women. Of course we will all respect her decision not to inform him of her real career and life here in Singapore, I cannot help but wonder what sort of toll such a big secret will take on their relationship. Perhaps Linah is right and she will be able to continue withholding her secret from Chip for the entire duration of the relationship, I cannot help but feel as though she has her work cut out for her knowing now that Riley and Margot are moving more publicly in the real world.

I arrive at the warehouse having had a fairly big day full of meetings, and hardly having much opportunity to see Chen, it was like we haven't seen each other since my little outburst on the floor of my office last week.

Tonight, the space inside the warehouse feels different somehow. As I make my way through the door there are less candles, less chatter, the entire vibe of the space feels different. A nagging feeling unfurls in my stomach as I begin to wonder if perhaps the invisible women will never be the same again. I spot Jia at her usual position behind the bar, although her cocktail shaking seems somewhat less enthusiastic than usual. I wander across and park myself on one of the high stools opposite her. She offers me a meek smile and cocks her head toward the stairs leading up to Margot's loft.

'What's going on there?' I ask quietly, peering curiously at the base of the stairs. Jia looks up and catches my eye, cocking one eyebrow.

'No clue, but Margot and Mei have been up there for a while. Linah hasn't arrived yet.' I stare at her, my mouth open in surprise. She nods knowingly, before turning back to her cocktails.

Perhaps Margot is willing to take a risk on designing something for Mei's wedding after all? Jia and I fall into comfortable conversation, discussing internal politics at HEH and news of Abbie's upcoming extended holiday.

'What are we going to do without her? I feel like every other day we are living through some saga that Abbie has to dig us out from?' I laugh, swirling the twizzle stick in my cocktail contemplatively.

'She'll only be gone eight weeks, and it isn't for a few months yet!' Jia playfully tosses a maraschino cherry across the bar toward me. 'I'll deny I ever said this, but I'm going to miss Chen a little bit when he leaves HEH.' I stare at her, mouth agape.

'I thought you hated him?' I frown. Jia shakes her head and laughs.

'Not entirely, besides, it is fun to have someone to exchange barbs with at the office. My last workplace was so dry; there was hardly a shred of personality between the executives.'

We are distracted from our conversation as Linah arrives, her hair tossed about from the wind, looking rather frazzled.

'Hi, Hi. I'm so sorry I'm late,' she offers, blowing air kisses to us both before dumping her handbag on the lounge and kicking her heels off.

'No apologies necessary, we were just catching up,' I smile at her as I hand over a martini glass. Linah sniffs it dubiously before eyeballing Jia.

'What's in it?'

'Nothing you'll hate, now drink up,' Jia grumbles before ducking around from behind the bar and walking to the bathroom. I turn to Linah and ask how her day was.

'Oh, terrible. I'm so tired of working with these assholes who don't understand the numbers and insist on making nonsensical statements about them!' She throws her free hand up in the air dramatically.

'Have you thought about going somewhere else? I can ask our finance team if we have any openings at HEH?' I offer, patting her arm gently.

'Thanks, Ava, but I've worked too hard in this firm to find myself out on my ass now. Besides, Chip wants to expand the ranch, so we need the money. I can't afford to take a pay cut now,' she sighs.

'More cattle, more land?' I cock an eyebrow at her as I sip my cocktail.

'More everything! He's decided to 'brand' everything, so now we need hats and belts and bumper stickers. God knows I love that man, but he makes me crazy some days,' she sighs, before taking a large gulp of her martini. 'Speaking of crazy men, how are Chen and Ryan?'

'Ha. Ha,' I state sarcastically, 'honestly at this stage I'm ready to give up and just be single forever. The other day I had to contend with Ryan asking me to marry him out of the blue and Chen...' I realise I'm talking much too loudly if Mei happened to walk in, 'Chen, kind of declared his love for me?' It sounds so bizarre when I say it like that.

'No! What did you say? What did you do?' Linah leans in closer in anticipation.

'What could I do? Chen is marrying Mei, and Ryan was only asking me to try and force my hand on returning to Australia.'

'Was he really?'

'Yes! I mean the conversation started out nicely enough but before I knew it, it turned into him ranting about me not wanting to come home. Of course, I don't want to go back yet. Things have been so unstable with HEH, and for better or for worse, he has to come to the realisation that HEH is my life now.' I stop to take a deep breath, 'end of monologue!' I laugh.

'I'm not about to launch into a lecture, because lord knows we all make our beds.' Linah looks at me nervously.

'Go ahead, get it out,' I smile empathetically at her.

'Maybe there is something in the simple life, and keeping the complicated life here separate from the simple life there?' She shrugs uncomfortably.

'I hear you, I do. It's just not very, me. I don't think I could find a way to compartmentalise my life that well. I find it hard enough to keep track of myself, let alone remembering who knows what and what I have to keep secret,' I sigh heavily.

If only it were really that simple. To just keep work and dating separate. The reality is, HEH is my baby now. No man will ever be able to take priority over the devotion and obligation I now feel for HEH. What Ryan seems to fail to understand is that HEH is not just a pay check for me. When I think of HEH, I think of all the staff and their families. I worry about their safety and their health. I worry about ensuring they are also living happy, fulfilled lives and that their work is fulfilling. I worry about what we prioritise and what impact HEH is having on the environment. There will never be another moment I spend on this earth where half of my thoughts aren't consumed with HEH.

Jia's return has me snap back to the present.

'Jia, do you find yourself thinking about HEH when you're not at work?' I frown across at her, sipping my cocktail.

'Are you kidding? I have to switch it off, or I'd lose my mind. That being said, the other day I was at the nail salon getting my mani/pedi, and I had to ask the poor woman to stop twice so I could answer my phone to take work calls,' she sighs, slicing up lime wedges for a tray of mojitos.

'When was this?' I laugh, feeling immediately guilty that Jia can't find five minutes of personal time at the moment.

'Oh, don't feel bad. It was 2 pm on Tuesday! It was just the only time I could get in at short notice. Unless I know, I am needed, I try not to look at my emails outside business hours. I do find that if I'm watching the news or listening to the radio though, my thoughts always drift to HEH and what impact the events may have on us.'

I sigh, relieved, 'I must say, I'm glad. I was starting to worry I was the only one who couldn't get HEH off the brain.'

The three of us divert the conversation to chat about celebrities and gossip until the dinner arrives.

'Ava, do you want to go upstairs and let the girls know foods here?' Linah smiles back at me as she makes her way toward the front door.

Upstairs, I find Margot's loft has been transformed. Never before had I seen so much lace and taffeta, chiffon and silk. The white fabrics spanned every possible shade, crisp white and ivory, all the way through to blush pinks and latte. I stand in awe as I peer at a myriad of sketches pinned to Margot's inspiration board. Some with huge skirts, others with mermaid tails and tight bodices. A couple of bohemian dresses stood out, covered in elegant lace with floral headbands and draped veils.

'Ladies?' I call, gazing more closely at lace samples pinned to one board. The intricate designs too beautiful to ignore, calling my fingers to them like a siren. Some had raised flowers and pearls, others beads and feathers. Movement behind me drags my attention away, as I spot Margot and Mei sneaking out from the back room.

'Margot, these are stunning!' I gasp, turning to grin broadly at her. 'Did you just come up with these?' Margot laughs, skipping over to me and embracing me warmly.

'I must admit, I've always been fascinated with bridal couture. Such elegance and room for creativity,' she sighs dreamily as she looks up at her sketches. Mei joins me on the other side, leaning in for a kiss on the cheek.

'She is incredibly talented, is she not?' Mei runs a gentle finger over a sample of ivory lace with pearls and silver inlay.

'Where did you find all of these fabrics? I've never seen lace like this?' I exclaim, pointing at a blush pink and gold sample.

'Italy, of course! $100 a sample, I'll admit, I cried a little bit when I clicked 'send' on the order. These samples cost me a mint, but my goodness wasn't it worth every penny?' The three of us stand there beholding the magnificence before us.

'Were you looking for us for any reason in particular?' Mei asks, turning toward me.

'Oh, yes! Dinner is here. I was so distracted, I forgot!' I laugh as our trio turn for the stairs. 'So Mei, are we allowed to know what you are thinking for your design or is that telling?'

Mei giggles as we descend the stairs. 'To be honest, I love every one of Margot's designs. We talked about going into stores together and trying on different styles. That way Margot can help me figure out what I want without having to make too many mock-ups!' I catch the glint in Margot's eye.

'What? It's not cheating! As long as we don't copy the design, there's nothing wrong with looking for inspiration,' she giggles nervously.

'I don't disagree! My grandmother always said, 'you don't shop to buy, you shop to see how they made it and make it yourself!' I laugh as we make our way to the dining table to settle in for dinner. I can hardly hide my relief that these two have made up. With the four of us gathered around the table, the space begins to feel warm and loving once again.

18

The next morning, after begrudgingly pasting on my face for the day, I make my way downstairs to find Gladys in the kitchen making Canadian waffles with bacon and maple syrup.

'Oh Gladys, some days I honestly wonder what I did in my life before I found you?' I sigh, dropping contentedly into a seat to sip my orange juice as she hits the button on the espresso machine. Seal puts his iPad down and turns to laugh at me.

'Life before Gladys? BG? I agree, I couldn't imagine it either,' his face contorts into a grin as he sips his coffee.

Xi quietly arrives via the elevator, mail in-hand, 'these came from downstairs.' He hands me the stack, neatly piled according to size. I can't help but smile; I wonder which of the gents on security cares about order and organisation. I'd love to meet him. I flip through the pile before coming to a stop at a snowy postcard. Mt Titlis, Engelberg, Switzerland.

'Oh, its a postcard from Elena!' I squeal, flipping it

over and reading it aloud, 'To my friends in Singapore, thank you for making my trip so special. To thank you and apologise for my son, please come visit me next chance, and I will show you the real Switzerland. Love Elena.'

I look up to catch Seal and Xi exchanging glances.

'No, we have to wait until we get HEH settled again! We are about to lose Chen; we can't go jetting off on a whim so close to his departure.'

'Spoilt sport,' Seal grumbles as Gladys passes him a plate piled high.

'I think it is very nice. She didn't have to send a postcard,' Gladys offers, handing me a plate and the maple syrup jug.

'Speaking of Mr Chen's departure, is everything ready for tomorrow?' Xi sits down on Seal's other side before pouring himself a glass of juice.

'Yes, I suppose so,' I pout, silently freaking out on the inside. I feel my stomach writhe, surprised no one else can hear it gurgling angrily.

'Do not worry, Miss Ava, and you will be fine. You know what you are doing,' Xi offers me a reassuring smile. As kind as it is of him to say, I am relieved to know Xi also spent time watching Winnie in this position. If anyone were to know what this job entails, it has to be Xi. If he thinks I can do it, maybe I should have a little more faith in myself. I was so confident that I knew what I was doing, and I fought Tony so hard to get here, I kind of forgot to think about what it would be like when I did. In psychology, they refer to it as imposter syndrome. This innate sense of fear that you are incapable of the task at hand and will be found out. I remind myself that I have handled situations for HEH and thus far haven't sunk the company. Perhaps my anxiety comes from the fear that now I will be exposed? I had spent this long in the shadows, invisible. I fought so hard to be seen, but why do I feel like I'm about to walk out there buck naked?

'Ava, you look like you just saw a ghost,' Seal nudges me with his elbow before reaching across to take the syrup from my hand, frozen mid pour.

'I suppose, it just dawned on me. Tomorrow. Tomorrow, the world will know I am the CEO of HEH. I fought so hard to get here with Tony and Chen, but now the real battle begins. If I thought proving to Chen and Tony that I was capable of running HEH was hard, how the hell am I meant to survive, proving it to all of Singapore? All of Asia?'

'I know what you need!' Seal states, jumping up from the counter. He walks briskly to the fridge, drags open the freezer door and withdraws a tub of ice cream. 'Can't have Canadian waffles without ice cream.' I can't help but smile at the dorky grin on his face. Even hidden behind his sunglasses, I see how hard he is working to distract my thoughts.

'Right you are, Seal. Thank you,' I nudge him with my shoulder as he sits back down beside me.

I'm about to shove an unladylike forkful of bacon into my mouth when my phone rings.

'Jia!' I answer cheerily, glad to see it is her number on the caller ID.

'Ava, are you coming into the office today?' She sounds flustered.

Oh dear. The last time Jia was this flustered, she had to tell Chen and I about Mr Evans.

'Yes, why? Please don't tell me there's another lovechild scandal or something?' I sigh heavily, placing my fork down on the plate sadly.

'No, no more love children that I am aware of. Tony's lawyer called. He wants to depose you.' I feel the blood drain from my face.

'Depose me?' I see Seal and Xi turn to stare at me.

'Yes, it is where they ask you questions 'on the record' in relation to Tony's case,' I hear a hint of exasperation in Jia's voice.

'I know what a deposition is, Jia,' I pout. I can almost hear Jia's eye roll down the phone.

'If you think that it will be like an episode of 'The Good Wife' or 'Bull' that you've seen on TV...' - dang it - 'I'd say its a fairly accurate depiction. Hollywood or not. They'll set up a recorder and ask you a series of questions to try and help build a case for Tony.'

'You'll be there too, right?' I feel my anxiety rising.

'Yes, Chen is also being deposed separately. We'll all be there.'

'Jia, do I need to get a lawyer who specialises in these kinds of cases?'

'You mean a criminal barrister?'

'I guess so?'

'No hun, you won't need one of those. You haven't done anything wrong.'

I sigh in relief. Legal matters make me so nervous. 'Thanks Jia, we'll be in soon.' I hang up the phone and catch the glances of Gladys, Seal and Xi.

'Don't worry, Miss Ava, Seal and I were deposed yesterday,' Xi offers supportively. I frown back at him, wondering where on earth I was during that. I voice the question to him.

'You were in the meeting with Miss Abbie and Mr Chen discussing the press conference tomorrow. It didn't seem like something to worry you about right now.' He bows his head guiltily.

'That was very considerate of you both. I suppose it makes sense for them to want to talk to me. I was the one he....' I can't bring myself to say it. Our assembly quietly returns to finishing breakfast, occasionally chattering about surface-level topics until the plates are cleared and I make my way upstairs to dress.

What the fuck do I wear for a deposition?

Inspiration suddenly hits me as I dig out my phone and google, 'The Good Wife deposition.' The images that appear are mostly of serious-looking cast members wearing an assortment of brown and grey suits and blazers. Hm, that's hardly inspiring.

I decide to opt for a navy silk jumpsuit and a Tagliatore double-breasted blazer. Add some sky-high nude pumps, and I'm ready to face the day. I grab my handbag and make my way back downstairs to join the others.

Arriving at the office, I barely have time to put my handbag down before Jia, and Chen walk in, their faces portraying the seriousness of the conversation we are about to have.

'Please tell me those faces are about the announcement tomorrow?' I hedge, praying there isn't some other major disaster I haven't yet heard about.

'Yes and no. I'm here to go through deposition preparation with you and Chen,' Jia sits herself down in the wingback chair, pointing to the sofa opposite her. I pick up my coffee, bless Sasha for having it ready, and make my way over to perch beside Chen. I can't help but notice the sensation his presence has on me. It feels like I haven't seen him in weeks, when in reality it can't have been longer than five days. Jia catches me staring at him as Chen obliviously fiddles with his phone.

We spend the next hour going through questions Chen and I are likely to be asked by Tony's lawyers, discussing how we will answer them and what type of detail to give, what to hold back. Jia finally wraps up the practice, telling Chen and I that she thinks we'll do fine, before leaving us to join another meeting.

Chen and I sit there quietly, feeling somewhat akin to having just been hit by a steamroller.

'Well, that was one way to start the morning?' I offer sarcastically, turning to face Chen. He cocks an eyebrow at me before grinning back.

'Yes, I suppose it was. At least it will mean the first 'Tony hurdle' will have been cleared. I'm just glad they're keeping the bastard in jail until his hearing.' Chen clenches his fists tightly. I see the veins on the back of his hands pop out.

'Apparently they felt he was too connected and had access to too many resources to be allowed to be left to his own devices. Knowing him, he'd absolutely have skipped the country to get away from facing what he did.'

'Did Tony ever confirm, how he killed Winnie or just that he did?' Chen frowns across at me. I shake my head in reply.

'No, just what he said that day in the lobby. But once they test the tea and the valerian, I'm sure they'll be able to get him to admit to it. He's too proud of what he did not to gloat about it to someone. I don't know if him telling us what he did counts as confession enough, if they can't prove how he did it?'

I shrug, suddenly caught wondering if there is some minuscule chance Tony could weasel his way out of this. Chen must feel my apprehension because he turns toward me, taking my hands in his.

'He can't hurt you again. You do know that, right?' He murmurs to me. I nod silently, unwilling to admit that 'knowing' and 'believing' are two entirely different things in my book. I lean back and cock an eyebrow at him, changing the subject.

'So, tomorrow we pull the ripcord,' I sigh. Chen nods slowly, chewing over his reply. 'I think, I can do this,' I state somewhat unconvincingly. I'm rewarded with a bright grin.

'I think, maybe I can become Chairman of Chen Industries.' We burst out laughing before standing and embracing one another warmly.

'Who'd have thought, back in the beginning, that we'd be here now?' Chen grins down at me, brushing a ginger lock behind my ear.

'Who indeed,' I agree. I notice the clock on the wall, realising the time. 'Ugh, I have to go. I have a meeting with the acquisitions team.' I cock an eyebrow at Chen, 'I'm going to miss having you in my meetings.'

'Miss my intellect, humour or wealth of knowledge?' Chen chuckles.

'Your distracting good looks,' I tease, tapping him on the nose with my index finger. 'But seriously, I have to go, and they'll be calling Sasha soon asking where I am.' Chen lifts his wrist to check the time on his watch.

'It's still five minutes to the hour. Are the teams expecting you to be there before the meeting starts? That's a dangerous precedent to set.'

'Believe it or not, I believe my employees' time is just as important as my own. If I expect them to be there 5 minutes before the meeting commences, then I ought to be there too.' Chen eyes me with surprise.

'An excellent point, Miss Elias, as always.'

The day seemed to crawl by, the anticipation of the deposition causing my stomach to knot relentlessly. My wee nerves got the better of me, causing me to duck to the bathroom multiple times for absolutely no reason.

When Jia eventually came to find me, I felt as though I was going to vomit.

'Just breathe, you'll be fine,' she whispers in my ear as we enter the room. Two men sat at the table, both with rather stern looks on their faces. Jia and I make our way around the table to sit facing the door. As I sit down, I begin to feel the blood pulsing inside my head. Now is not the time to get a migraine! As the men begin to introduce themselves and launch into a spiel about what their expectations are, I spot movement out the door. Through the glass pane, I spot Chen carrying a chair. He places it a few metres back from the door before sitting down and smiling reassuringly back at me. In an extremely uncharacteristic move, he gives me two thumbs up, before digging his phone out to answer a call. All of a sudden, the world seems to balance out. I feel my blood pressure recede, the pounding in my head begins to fade, and I feel as though I can conquer anything. The thought makes me smile, Chen helps me feel calm. I read a quote somewhere that said, 'the right man helps you feel like you can conquer the world! Wait, no, that's wine. Wine does that.' It takes everything I have not to giggle. Jia would absolutely think I'd lost the plot. Not to mention these suits.

The deposition proceeds similarly to what I was expecting. They asked questions, I answered them to the best of my ability. Jia objected where necessary and pointed out items to be noted. I felt much more at ease with her by my side and watching her in action was awe inspiring. Damn girl, this woman is a law-yer!

When the suits eventually announced they were finished with me, Jia walks me to the door. She gives my arm a quick squeeze of encouragement before ushering Chen in. I grin up at him as I take my place in his seat, watching him settle in through the glass. When he looks up and catches my eye, I give him the thumbs up and wink playfully. Once the interview begins, I pull out my phone and check my emails. All I can say is thank god for Sasha. She digs out the ones she can action, only flagging my little 'Ava' ones that she can't. That being said, in the 45 minutes I was being deposed, Sasha flagged 20 new emails for me. Mostly just large purchases and contracts from the executive directors for my sign off.

A sudden movement inside the meeting room catches my attention, as I see Chen half stand and point, a somewhat accusatory, finger at the suits. I'm beginning to wonder what set him off, when my phone rings. I look down at the caller ID, seeing that it is Ryan. Not ready to deal with another of his ranting complaints about my life in Singapore, I decide to let it go to voicemail. I look back up to see Chen has simmered down, although perched right on the edge of his seat. I can only imagine they are asking him about his involvement in all of Tony's schemes. It makes sense considering it was the reason Tony brought him on in the first place. That doesn't make it any easier for Chen though, having to explain why he took the job and that he had no knowledge of what Tony was really up to.

After another 10 minutes, the questioning seems to strike another chord. Chen stands up abruptly, with a face of pure thunder. I can almost feel his rage from here. Perhaps they're asking about the ball where Tony hit me for catching him trying to sell HEH land, or about the main reason they're here; the lobby incident. I watch Jia reach a hand out to place on Chen's forearm, trying to encourage him back into his chair. I can't decide if I should stay to show him my support, or go, so he doesn't feel like he's being scrutinised for his reactions. He seems to take a deep breath before returning to his seat. I can see from Jia's expression beside him that she's none too impressed with the line of questioning from the suits.

The conversation seems to settle in after that, and 15 minutes later, I see Chen and Jia stand somewhat tersely before exiting the room. Chen offers me a shy smile before making his excuses and heading to the elevator. Jia and I wait until we watch the suits leave the room, and join the waiting member of security show them back down to the lobby. The second they are out of earshot, Jia rounds on me.

'Did you know?!' She grinds out; I can't tell if in anticipation or frustration. I frown back at her, unsure what she's referring to. She elaborates, 'did you know how deeply Chen feels about you?' She must see the recognition in my face, because she immediately grins like the Cheshire Cat. 'I know you'd said he'd declared his hand, but my god Ava, that back there was not a man in love. That was a man who would crawl over broken glass for you.' I'm in the process of figuring out how to answer her when my phone begins to ring. I look down to check the caller ID and Ryan's face appears on the screen again. I sigh heavily, lifting one finger to Jia, asking her to wait one second.

'Ryan?' I answer, a little more gruffly than I'd intended.

'Ava?' Ryan's voice sounds worried on the other end, causing me to frown to myself. 'Are you alright?'

'I don't understand. Why wouldn't I be?' Jia looks at me; her confusion no doubt mirroring my own.

'I just saw on the news that Tony is being investigated for murder, what the hell happened?' Ryan's tone reaches near hysterical. It suddenly dawns on me that I might have forgotten to text Ryan to update him on the goings-on concerning the investigation into Winnie's death. I don't see why it matters, the last time we spoke, he threw all his toys out the pram.

'Ah, yes. Tony is being investigated for murder,' I confirm, unsure what else to add. Jia raises an eyebrow at me, as though asking for an explanation.

'What the hell, Ava? We only spoke the other day, and you never mentioned it?' Ryan's accusatory tone hits a nerve.

'Last time we spoke, Ryan, you launched into a tirade and to be quite frank with you, as a result it completely slipped my mind. You made it clear that you wanted distance, so I don't see what would possess me to pick up the phone and call you when you've made it perfectly obvious that you don't want to hear from me,' I state bluntly, Jia's eyebrows shoot up in surprise before me.

'I'm sorry for caring!' Ryan all but shouts down the phone before the line goes dead. I stare at the phone in my hands, wondering where on earth my relationships went so badly tits up. Jia's priceless face catches my attention.

'Yes?' I smirk, unsure what else to say. She offers me a coy smile.

'I'd say it's about time these boys learn, you bite back.'

That night, I find myself restlessly wandering back and forth in the kitchen stuck in a routine from hell. Open pantry door, peer in pantry, find nothing appealing to eat, close pantry door. Open refrigerator door, peer in refrigerator, find nothing appealing to eat, close refrigerator door. It must have been after the tenth cycle that Gladys sighs heavily from the doorway, catching my attention.

'Can I make you something, Miss?' She eyes me with concern. I shrug, unsure what I feel like. Or if I'm even hungry. 'Why don't I make you some cookie dough?' I smile back, thinking that she may be right on the money there. I make my way to the fridge and withdraw the jug of orange juice, before finally sitting down at the island to watch Gladys work. Only a few minutes later, I hear the door alarm go. Gladys and I exchange a look, both peering at the clock on the wall, wondering who could be visiting at this hour.

I buzz up the elevator and a few minutes later, Tari walks into the kitchen. I jump up and ensconce her in a warm hug. Relief washes through me as I suddenly realise, a visit from her is exactly what I needed. She says hello to Gladys before taking a seat beside me at the island.

'What brings you here?' I grin across at her, immediately feeling my mood lift.

'Well, I had a thought tonight on shift and thought I'd come and share it with you.' She stands and mysteriously takes my hand, luring me toward Winnie's study. I turn back to wink at Gladys, checking she knows I'm coming back for my cookie dough.

'I remembered something I had read in one of Winnie's diaries and I thought you might be a little nervous about tomorrow. I don't know if it will help, but I wanted to read it to you anyway,' she points me toward the sofa before turning back to the bookshelves and withdrawing two books. One from the beginning of Winnie's writing and one from a few years later. I sit quietly, entranced as I watch Tari flip through the pages, scanning the characters before her. She eventually stops and begins to read.

'Today I made a life altering decision. One I do not take lightly, and am terrified in equal measures with excitement. I have decided I am no longer satisfied with working on the docks. I want to build an empire and live grandly in wealth and splendour. I feel a little silly writing this, but I believe you must dream big if you wish to achieve your goals. And without further adieu, here it is; today, I took out a loan to start a company with a ship of my own. I shall start with one, as it is all I can afford, but over time I intend to see it grow.' Tari looks up at me a broad grin on her face.

'That's where it all started. Just one boat. I know he wrote 'ship' here but later on he does admit it was just a big boat.' I find myself grinning back at her before resting my head back on the sofa and listening to her continue reading. She shuffles through the second diary, before launching back in.

'What a difference time and reflection make? I have realised the error in my thinking; that building an empire can be borne by one man. It takes many hands to build anything worth nurturing, and I have come to understand that I too must find myself an army. Huynh Enterprises Holdings may have started out as my business, but I cannot bear it alone. My only hope is, should I ever have an heir to inherit whatever is to become of HEH, that the integrity of our humble origins is never forgotten.' I reach over and wrap my arms around Tari, unable to articulate just how much it means to me to hear Winnie's thoughts on HEH's beginnings.

'Thank you, that is exactly what I needed to hear,' I sigh, feeling a weight lift from my shoulders. Tari leans her head against mine, humming quietly to herself.

'What was Gladys cooking at this time of night?' Tari leans back to look at me. I grin cheekily, feeling as though I've been caught with my hand in the cookie jar.

'Cookie   dough.   Want   to   share?'

19

I roll over in bed on the morning of the announcement and feel the anxiety clench in my stomach.

Am I ready for this? The short answer is, I no longer have a choice.

I roll out of bed and make my way to the shower. I'm about to step into the water when I hear my alarm go off. Sighing heavily, I decide on a short shower, before making my way back to my bedside table wrapped in a towel. Standing there quietly; I contemplate my future. I was so certain when I first came to Singapore, certain that I could run HEH successfully, certain that I wouldn't make an embarrassment of myself. Why, after having to fight so hard to get here, do I suddenly feel unsure?

I sit on the edge of the bed, leaning over to pluck Winnie's ring from its place in the box of Winnie's gold letters, and hold it lovingly.

'Winnie. It feels like a lifetime ago that I read your letters and found myself full of courage and optimism for the future. A future you envisioned, and entrusted to me. Today, I swear to you, I will do my darndest to honour your legacy.' As I sit there, I'm suddenly struck with inspiration. I grab my purse and withdraw Monty, before making my way to Winnie's office and rifling through the drawers and cupboards in search of paper and an envelope. I'm going to write myself a letter, so that future me has someone to offer her guidance and support whenever the next major hurdle arises. As I shuffle through papers and little boxes of knickknacks, I come across a leather drawstring bag. How intriguing!

I extract the bag from the back of the drawer and dust it off. Pulling it open I find what appears to be one of Winnie's undated diaries and a rather fancy with-compliments card. I peer at the gold embossed card, and decipher the elaborate script, 'Until next time, Mr Huynh'. I frown down at the card, before focussing on the diary. Lifting the leatherbound relic delicately, I flip through the pages only to find them blank.

This must be the company Winnie ordered his diaries from, and he had this one stashed away for the new year. I feel my heart warm and after a moment of indecision, I sit down, open the journal to the first page, and begin to write.

'Good Morning, Supreme Leader. Are you all set for the media scrum?' Seal teases, spearing a piece of watermelon with his fork at the kitchen bench. I've just walked into the kitchen, feeling a little lighter and a little more prepared for what the day has in store for me.

'Word of this press conference has spread across

Asia; even my mum called last night to ask if she'd be able to watch it somewhere from Australia,' I shrug and sit down beside Seal, 'I'm not sure the HEH lawn is going to be big enough to hold the media.'

'Morning all,' Xi chirps as he enters the kitchen, heads straight for the coffee machine. He stops and turns to face us all as the machine brews away in the background. 'What are you talking about?'

'How many of the media we expect at the turnout today,' I smile, pouring myself an orange juice. Gladys turns toward us from the stove, a large pot of stewed fruits and berries in her hands.

'My warm berry breakfast compote,' she announces proudly. The four of us sit and eat comfortably, chatting lightly about Christmas shopping and summer vacations. Before I depart the table, I take a moment to thank the team for their help and support. Lord knows where I'd be without them!

I head back upstairs to pick out an outfit for today's press conference. This may be the most important day of my career. Possibly my life. I need to look like I know what the fuck I'm doing. I stand before my wardrobe, the array of colours popping out at me. Do I opt for something bright and cheery, or something dark to signify that I'm taking this seriously? I reach my fingers up at the open racks, stroking down cotton, silk, chiffon.

Hm, better not put on a ballgown, even though all I want to do right now is play dress up and pretend I'm a princess. Run through the halls of an abandoned castle wearing a tiara with not a care in the world.

The sound of my phone ringing drags me from my reverie. I make my way out of the wardrobe to pick it up off my bed.

'Hi, Jia,' I sigh, 'what are you wearing today?'

'I was hoping you'd ask that. I'm downstairs,' I can hear the grin in her voice.

'Oh! Please come up! I need your help!' I all but wail down the phone as I run toward the elevator. Pacing back and forth before the doors impatiently, I can barely contain my relief at having Jia here with me for the morning. The doors open before me at a glacial pace, revealing Jia and three faces I was not expecting. I feel hot tears swimming as I rush forward to embrace Tari, Margot and Linah.

'You guys didn't tell me you were coming!' I cry, squeezing them tightly.

'We wanted to surprise you!' Linah grins, leaning back and wiping away a teardrop.

'Let's get you into a kick ass outfit, huh?' Margot takes my hand and leads me back down the hallway.

'We know how sticky the weather is outside, so I suggest,' Margot pauses for dramatic effect before pulling a dress from the rack, 'the Ted Baker Masquerade Wrap Dress.' The navy printed pattern is stunning, with light blue and gold detailing. I grin up at her, nodding enthusiastically.

'I love it!' I immediately jump up to put it on. A few minutes later, Jia announces that we must head into HEH to start the day. I already knew, having seen the schedule of events, that I was in for quite a long day.

The scrum of media had already begun to swarm

HEH as we arrived. Thankfully, we managed to get the cars close enough to the door to sneak in relatively unscathed. Abbie meets us in the lobby, before riding up in the elevator. The usually spacious interior feeling somewhat cramped with our numbers. The lobby of the executive floor has been overrun with HEH's PR and media team, and what appears to be portable hair and makeup specialists.

After running through the schedule for the day with Sasha and Abbie, am guided through hairstyling and makeup. I stare at my reflection in the mirror. The team have done a marvellous job; my skin glows without looking cake-faced, my glossy ginger curls piled in a high ponytail that cascades down my back. Paired with the dress Margot picked out, I look beautiful and approachable whilst maintaining a standard of professionalism and elegance. I smile down at Winnie's ring as my nerves begin to settle in the pit of my stomach.

When Abbie has finished with me for the meantime, I make my way into the office to check emails and centre myself. I'm midway through replying to my head of finance when Sasha makes her way in quietly.

'I brought you some peppermint tea, in case you were feeling a little jittery,' she smiles at me kindly as she places it on the coaster.

'That is incredibly thoughtful of you, Sasha. Thank you.' She leaves just as quietly as she came. Having answered as many emails as my brain will allow, I stand and begin pacing restlessly back and forth before the window. After two laps, I stop momentarily to kick off my heels, wondering for the life of me why I had been wearing them all morning already.

The sound of the door opening behind me catches my attention, and I turn to see Jia standing on the precipice, holding a large bouquet of flowers.

'What the?' I frown, making my way over to her.

'There's a card, but the others wouldn't let me sneak a look,' she laughs, handing the plume over. I thank her as she leaves, eyeing the flowers curiously. My family sent me a congratulatory bottle of champagne to the penthouse, so I am at a loss as to who these could be from. I pick up the card and withdraw it from the envelope. The text on the front makes me laugh, 'Congratulations on your promotion!'. I open the card and read the printed text, 'To Ava, thinking of you on your big day. PS. Sorry for the card, it was the only one I could pick online that wasn't birthday or wedding related. -Ryan'. I stare at the notecard. What am I meant to do with that? A range of confused emotions swirl up inside me. I sigh heavily, placing the card down beside the flowers before sipping my tea pensively. Sighing again, I realise I need to pee and begrudgingly make my way to the ensuite. At the basin, I check my watch, realising it'll be time to get going soon. I stare at my reflection in the mirror, chanting to myself over and over in my head, you can do this.

Opening the door to the bathroom, I halt, realising someone is standing by Winnie's desk. Before me, like a chiselled statue in a three-piece suit, I watch as Chen smirks at the notecard. It looks so tiny in his hands.

'Didn't your mother ever tell you it's rude to pry?' I scold him playfully, making my way back into the room. Chen eyes me nervously, clearly embarrassed at being caught in the act of snooping. I make my way over to him, grinning cheekily. 'I am kidding, you know.' He seems to let out a sigh of relief.

'I came to wish you luck. And to impart an old family custom, if you'll allow me to?' I realise at this proximity, just how nervous Chen seems.

'Are you alright?' I ask, peering at him closely before acquiescing, 'please, be my guest.' He seems to relax infinitesimally, as he raises his other hand to present me with a large square jewellery box. I eye him dubiously, beginning to wonder if we're about to cross a line. He waits patiently, watching me closely.

I hesitantly open the box, to reveal a single gold pearl hanging from a delicate platinum chain. I find myself holding my breath as I stare at the stunning piece.

'It is a Myanmar golden pearl, from the South Sea. Ancient Chinese legend tells a story of how pearls were once grown inside the heads of dragons, and in order to own one, one must sleigh the dragon. It is believed that they symbolise wisdom, which one gains through experience,' I look up to see Chen watching me anxiously, 'do you like it?' He breathes.

'It's beautiful! Thank you, Chen. But is it appropriate for you to be giving me such a gift?' I feel guilt unfurling in my stomach. Chen chuckles, placing the box down on Winnie's desk as he lifts the chain gently.

'Amongst ancient families, it is traditional to offer a sign of thanks to our leaders. If Winnie were still here, I'm sure he would have done the same, as you now carry on the Huynh family name,' he grins down at me reassuringly. I turn around slowly, as Chen unlatches the clasp and fixes the chain around my neck. I beam up at him before making my way to the bathroom to see it for myself. Staring into the mirror, I reach my hand up to touch the pearl, watching Winnie's ring glint in the light beside it. Chen appears behind me, as we stand mere centimetres apart. We stay there watching one another, the tension palpable until eventually, Chen leans forward and places a kiss on my hair, before turning and quietly departing the room.

The moment arrives for me to be ushered from the office and down to the media event, where the others are already gathered. I'm surprised, however, when Abbie hits the button for the restaurant floor. I frown at her in surprise, curious as to what she has planned. We disembark, to a large crowd assembled around the elevator bay. I see Tari, the Invisible Women, Chen, Sasha, the executives, and what appears to be most members of staff, holding champagne glasses. A young waitress appears from the crowd, carrying a tray with two flutes for Abbie and I.

I watch Chen step forward, raising his glass in my direction.

'Ladies and Gentlemen of Huynh Enterprises Holdings, I give you your fearless new CEO, Miss Ava Elias!' The entire room erupts into a cacophony of 'cheers', hoots and whistles. I can't wipe the grin from my face as I sip my glass, filled with beautiful pink bubbles. I'm about to step away when suddenly calls of 'speech' begin to ring throughout the room. I laugh nervously before conceding defeat.

'Okay! Okay! Thank you, Mr Chen. We wish you well in your new adventure at Chen Industries,' I raise my glass in a toast to Chen.

'Cheers!' Echoes about the space.

'Most of you already know me, but for those of you who do not; I'm Ava. It is my most tremendous honour to be working with you all in supporting Winnie's legacy. I look forward to sharing the future of Huynh Enterprises Holdings, with each and every one of you.' A chorus of 'hear, hear' ripples throughout the room before the gathering breaks up. Staffers come past to offer their welcome before moving on to chatter amongst themselves. A few minutes later, Abbie appears at my elbow to excuse me from the throng.

'It's time,' she smiles at me encouragingly, eyeing my drink.

'Is that a 'down it, because you'll need it' look?' I laugh nervously as she shakes her head.

'No, I was just thinking the pink champagne matches your ring. It's exquisite.' She places a hand at my back as we farewell the staff and begin the procession to the lobby.

The crush of people occupying the front lawn is terrifying. There doesn't appear to be a single inch of the car park left vacant. Chen and I make our way toward the podium as the rest of our party are ushered to a reserved viewing space. Applause and cheers erupt as Chen approaches the podium. Good lord, this man really does get the rock star treatment wherever he goes. He grins widely down at the crowd, waving enthusiastically.

'Thank you, thank you. Ladies and Gentlemen, I stand before you today and give thanks on behalf of Huynh Enterprises Holdings for the support we've received these past months. It has not gone unnoticed,' he pauses to offer a short round of applause. 'It is my great honour to have served as CEO of HEH, and it is an experience I will forever be thankful for. I leave you in the strong hands of a woman, Mr Huynh Li personally selected to lead Huynh Enterprises Holdings into the future.'

'I'd like to welcome to the podium, Miss Ava Elias,' Chen holds his hand out to me. I place my hand in his and cling to it for dear life. Stepping forward, I look down into the crowd, smiling and nodding. I take a deep breath, looking out at the sea of faces before me; some with notepads and recorders, others hidden behind cameras and lighting stands, all watching me eagerly. My eyes come to rest on a small huddle of faces, all beaming up at me. Jia, Linah, Margot, Tari, Xi, Seal and Sasha. I spot Mei down below, standing beside a rather stern looking Mrs Chen. She gives me a brief smile and a sneaky thumbs up before receiving a quiet admonishment from Mrs Chen. I give them all a wide smile as I take a deep breath. I look down at Winnie's ring, silently asking him for strength.

'Thank you, Mr Chen. Good Morning ladies, gentlemen and members of the press.

'My name is Ava Elias. Since Mr Huynh's tragic and untimely passing, I have been, and from this day forth will continue to be publicly; the CEO of Huynh Enterprises   Holdings.'.

20

A week later, having spent 20 minutes pacing back and forth before the window in Winnie's office, looking out across the financial district, I hang up from a call with Mr Peng. He called to discuss an alleged security incident at the London office. I look up and see an unexpected face in the doorway.

'What are you doing here?' I laugh as Chen strides into the room. 'I would have thought security cancelled your pass last week?' Chen grins broadly at me, undeterred.

'They know me, they let me in,' he chuckles, coming to a stop before me as I lean back against the desk.

'What can I do for you, Mr Chairman?' I cock an eyebrow at him playfully. He sighs, embarrassed and runs a hand through his hair.

'How long do you think it'll take me to get used to that?' He laughs. I shake my head, shrugging. 'I came here to invite you to lunch. In a thinly veiled guise to show off my 'new digs'.' He grins cheekily down at me.

'You're inviting me into enemy territory!' I shoot him a look as though scandalised by his proposal, 'I'll just grab my bag.'

'You seem to be settling in well, the press received you extremely well, if you want my opinion,' Chen smiles proudly. He makes his way around the desk to peer out the window, taking in the financial district buzzing below. 'I already miss being in the centre of town, everything was so easily accessible here.' I join him at the window, turning to smile up at him.

'You're always welcome to visit,' I laugh.

On the way out, I flag with Sasha that I'm headed out for a few hours. She controls her face until Chen passes, only to throw me a look of delight behind his back. I can't help but grin back, anticipation blooming in my stomach.

Climbing into the back of the BBSUV downstairs, Xi politely holds his tongue. Seal, on the other hand, gives me a knowing look as he shuts my door before climbing in beside Xi in the front. The four of us spent the short trip in relative quiet, Chen and I occasionally exchanging looks in the back seat.

'Why is it that I always feel like I'm about to be chastised, whenever I'm in an enclosed space with those two?' Chen chuckles quietly to me as we enter the lobby of Chen Industries.

The vast space before me, takes my breath away. The gargantuan room feels like an upmarket hotel from another era; images of the Ritz in London come to mind. Gold detailing everywhere, soft, comfortable furnishings, crisp marble tiles with enormous middle eastern rugs splayed everywhere. Colossal flower pots stand around the room; their bright blooms bathing the space in an array of sweet scents. I stand there beguiled and entirely confused by the furnishings. My trance is broken, only by a group of men entering the space carrying an enormous white spruce tree. We watch in awe as the group manoeuvre the tree into the centre of the room before erecting it, where it stands just centimetres shy of the chandelier.

'Is that a Christmas tree?' I stare bewildered. There are so very many things about this space that do not make sense to me. I always assumed CI would be cold and clinical. Clean and no fuss. This space feels luxurious, to the point of excess.

'Yes, a White Spruce, shipped, especially from Canada. My mother always insists on putting the tree up early. She says there is no point paying for something festive only to have it on display for a week,' Chen whispers as we watch people from all directions scamper around to collect fallen pine needles from the floor.

Once safely in the elevator, I decide to hedge my bets and ask Chen about the furnishings in the lobby.

'Uh, care to explain?' I peer up at him quizzically. He turns to frown at me in confusion. I wave my hand around the general vicinity of the elevator, indicating to the elaborate mirrored surfaces and the pressed-metal button panel. 'I'm a little surprised there isn't a chaise lounge in here too.'

'Ah, that,' Chen chuckles, scratching his chin, 'my mother has quite the taste for expensive, well, everything to be honest. When they built CI headquarters, my father relinquished design control to my mother and what you see is the result.' He shrugs, undeterred by my question.

'This place is insane. You know that, right?' I giggle, peering at the detail on the gilded mirror beside me.

'Why were you surprised about the Christmas tree?' Chen smiles down at me, tilting his head to the side like a puppy. I frown up at him, confused.

'Well, partly, I suppose because I had forgotten the date. I have no idea where this year has gone.'

'And the other part?' Chen grins at me curiously as we disembark the elevator.

'It might sound insensitive, but I wasn't sure how many Christian holidays are celebrated here,' I shrug, unsure how else to phrase it. Chen laughs out loud, leading me down yet another ornately wallpapered corridor.

'Singapore is fairly westernised these days, we celebrate all the Christian holidays. We also celebrate a variety of holidays from other faiths too. We're very inclusive like that,' he grins. He comes to a stop before large mahogany double doors. 'This is me.'

In gold detailing the entrance stands marked 'Chairman of the Board'.

'That's going to cost a pretty penny to change whenever you get a Chairwoman,' I cock an eyebrow at Chen as he opens the door.

'You're already planning on turfing me out of office?' He chuckles.

The office beyond reminds me of a classic 1920s speakeasy bar. Stunning dark timber panelling runs halfway up the walls, spanning the entire circumference of the room. One wall is occupied floor to ceiling with bookcases, complete with a rolling ladder. Another wall contains similar shelving but is covered in downlights showcasing all manner of decanters and brandy balloon glasses. Dark leather chesterfield couches sit beautifully nestled in one half of the room, the other taken up by a behemoth of a Victorian mahogany desk. Chen watches me carefully as I take in the room, rooted to the spot.

'Thoughts?' He hedges quietly.

'What, no cigar room?' I tease, my trance broken, as I step further into the room. I feel rather than see Chen's sigh of relief beside me.

'It's on the 'entertainment' floor,' he states deadpan. I turn to stare at him, unable to detect any sarcasm. 'I can show you if you like? When we tour the rest of the building?'

'You're serious? A cigar room? What else does this place boast? An indoor pool? Spa services? Laundromat?' I pout, knowing I sound like a child but still feeling as though on some level, HEH and CI are in competition.

'I prefer Winnie's office, if I'm honest. But my mother is never to know that. Besides, other than the cigar room, you know HEH has all the same facilities we do here. CI doesn't have a helipad either,' he points to the roof. I grin across at him, grateful he isn't taking my mood too seriously.

'How did that happen?' I feign innocent curiosity. In reality, I'm dying to know.

'Turns out, the block wasn't zoned appropriately for it when the land was sold. My father didn't learn of it until the architects were going over the final plans. Naturally, those responsible were immediately fired,' he shrugs as he wanders the space beside me.

'Naturally,' I offer sarcastically, rolling my eyes. 'Those poor people, I can't imagine suffering the wroth that would have been Mr Chen Senior.'

'Strangely enough, I miss it sometimes. I have moments when I realise I will never fight with him again. We will never clash heads or have a difference of opinion. Those were the most common interactions we ever had,' Chen's voice darkens, his loss apparent. 'Sometimes I would pick arguments with him, just so we had something to talk about.' He hangs his head, reaching one arm out to touch the back of his fathers leather chair, perched behind the desk. Unsure how else to console Chen, I step over to him and wrap my arms quietly around his waist. We stand there for what feels like an age, wrapped in each other's arms. Eventually my stomach grumbles so loudly between us, it causes Chen to chuckle and pull away. 'I take it that is lunchtime for Miss Ava?' He grins down at me.

'Please! Apparently I'm starving!' I laugh as Chen makes his way to his desk. He picks up the phone and asks the person on the other end to place the lunch order. As he hangs up, I cock my head to the side, asking, 'Do I get to find out what we're eating?' I make my way toward the shelves full of decanters, soaking in the detail on the glassware.

'It's a surprise,' Chen states playfully, coming to join me and lounging in one of the armchairs.

'I hope you'll be happy here,' I offer sincerely, turning to watch him. 'I really mean that.' Chen's replying smile melts my heart.

'Come, let me show you the rest of the building while we wait for lunch.'

After we've eaten lunch, an assortment of fresh dishes from the market and litres of lime juice, Chen and I pack up the containers on the coffee table between us. I sigh contentedly, laying back on the lounge, feeling thankful that I wore elasticised clothes today.

'Thank you for lunch and the tour. It has been such a lovely few hours, but sadly the real world beckons,' I shrug, smiling across at Chen. I'm about to stand and collect my purse when the main door is unexpectedly thrown open. Chen and I both swivel to eye an older woman with a face of thunder. Mrs Chen. She looks as stern as a drill Sargent, all sharp-angled clothes and dark gaze.

'What is the meaning of this?' She bellows. I'm immediately confused. Is she upset that I'm here because I'm from HEH or because I'm not his betrothed? I stand up with the intention of introducing myself, seeing as I never had the opportunity at the HEH ball. The withering stare that falls upon me, kills any notion of polite banter. I turn to eye Chen, uncertain what I should do. He stands there, mute; I cannot tell if from shock or fear, but he says nothing.

'This is not your childhood treehouse! You do not get to invite just anyone in here to show of your toys!' Mrs Chen yowls, stepping decisively into the room toward me. 'Out! Out, Out, Out!' She ushers me out the door in such a hurry; I suddenly find myself standing on the other side of the mahogany timber in the middle of an empty hallway. The sound of Mrs Chen's raised voice continues to reverberate through the door, although too distorted for me to discern her exact words.

Well that was sufficiently awkward.

I suddenly realise I no longer possess my handbag.

I stand there uncomfortably, uncertain what to do next.

Do I knock? Will she just ignore me? Will Chen find it and bring it to the penthouse later? Maybe he's under surveillance and won't be allowed to come to the penthouse anymore?

I resign myself to returning to the lobby, assuming Xi and Seal will be around somewhere nearby waiting for me. If they don't hear from me, they will eventually come back to find out where I ended up. I make my way to the lobby, feeling oddly naked without my phone or wallet. As the elevator doors open to the hall, I notice immediately that Xi and Seal aren't sitting around waiting for me. I make my way to the complimentary coffee cart in the back corner of the room and decide to park myself with a superior view of the Christmas tree being decorated. I sit there and watch as box upon box of decorations are carried in. There were beautiful glass ornaments, baubles, strings of pearls, fat fluffy tinsel in an array of colours, metallics and shapes. I watch in awe as nimble-fingered staff open and unravel a long string of elaborate glass snowflake-shaped lights. Christmas is by far, my favourite holiday. I love the food, the decorations, spending time with family and friends. It has always been a dream of mine to have a white Christmas in the northern hemisphere. I may spend several months in the snow each year when I'm at home, but because the seasons fall differently, I'll never have a winter Christmas at Dinner Plain. The thought strikes me with inspiration, perhaps next time I'm back, I'll host a Christmas in July. I don't see why we should miss out on all the fun winter-themed Christmas traditions because our festive season falls in Summertime. I can already taste the pumpkin pie, gingerbread men, spiced mulled wine, warm sticky date puddings with butterscotch sauce, egg nog; oh the list is endless.

As I sit there ensconced in thought about the delights that are Christmas, I am completely oblivious to Seal and Xi's arrival. Having both realised I am too absorbed watching the delicate decorations being painstakingly hung, one by one, they opt to seat themselves either side of me on the sofa.

'Isn't it beautiful?' I whisper, in awe. Seal and Xi exchange a glance before settling back and watching with me. 'We need to think about a tree for the penthouse. I'd completely lost track of time. What do you both do for Christmas?'

'Traditionally, Miss Ava, HEH gives employees two weeks off over Christmas and New Year, working with a skeleton staff through that time,' Xi explains. I nod my understanding. 'I take the time to spend with my daughter and my family. Will you go back to the USA Seal?'

Seal nods in acknowledgement, stating nervously, 'I was going to mention it, I swear.' I smile across at him, patting his arm beside me.

'Don't sweat it Seal; I have no problem with you taking some time off to go home and see your family.' I feel him relax beside me as relief washes over him.

'Thanks, Ava.' We sit there for another 10 minutes in peace, watching the worker bee team before us decorating the tree in record time. When I eventually come to the realisation that Chen isn't coming down with my purse anytime soon, I suggest to the gents that we head home.

Gladys and I sit down to enjoy a dinner of beef ragout pappardelle, just as the door goes. I look across at Gladys, mid-sip of my shiraz, contemplating ignoring it and pretending I didn't hear the buzzer. Realising that it might be Chen, returning my handbag, I decide I'd best go and check. Begrudgingly, I drag my ass to the screen and sure enough, there stood Chen in his giant celebrity aviators and designer athleisure. I mash the button to open the front gate, allowing him access to the elevator lobby.

'Should I leave you, Miss Ava?' Gladys peers at me from the table. I shake my head and make my way into the kitchen to grab another bowl for Chen.

'Not at all, I'll just grab him another place setting, just in case he wants to join us,' I'm relieved to see a smile on her face as I return to the table. A few minutes later and Chen arrives, my purse in hand.

'Thank you!' I grin up at him as I check the contents are all accounted for.

'Believe it or not, I did not steal anything from it, Miss Elias,' Chen chides lightly. I peer up at him cynically, feigning distrust before laughing and inviting him to join us for dinner.

'I can't stay too late, my mother has me on a curfew,' he chuckles humourlessly. I eye him curiously, knowing full well he isn't joking. That woman was scary.

'I'd not want to cross her, that's for sure,' I murmur, stuffing my face full of pasta. Out of nowhere, Gladys jumps up and blurts, 'I forgot the garlic bread!' She screams out of the dining room and into the kitchen. The smell of fresh bread wafts toward us as she takes it from the oven. It smells divine.

'Thank goodness. It's perfect!' She smiles proudly as she carries it in on a timber board with a large serrated knife.

'My compliments to the chef,' Chen smiles across at her as she returns to her seat. Gladys' cheeks warm as she glows under his praise. I'm glad to know I'm not the only person he has that effect on.

The three of us fall into easy conversation as we indulge our way through the pasta, bread, and before we know it, Gladys has departed to the kitchen to collect dessert.

'I'm sorry, we don't usually have desserts, I eat way too much otherwise.' I peer after Gladys, wondering eagerly what she has prepared for us. I don't have to wait long before Gladys returns carrying a tray with dessert size bowls of cream and a large bowl of dark chocolate mousse. I feel my mouth immediately begin to water.

'Gladys, do you know how long it has been since I ate chocolate mousse?' I exclaim, delighted to see the top covered in chocolate shavings. Chen grins across at me broadly, clearly enjoying my childish joy.

'If I knew desserts made you this happy, I'd have brought more of them to you at HEH,' he chuckles.

'Why do you think these days, Jia always comes to my office with doughnuts or cinnamon scrolls when she is delivering me bad news?' I laugh at him as Gladys scoops me a giant serving of the fluffy delight. I'm so excited to eat it I don't wait politely for everyone to be served, I just dig straight in. It is the most deliciously fluffy, creamy, chocolatey cloud I've ever eaten.

'Gladys, you spoil me,' I pat her arm beside me. 'I

meant to ask you, what do you normally do for Christmas? Do you go home to see your family?' Gladys looks at me in surprise.

'Well, I do have family, but Mr Huynh liked to spend the Christmas holiday here. I can't remember the last time I didn't work a Christmas,' she looks up at me wide-eyed, 'that's not to say that I wasn't very happy to work Christmas, and Mr Huynh did give me lots of holidays at other times of the year...'

'I completely understand. Well, this year I think I'm going to go home to spend it with my family in Australia. I owe them a lot of explanations about Chen's departure and the fact that they'll probably be seeing much less of me over the next 12 months. I'd be happy for you to take as much time as you like. I can fend for myself for a bit. It'll do me good to keep in practice anyway.'

'We can discuss it another time Miss Ava, for now, I will leave you and Mr Chen to talk.' Gladys picks up her bowl and departs the table. I turn to eyeball Chen, unsure if he is going to be the first to talk.

He sighs heavily, 'I owe you an apology, for my mother.' He peers across at me nervously. I nod contemplatively.

'Was she angry because it was me, or because I wasn't Mei?' I cock an eyebrow at him. He runs a nervous hand through his hair.

'Both. She is not a naive woman; she can see how I change around you,' Chen sighs. I find myself frowning deeply at that statement, and it doesn't pass Chen unnoticed. He raises a hand to press one finger between my eyebrows over my deep frown line. 'What?'

'How does your mother know what you're like

when you're with me? She's never even met me.' I pout, frustrated to be judged so harshly by a woman I don't know. Chen chuckles darkly, patting my hair gently.

'She has seen how much I've changed since you came to Singapore. You've turned my world upside down, Ava. I find myself seeing things through a different lens, and that terrifies my mother. We aren't raised here to think independently and have our own ideas and opinions.' I peer at him sceptically, still unsure I believe his explanation is enough to justify his mother's venom. 'My mother is having to contend with a son, returned from the USA to head a 'rival' company,' I interrupt him at this point.

'Which your father pushed you into via Tony.'

'Yes. I return to Singapore and move straight in with HEH. Then after being exposed to you, suddenly I'm talking back with my own theories and expectations of the business and of life. Gone is the 'yes man' my mother raised. It doesn't take a genius to figure out what the common denominator is,' he laughs, bopping me on the nose with his index finger. 'If I am being honest with myself, I'm not sure I really like who I was before I met you. Some days, I am so ashamed of my previous behaviour, I can barely function.' Chen hangs his head, avoiding making eye contact.

'We all have those moments in our lives that we aren't particularly proud of. I once had an argument with someone at a supermarket over a ticket at the deli counter,' I whisper, embarrassed. Chen's head snaps up, eyeing me curiously. I shrug, 'I couldn't for the life of me tell you why. I remember at the time feeling so justified in my actions, and the moment it was over, I felt so stupid.' I place a hand on his forearm and squeeze it gently once. 'My point is, we all do stupid shit that we regret. Those actions are not what make us who we are, but more what help shape us; because we realise who we don't want to be.' Chen smiles hesitantly at me.

'I guess that means you realised that day you never again wish to be the person who argues over supermarket deli tickets?' He smirks. I nod guiltily.

'Exactly. I am ashamed to know that I was ever capable of such inconsiderate behaviour, but I know now that I will never be that person again,' I sigh, 'and that has to be enough for me; otherwise I'll beat myself up over it for the rest of my life.'

'So what you're saying is, I need to forgive myself for who I was and work toward being a better person in future?' He grins at me. I nod gently, sweeping his silky fringe back behind his ear. 'I will work on that.'

'Now we must face our demons separately, you at CI and me at HEH. We made a pretty good team, didn't we?' I smile wryly. Chen nods contemplatively. 'I don't think I ever thanked you properly for being my beard. I know in the beginning it wasn't what I'd planned, but I've learned so much from you. Thank you for caring for HEH like it was your own.' I feel myself welling up at the thought of how much Chen looked after the team at HEH. How well he looked after me.

'I meant what I said Ava. I'll always be here for you. No matter what I'm dealing with. I'm only ever a phone call away; I promise you that,' Chen's voice waivers, laden with everything he cannot say. I reach up to stroke his cheek, 'Me too, Chen. Me too,' I whisper.

A quiet buzzing drags me from a deep sleep, having fallen exhausted into bed following Chen's belated departure. I roll over, stretching languidly across the mattress, mildly irritated at being woken and stare at my phone on the bedside table. The flashing and vibrating stops momentarily, long enough for me to notice five missed calls from Mei. It's after 1 am.

My stomach drops. *Does she know?* I momentarily lament not throwing Chen from the penthouse the minute he kissed me at the elevator, but in that moment, all I wanted was be ensconced in his passion. I feel a wave of guilt surge over me, leaving me wanting nothing more than to wash the smell of Chen and sex off me. *How could she know?* Could she really be upset enough to call me at this hour? *Also, talk about glass houses.* I watch my phone anxiously, fearing that it may grow fangs and bite me at any minute. Suddenly, the screen lights up, and the handset begins to vibrate again. I take one ragged breath, pick up the phone and hit 'answer'.

'Mei?' Nothing.

The line goes dead.

Well. Fuck.

Coming Soon

The Invisible

BOOK III
THE INVISIBLE SERIES